WORLD OF HEROES: THE UNTOLD SECRET ORIGIN OF THE NEW FIGHTERS

SUPERHEROES FOR THE SOCIAL MEDIA ERA

Many long years have passed since superspeedster Jack Quick mothballed his costume, but when he receives a desperate call from a troubled former teammate, Jack has no choice but to don his running suit, dash to his old friend's side, and put the call out to reform their old team, the Fighters.

However, little is as it appears in this strange world of heroes and villains—and when the new breed fails to live up to the old guard, will Jack side with his old friend or choose justice?

An exciting superhero story in the tradition of your favorite comic book heroes like *Justice League*, *The Avengers*, *The Flash* and *S.H.I.E.L.D.*, **WORLD OF HEROES: The Untold Secret Origin of the New Fighters** is an action-packed adventure tale of powers, costumes, capes and justice for all!

WORLD OF HEROES: THE UNTOLD SECRET ORIGIN OF THE NEW FIGHTERS

The Complete Novel

A. J. PAYLER

Copyright © 2016 by A. J. Payler

Originally released under the name Marc Allan Moore.

All rights reserved. The moral right of the author has been asserted. No part of this book may be reproduced in any form or by any electronic or mechanical means, including information storage and retrieval systems, without written permission from the author, except for the use of brief quotations in a book review.

This is a work of fiction. Names, characters, places, and incidents either are the product of the author's imagination or are used fictitiously. Any resemblance to actual persons, living or dead, events, or locales is entirely coincidental.

Cover image © rudall30

CONTENTS

1. Episode One: From Out Of Oblivion   1
2. Episode Two: Heroes Assembled   43
3. Episode Three: The Villain Revealed   73
4. Episode Four: The Circle Tightens   99
5. Episode Five: Nobody's Children   141
6. Episode Six: After All   163
   Epilogue   185

   About the Author   189
   Also by A. J. Payler   191

EPISODE ONE: FROM OUT OF OBLIVION

WEDNESDAY MORNING, 7 AM

The signalphone at my bedside shouldn't be ringing at all. I only keep it there for the sake of nostalgia; it wasn't designed to work with the phone lines of forty years ago, let alone modern digital cabling.

I pick up the phone and turn it upside down: still not plugged into anything. The ringing doesn't even waver.

Ten rings later I finally succumb and lift the handset off its cradle. What am I going to do, disconnect it?

"Hel-"

"JACK QUICK. YOU ARE SUMMONED."

Ugh, that voice: flat and humorless, far too loud, and tinged with metallic resonance. Somehow, the absence of the familiar distortion of ordinary voice transmission is the worst part; Master Mystic literally sounds like he's speaking a hair away from my ear. So creepy.

"Good to hear from you too, M&M. Keeping the old mantle dusted?"

"JACK QUICK, this is NO occasion for levity. The FATE of the very UNIVERSE ITSELF is at—"

"—at stake, got it got it. Any reasonable person suddenly awakened by your intonations after twenty-five years would have jumped to that assumption. Maybe you'd realize that if your Mystic aspect retained some vestige of human personality."

"JACK QUICK, you TRY the patience—".

"After all, it's not like you ever call just to gossip about girls. Or boys, for that matter."

"—of Grantu. Nigh TWENTY-EIGHT YEARS have elapsed since last the call of destiny summoned FATE'S FIGHTERS, yet NOW we must reunite to prevent UNIVERSAL CALAMITY. YOU, Jack Quick—"

"Okay, okay, okay. Where and when?" I should know better than to bother trying to mess with the old buckethead. Thirty years on and he still doesn't have any idea how people work.

"Where the FABRIC of existence THINS, at the hour of HIGHEST—"

"Your place at noon. Got it."

I keep listening as though expecting Mystic to acknowledge my sick burn. After a minute I realize I'm just sitting alone on my bed, holding a broken handset to my head. I know Mystic's ethereal transmissions don't, like, end with a click, but perhaps his total disregard for the rules of human interaction should stop short of hanging up without saying goodbye. Life isn't a movie, after all.

My temples are pounding and my stomach hurts. I guess I've got to dig the costume out. And as annoying as he can be, now I wish I'd let Mystic rattle on for a while, since thanks to my futile display of rebellion I don't have any idea what's actually going on. Never could resist a good line—or a bad one, as my ex-wife would testify. If I have a weakness, it's not knowing when to keep my mouth shut. That and antimatter radiation.

I hoist myself off the bed and catch a glimpse of my reflection in the bedroom mirror. I feel as old as I am. *Congratulations, Jack: by all indications, you've learned absolutely nothing since Sloan took off.*

* * *

Yeesh, this attic is a disaster area. I used to be big into keeping souvenirs, which I invariably referred to grandiosely as 'trophies' from my 'adventures'. I even allowed myself to fantasize that someday, someone would open a Jack Quick Museum. Surveying the dusty pile of junk before me, the idea makes me blanch. Sure, in its time the Reflektor's Mirror Mauser was a deadly weapon, but it still looks like a toy plastic piece of junk. The thing won't even light a room without a chunk of highly enriched uranium in the grip, and there's zero chance Reflektor knew the first thing about proper radiation shielding.

Broken superweapons, torn pieces of capes, full-head rubber masks...even I don't remember where half of this crap came from. Why would anyone else want it? Even artifacts of genuinely memorable events molder unsold ever since the bottom fell out of the super-collectibles market. The problem is, there's always something new coming around the corner, so no one seems to have any interest in looking back anymore—wistfully or otherwise.

Partially concealed beneath the Axis Agent's swastikoat—that's really what he called it—a half-crushed box labeled 'JQ costumes' seems to offer my best chance of finding what I'm looking for. I pull it out and sit crosslegged on the floor before it, sifting through its contents while my face wrinkles with distaste. I'd entirely forgotten some of these designs: back in the day, I was always trying to keep my look fresh by incorporating the latest, hippest trends; in retrospect, this only served to ensure my new outfits were dated on arrival. Generally, as soon as a new uniform got a tear I'd show up to the next team meeting sporting my 'classic' look, muttering about the time and expense involved in fixing superfiber weaves and complaining how nothing holds up the way it used to. It's a testament to my former teammates' patience that they called me out so rarely on it.

After taking stock, I determine that the box contains six identical classic costumes in various stages of wear and four passing variations, each missing one crucial accessory except the last, a never-worn ensemble gifted to me by a well-meaning colleague who fancied herself a clothing designer. Holding it against my body, I'm reminded how good a thing it was that Sue's husband had money. Then again, maybe if Sue had actually needed to earn a living instead of frittering her designing ability away on overcapitalized hobbies, who knows what might have happened?

Eh, most likely the same thing that happened anyway: this thing is fucking hideous. Shuddering, I ball up the offending ensemble, return it to its cardboard wardrobe and extract the least-tattered classic-look outfit. There's some scuffing on the boots and a small rip in the left arm where someone managed to tag me on my last time out—I want to say Scimitar Sultan—but it looks otherwise passable.

I swap out the costume's boots for a less-worn pair and turn to clamber back downstairs, but the sight of the large, dusty frame leaning against the wall stops me in my tracks. I wipe my hand across the glass, and the whole gang grins back at me from behind the faded matting. Our old group portrait: fatefully taken just a few weeks before everything started going south on us, it hung in my office for years, but I stuck it up here after it started to become too depressing. Looking at it now, I remember why. I turn the portrait to the wall, click the light off and clamber down the steps, clutching my balled-up uniform to my side.

* * *

Well, it could fit a lot worse. Granted, it could also fit a lot better, but that might have required some effort on my part, either to maintain myself at the costume's dimensions or to conform it to my present shape. I'm just lucky my powers kept my metabolism chugging along as the years passed, or I wouldn't have a prayer of squeezing back into the damned thing.

A couple of staples do fine to close up the hole in the arm for now, I slip the boots on, and…I look like a second-rate Jack Quick cosplayer. It's not just the fit; costumes today have gotten so elaborate and detailed that my old running suit simply doesn't make the grade anymore. Hell, these days even casual cosplayers put far more time and attention into their outfits than I ever did, and it shows.

Oh, well. No time to worry about it now, and no point in

pretending I ever developed any sense of either fashion or shame. All the uniform really has to do is identify me as an ostensible professional, and if anyone out there remembers me at all, it'd be dressed like this.

I take a deep breath, check my hidden inside pockets for my keys, wallet, and phone, and brace myself to race off—but as I pass through the foyer, I catch a microsecond glimpse of my reflection, and a torrent of images cascades through my mind: the case of the crying knight, the mystery of the modern monk, the time we all got turned into pirates, and a dozen others.

The experience depletes me unexpectedly. I brace my forearm against the doorway and look down as if double-checking my boots, but I'm really just trying to breathe. I stand there for a full minute, long enough to transition awkwardly from fake boot check to fake stretches for my nonexistent onlookers' benefit.

Not until I take my first step down the road toward Master Mystic's hidden fortress do I know what I'm going to do. It's not until the half-mile mark that I'm totally sure I'm not going to turn around and go back to bed.

* * *

Mystic's fortress looks exactly the same. I shouldn't be surprised—I'm told it technically exists outside our plane of reality, whatever that means—but the fact that it hasn't changed one bit in nearly three decades is somehow both comforting and extremely disconcerting.

After taking a second to check my reflection in the courtyard's scrying pool—not gazing too deeply, lest the pool gaze into me—I proceed up to the tower's entryway and lift the massive iron door knocker. Before I release it, the withered face sculpted into the knocker's surface twists to life, speaking haughtily: "What mortal soul dares disturb the mystic fortress of the master?!?"

I roll my eyes. "It's Jack Quick, Ken."

The face smiles. "Oh, Jack! Wow, long time, yeah? Got to be what, twenty years?"

"Almost twenty-eight, according to your boss."

"Man, time flies, huh? At least it does when you're stuck to a door. Hahaha! So how've you been?"

Damn it. "Oh, pretty good, pretty good. You?"

"You know. Still a cursed door knocker, hahaha! So I guess the master summoned you, huh?"

"Sure did."

"God forbid he tells me anything. Not like I'm starved for conversation up here, haha!"

"You did try and destroy the universe, Ken."

"Come on, Jack, don't do me like that. That was like, forever ago!"

"Sorry, Ken, just stating the facts. No offense intended. So, am I good to enter?"

"Yeah, yeah, go on." The door swung open. "Hey, if you get a chance put in a good word for me, will you?"

"I'll try," I say. I won't.

"Mucho thanks, dude! See you later!"

The door shuts behind me. For just a moment, I'm engulfed in blessed, silent darkness. Then, seemingly of their own volition, half a dozen torches burst into flame around the room's perimeter to reveal a dismaying tableau: overflowing trash cans; tomes, codices, and scrolls piled in disarray; stale, oxygen-deficient air; and dust-covered cobwebs covering every corner of the eighteen-foot ceiling. A lone recycling bin groans under what must be a year's worth of unread magazines; a roll-top desk shoved against one wall inelegantly cradles a laptop so old I'd bet my net worth against the manufacturer's ability to service the machine—assuming the company still exists. Shockingly, the room seems relatively free of mold and mildew; I take this as a sign of professional courtesy extended toward more potent forces of entropy.

Spaced evenly around the massive circular table sit eight high-backed chairs, just as they were the last time I was here. Slumped in one is a pile of laundry that vaguely resembles the man I came to see. I lightly tap one shoulder and Nelson lurches awake, flailing wildly at unseen demons. After a moment, his watery eyes focus and settle on me:

"...Jack? Jack Quick?"

It rattles off my tongue before I can stop: "In the flesh—and quick as a flash." Remembering how I used to see every conversation as an opportunity to crowbar in my terrible catchphrase, I cringe, choking back the urge to apologize before continuing: "You...called me, didn't you, Nelson?"

"I..." Nelson looks around as if reacquainting himself with his own home. "I'm sorry, Jack, things aren't what they were when you were around."

"I'm around now."

"You know what I mean," he says, but I'm not sure I do. From the looks of things, Ingrid must have left some time ago. I'm pondering whether Nelson's state of dishevelment preceded or was precipitated by her departure when he clears his throat, lurches over to the desk, and taps a few keys, mumbling inaudibly to himself. After a few moments, he laughs bitterly and turns to face me: "So, you got the Summons Sorcerous and came dashing right over, huh?"

"You...don't know?"

The sarcasm in Nelson's voice is corrosive. "Like I said, Jack, things here aren't what they were. The 'Master' and I aren't on speaking terms of late, so forgive me if I'm not a hundred percent up to date." He disappears beneath the table for a moment and emerges clutching the mantle of Grantu, addressing it like a fifth-year senior in a high-school production of *Hamlet*: "Isn't that right, you controlling piece of shit?" Gritting his teeth, he grips the mantle with both hands as if to rend it, but instead he sighs, discards it on the table, and collapses back in his chair.

"Nelson, I don't know what's going on with you, but—"

"Well, whose fault is that? Twenty fucking years without a call, email, or even a Christmas card. None of you fuckers really cared about me. No one ever listened; you were just waiting for your chance to talk. My life was slipping away and nobody gave a crap!"

"Look, man...I'm sorry. I can't speak for the others, but I thought you just didn't want to be bothered. You always seemed so serious and focused, I was just afraid to—"

"Not me! Not me! Him! Him!"

"Ok, but...I didn't..." I trail off as Nelson mutters inaudible obscenities at the floor; he clearly isn't hearing me.

Now, I don't have any choice. Telling myself Nelson would understand and forgive me if he was capable, I race around the table, snatch the mantle of Grantu from Nelson's grasp, and slam it down across his shoulders before he even realizes I've moved. Even with my speed, I barely have time to turn away as magical lightning arcs across his body and Nelson screams in agony. Shielding my eyes against the blinding glare, I watch afterimages of my silhouette flicker against the wall until the light sputters and dies, then turn around.

No longer slumped over, Nelson's already taller than most at his full two meter height, but now that he's hovering eighteen inches above the floor, arms crossed, eyes ablaze with blue fire, he casts a far more imposing figure. Nelson's shabby sweats have vanished, replaced by the golden armor of Master Mystic, and rather than Nelson's barely coherent babble, it's Mystic's booming voice that fills the room.

"MY GRATITUDE for the CELERITY of your actions, Jack Quick."

"Yeah, well, that's great and all, but I really hope there's something behind this, since I'm the one who's going to have to explain it later."

"Jack Quick, you MUST appreciate the—"

"Look, if you really want to show me your gratitude, how about taking the volume down? Seriously. You can traverse gaps between dimensions but you can't modulate your voice?"

"Jack Quick, you FORGET your PLACE."

"That's another thing—you've lived among humans since before we had agriculture, and you still think 'overbearingly highhanded' is the way to go? Come on. I know this act impresses the rubes but I've known you—both of you—way too long for this shit."

Mystic floats silently for half a minute, then lowers himself to the floor. He still towers over me, of course, but only the way a normal six-foot-six guy would.

"My apologies, Jack Quick. I allowed the gravity of the situation to affect my manner of bearing. I assure you, no disrespect was intended.

But as you know, among my duties is that of protecting the universe against extradimensional incursions, manning this guard tower along the wall separating order from chaos. From this vantage point here in my occult outpost, I discovered the approaching calamity, and it is to this place I must summon those whom I pray will stand by my side against the tide of approaching evil—for though I know not in what manner we might carry the day, I know only that prevail we must."

Ugh, this guy. Don't think I didn't notice that ever-so-brief apology dovetailing directly into self-aggrandizing overexplanation, but this isn't my first go-round with the Master. Pick your battles and all that.

"Yeah, I was here when you eternally banished the Old Ones from this plane—both times. Is it them again?"

"Nay, Jack Quick. But in the course of performing my duties, I have discovered that something potentially catastrophic is coming."

"Please don't say 'performing my duties' again. So is it Dr. Devastation? Organico?"

"It is like no opponent we have previously faced, Jack Quick. I cannot say what it truly is, for this universe contains places that cannot be seen and things that cannot be known even by one such as myself, the last remaining master of myriad ancient arts unknowable by mankind. I know not what form it shall take or precisely when it will strike, but the severity of the disturbance in the fabric of reality tells me this: in the wake of this event, everything we know and hold dear may well be destroyed or irrevocably altered for all eternity."

"So...not the Grappler Gang, then."

"Jack Quick, your levity is inappropriate in this time of dire need. For what we must—"

"Look, Mystic, we all have our own ways of coping: some people get rudely imperious, I make bad jokes. But look, if this is really such a big deal, then why me?"

Mystic's gaze brushes the seven dusty chairs around the table. "Jack Quick, you were not the only soul to receive the Summons Sorcerous. I can but presume our former colleagues found themselves either unwilling or unable to answer the call to action. I cannot make their decisions for them, nor predict how this inaction will reflect upon their character when the last trumpet blows, but I accept their choices—though I allow that their absences will be keenly felt."

This news is a brick in my stomach. I brace myself against the chair inscribed with my logo, gasping for air as I pray the nausea passes. "Oh geez, man, come on. If this is really some cosmic-level deal, there's no way. I mean, I run fast, you know? I'm a guy who runs fast. And you...well, we're both out of practice and out of shape. I'm not even sure we could handle the Grappler Gang right now. And based on what you're telling me, I'm guessing there's no way this is a thing you and I have a ghost of a prayer of handling all on our lonesome. Right?"

Eyes of cerulean flame stare blankly through me. I don't hear an answer.

* * *

I guess I didn't want to admit it either to Master Mystic or myself, but some part of me was really hoping Sloan would be here. I don't think it's a coincidence how our relationship got a lot more difficult once the group dissolved: group dynamics brought out our commonalities, but I've never been great in one-on-one situations. Besides, eight weirdos is a gang; two is just a couple.

"What is the meaning of 'histakes', Jack Quick?"

"That's 'hi-stakes'. See? That's a dash. Every character counts in a headline." I can't tell whether he understands any better. To Mystic, newspaper printing is still relatively new technology.

"And here, a 'g' and an 'r' followed by the number eight?"

"That's supposed to be 'great', Mystic."

"Ah, then the number four here is intended similarly to be pronounced aloud." He's blessedly silent as he scans the remaining copy before concluding, "I believe a word is misspelled in the concluding paragraph, but whether by design I cannot say. Otherwise, this should suffice for our purposes."

He hands the paper back to me:

. . .

ESTABLISHED SUPERTEAM RECRUITING 4 HI-STAKES MISSION - GR8 OPPORTUNITY

Experienced, well-known classic superteam regrouping with new lineup, looking to fill several positions. POWERED INDIVIDUALS ONLY PLEASE (super-science & 'magic' ok).

Looking to begin mission ASAP, must be available to start immediately. Great opportunity for talented up-and-comers & a chance to larn from the best.

I write an 'e' beneath 'larn' and seat myself before the decrepit computer to post the ad. "What contact should I put for replies? Do you have an email address or a normal phone number—you know, one that doesn't require casting a spell to contact? I mean, I'm sure Nelson does, but your better half doesn't seem to be at his best right now."

"You are correct, Jack Quick. Of late, my host's incalcitrance has resulted in a number of petty indignities. He must not be entrusted with dominion over such critical communications."

"All right. I'm going to sign up for a free email account for you, okay? Here, I'm writing the login and password on this piece of paper; change the password to something you can remember as soon as you get a chance. Now, once people start replying to the ad we can weed out the losers, set up some auditions, and we'll be back in action."

"This seems…indirect."

"Well, Mystic, you can't just gather a bunch of people with crazy powers and outrageous costumes together and go around beating people up anymore. Everything's more organized than it was back in our day. You know how it is: too many jagoffs started thinking they were too special to follow the rules, so now the rules are laws that apply to everybody. Before either of us can even get a cat out of a tree we need to get legally recertified for field operations—otherwise we look like the bad guys, they bring the big guns down on us, and this whole thing is done before you can pull a rabbit out of a hat. Hopefully whatever cachet we have left over helps expedite the process, but to that end, while you're sifting through ad responses, I'll be doing some direct recruiting the old-fashioned way."

"Buying slaves?"

"What? No! Why would you say that?"

"Very direct. Very old-fashioned."

"Well, that was a long time ago."

"Is that not that what 'old-fashioned' means?"

"You know what? Maybe you shouldn't say anything to anyone who responds to the ad."

* * *

I haven't ever visited Sloan's studio before. Never asked, never been invited. Still, everybody there seems to recognize me, from security waving me through the front gate to the office drones muttering in my wake. Believe me when I tell you: this is not typical. At the best of times, my appearance will garner the cocked head of dim recognition, but most of the time I'm thoroughly anonymous. Granted, these are my ex-wife's offices, but if even her youngest underlings and interns recognize me on sight, it's an encouraging sign.

I've nearly reached her assistant's desk when I finally spot my reflection in the thick glass walls surrounding her office, and it hits me: of course they recognize me, I'm wearing the costume. I feel like finding a side door and slinking out without saying a word, but she already knows I'm here. Oh well, there was no way I was getting out of this without embarrassing myself at some point. At least it's out of the way.

"Go right ahead in, Mr. Quick. She's expecting you." Sloan's assistant wears the broadest, whitest smile I've ever seen on a man.

I'm sure she is, I think. I'll admit to being a little dazzled at the opulence of Sloan's office: it's like a robber baron's den as designed by a neofuturist art collective. The chairs are so elegant I'm not sure whether they're meant for sitting or merely admiring, so I stand. One wall is completely covered with framed pictures featuring Sloan standing next to the world's most famous people, from heads of state and A-list actors to Action Man and Sister Sensation; the opposite wall is dominated by a floor-to-ceiling transparent screen flashing dozens of transmissions from all over the world.

Sloan glowers at me from behind her desk, clutching the telephone to her ear so tightly I'm legitimately concerned it'll break off in her hand. She mutters, "Never mind, he's here now, I'll handle it. No, Jon, please don't come down, I'll see you tonight. Okay. Love you too."

She hangs up the phone and looks me straight in the eye, her jaw set: "Jack. Perfect timing as always. Thanks for keeping it low-key, the costume is a big help there."

"Come on, Sloan, cut me a break. You know I wouldn't have come if it wasn't important."

"You wouldn't have come if it wasn't important to you, but that's about as far as that goes. Either way, let me save us both some time and cut to the chase: I'm not going with you, and I'm not interested in rejoining the Fighters for any reason."

"Sloan, just let me expla—"

"Don't try to tell me that isn't why you're here, Jack."

"Okay, but it's not what you think."

"Oh, isn't it? So you didn't get a call from Captain Creepy, dig that costume out of your attic, and come racing right over to see if we couldn't bring back the quote-unquote 'good old days', then? Give me a little credit."

"Look, I know you've moved on. This isn't about that, it's something bigger than us. If we don't get every helping hand we can..."

"What, Jack? The sun goes out? Time implodes? The universe disintegrates? Well, newsflash: I don't care. That's right! You know what's important to me? The staff of two-hundred-plus people out there who don't get paid unless I somehow manage to produce a show today. People I care about, people who depend on me. And sure, if the sun somehow stops shining then yeah, I guess I'll have to deal with it then, but I trust you'll forgive me if I don't hold my breath in the meantime."

"Damn it, Sloan, just listen for a minute. Please, just give me a chance."

She removes her glasses—when did she get glasses?—and rubs the bridge of her nose. "All right, Jack, fine—go ahead. Tell me specifically how me squeezing into a thirty-year old outfit and hitting things with a metal torch is going to help."

"It's..." I catch a reflected glimpse of myself in the surface of one of the many awards filling the shelves behind Sloan's desk, and my mouth closes without another word. I meet her eyes, and she meets mine.

"Look, Jack, I'm sorry for getting cross with you. But you show up here out of the blue and disrupt everything, and the truth is that none of this really has anything to do with me. I get where you're coming from, I really do. But I'm not American Rose anymore, and I'm not interested in putting the band back together. I don't even have the costumes, for god's sake. They were auctioned for charity years ago."

"I'm...I'm sorry too, Sloan. I'll leave."

"Hold on a minute, Jack." She comes around from behind her desk and places her hand on my arm. "Look, I know you miss those days. But they weren't as good for me, and I'm a different person now. A happier person. But I do still care about you, and I want you to be happy too." She bites her lip and looks up at me. "I...I can tell you're not happy. And I know you haven't been happy in a long time. But I can't go back. I just can't. And even if I could, it wouldn't magically put things back the way they were."

"I get it. I was stupid to come here."

"No, Jack...well, yeah. Just call ahead next time, okay? Maybe you could even be on the show as a guest. You know, once you clear up whatever it is you and Mystic are working on."

"Yeah, okay." *Like that's ever going to happen. Fuck. Now what?*

She extends her arms. "Oh...come here, Jack." We hug, and for a moment everything is all right. I try to remember the feeling, to make it last, to live in this moment.

She breaks the hug, holds me by the shoulders, and looks into my eyes. "Hey, it's all going to work out okay. It always does. Right?"

"R-right."

"There you go." She punches me lightly on the arm. The gesture feels awkward and mismatched, but her intent is clear. "Are you all right?"

I start to answer, but I'm interrupted by a loud knock on the door and a muffled voice: "Sloan? Is everything okay in there?"

Sloan wipes her eyes with one hand before clearing her throat and enunciating: "Yes, Jon—come in."

The door opens and in strides Jonathan Theriot, Sloan's new—well, current, not new—husband and head of security. He looks mistrustfully at me, then to Sloan. She nods at him almost imperceptibly.

"We've just finished up here. Right, Jack?"

"Yeah."

"Well, Mr. Quick, in that case, allow me to show you the best way out of the building. If you'll follow me?" I look over my shoulder as Theriot leads me from the room: Sloan is already back behind her desk, as perfectly composed as when I entered, back at business. Sloan's assistant smirks triumphantly as we pass and Jon shoots me a sideways glance, checking to see if I'll react, but I won't give them the satisfaction. I just keep my eyes forward, as expressionless as possible.

Jon guides me down a side hallway filled with lighting equipment. I'm guessing this isn't so much the quickest exit as the most discreet.

Theriot clears his throat. "So, I see you're flying the colors again, Jack."

"Yeah. It's a whole thing."

"I bet."

"No, really, Jon. I didn't come here to try to win Sloan back or anything like that."

For a moment Theriot looks at me like I'm crazy, then breaks out laughing and claps me on the back. "Hahahaha! Oh fuck, man, you haven't changed a bit. That's the last fucking thing I'm worried about. I mean, don't get me wrong; I'd beat you until your own mother wouldn't recognize you if I really thought that was what you were after. But seeing you, knowing how you are—I know how it works. You're worried about some impending disaster, and you're trying to do whatever you can to fix it. I can hardly blame a guy for that. I don't agree with how you went about it, but I know what's it's like to care about something so much that you lose sight of everything else."

"Well...okay. Long as you're not mad."

"Mad? Oh, I'm plenty mad. Speaking frankly, I could do without ever seeing your weasel face again, not to mention being put in the position of having to escort my wife's ex out of the building. You'd just better pray there aren't any photographers hanging around out in the alley today."

He pushes an undistinguished metal door open, waves me through, and pulls a cigarette pack from his jacket pocket. "Don't tell the old lady. Want one?"

I do, but I shake my head no. He shrugs. "Suit yourself." He takes a deep drag, releases a slow, steady plume of smoke, and shakes his head. "Look, if I get this right, you're serious about getting the costume thing going again and you need help. But you understand Sloan isn't the one to do it, yeah?"

"Yeah, no, I know. I wasn't thinking, Jon."

"You sure weren't. But look: we had this woman on the show a while ago. Wealthy businesswoman, feel-good success story—woman-owned and run company, gives female ex-cons a fresh start, that sort of thing. Anyway, interview goes along fine, she's chatting with Sloan during the breaks, and it turns out she's one of these super-wannabes. Got powers of some sort, a costume, the whole deal. Even a sidekick. Who the hell has a sidekick anymore? Sloan just smiled and waited out the taping, but afterwards she went off for an hour about how the woman kept pumping her for tips on getting into the costume game, stories about her American Rose days and so forth, wouldn't take no for an answer. Sound familiar, yeah?"

"Little bit."

"Anyway, long story short: if you're interested, I can pass on your contact info, maybe see if what you've got going on might be the kind of thing she's looking for."

"Jon, that sounds great. I'll take you up on that."

"Hey, no skin off my ass. She won't be back on the show either way. But who knows—two birds, one stone, all that good shit."

"I really appreciate it, man. And hey, thanks for...well, thanks for believing me."

Mid-inhalation he wheels around, glaring, the end of his cigarette glowing bright red.

"Believe you? No, Jack, I believe you believe this is some big important mission to save humanity or whatever, but outside of that, no, I don't believe you. I can't." He takes one last drag and tosses his cigarette into a coffee can full of identical butts.

I begin to respond; Jon holds up a finger to stop me before continuing: "But! The fact is I love that woman—and the kids—so much, so fucking much, and I know what it'd do to them if anything serious ever happened to you. But you and me? Let's be men here, and let there be no mistake between us. I'll help you out here because of what you mean to Sloan and the kids, but don't interpret that to mean I personally give a fuck or believe in you or anything. Because I do not."

"I get it, Jon. But thank you anyway."

"Thank me by getting the fuck out of here and not coming back." The door latches behind him and he's gone.

* * *

Racing away from Sloan's studio, I'm grateful once more for the solitude my abilities provide. When I'm running the world contracts, as pace by pace the road ahead becomes the road behind. The air rushing by my head drowns my thoughts out until nothing remains but the determination to keep putting one leg in front of the other. The objectivity is comforting: one kilometer is always one kilometer. Didn't get enough sleep? Pulled a leg muscle? Burned by an errant flame blast? Doesn't matter, still thirteen hundred steps to get through each kilometer. Few people will ever know how therapeutic it is to run until the road literally runs out.

Of course, the location of Mystic's tower—okay, fine, the Earthly manifestation of what our consciousnesses perceive as Mystic's tower in three-dimensional space—has been kept a secret among the Fighters for decades. Along with Mystic's defensive spells, this helps prevent unfortunate hunters from randomly stumbling into a dimensional portal to the nether realms or interrupting an astral battle for the soul of mankind.

For these reasons and more, I'm dumbfounded to find at least a dozen people milling about outside the tower. A teenaged boy wearing an asymmetrical haircut and a black leather trenchcoat points: "Jack Quick! Holy shit, it's really him! See babe, I told you—if he's here, it's got to be real!"

A pair of identical-looking girls not older than fifteen exchange glances and speak in unison: "Who's Jack Quick?"

"He was one of the originals! Don't you scuts know anything?"

Their eyes roll and return to their phones.

Haircut boy comes rushing up to me, with a few visibly less-impressed stragglers trailing behind. "Man, ignore them, Jack. You the man!" He juts his chest out, extends his hand, and introduces himself: "I'm Edge!"

It sounds like he's been practicing it for a while. "Uh, Edge? Nice to meet you and all, but what are you doing here?"

"You not here answering the ad? I's starting to think this was just some sort of prank 'til you showed up. Hey, can I get a picture?" I don't answer, but he hands his phone to a sulky dark-haired girl and leans in next to me anyway. "Thanks! Jack, you a for-sure shoe-in with the wayback bonafides you got. When you get in, you give me the nod, yeah?"

"Tell me how you found out about this and I'll think about it."

Haircut looks at me sideways. "Huh, you think you got the invite exclusivo? Naw, bro, it's all about it online, top of page lotsa sites. My girl here even called me in sick to get us over here pronto." Sulky shoots Haircut a look; his eyes widen and his lips babble: "Not that I don't got drive, dude. I give a hundred and ten percent and I never give up. I get it done!"

"Thanks. You've been a big help." I clap him on the back and give his girlfriend a thumbs-up before speeding up to the door.

"Jack, thank gods—a familiar face! What's with all these spring break refugees? Years without a visit, then you show up, and next thing I know I got the entire cast of *Saved By The Bell* banging on my face all morning. That kid with the dumbass haircut knocked every ten minutes for an hour before he got a clue."

"That show was cancelled before any of these people were born, Ken."

"Oh gee, I'm sorry. I don't get much opportunity to update my pop culture references what with being nailed to a door. Next time bring me a damn *People Magazine* if you're so concerned."

"So haircut boy's been here awhile?"

"Yup. That quiet kid in the glasses was first though. Didn't even knock."

"And you haven't let any of them in?"

"Shit, no. I'm not even supposed to let anyone hear me talk without Master Mystic's say-so. The 'scary magic door' bit is reserved for potential threats, and this lot...well, you saw them."

"All right, Ken. I'm going to head in and see what the Master hath wrought. Don't let anyone else in until I find out what the hell's going on."

"I don't take orders from you, numbnuts."

"You won't be taking orders from anyone if I have Mystic turn you into a toilet plunger. Just do it, yeah?"

I slam the door a little harder than necessary and a few seconds later I'm rewarded with the sound of vigorous door knocker abuse. Unfortunately, things on this side of the door aren't making much more sense.

"JACK QUICK! THANKS TO YOUR CUNNING RECRUITMENT STRATEGY, SOON VICTORY SHALL BE WITHIN OUR GRASP."

Well, at least he's not hovering. "Modulate please, Mystic, modulate. And what now?"

"Your strategy was a success, Jack Quick. Within mere minutes of your egress from the tower, your advertisement garnered response from one whose power and abilities shall no doubt allow us to triumph in beating back the darkness: none other than he who is known as the Action Man."

Oh, boy. "Action Man, you say?"

"Aye. And surely it is undeniable that with such a titan of truth so swiftly behind our cause, surely our efforts are destined to culminate in triumph."

"Didn't I say not to talk to anybody until I got back? I could swear I did."

"Oh, I spoke not with the Man of Action. As his initial contact rightly pointed out, such trivialities as auditioning or formal application would be a grievous waste of time for the preeminent superhuman of the modern age. Bearing your words in mind, as well as the immense gravity of the impending event we shall soon face, I immediately sent him the location of my Fortress Mystic, in return for which he avowed to join us as soon as he is able. Gird yourself for action, Jack Quick—for at any second, the battle shall surely be well joined!"

"Yeah, well, don't go printing up new roster announcements yet. What makes you think it was Action Man responding to the ad?"

"He identified himself, Jack Quick. It is well known that Action Man adheres to a strict moral code prohibiting misidentifications and all other such frauds."

"Right, right, that makes perfect sense. One last question: have you looked outside since I left, or taken notice of that banging on the door?"

"I have, Jack Quick, and I must confess that resisting the temptation to edify these mortals regarding the folly of disturbing the Fortress Mystic without leave has been difficult. However, in keeping with your admonitions, I have remained silent ere your return."

I sigh deeply. "All right. Come with me and let's get this cleared up as neatly as possible."

I lead Mystic to the door and kick it open with as much force as I care to muster. It flies back against the wall and I hear Ken mutter a barely-audible "Ow," as it hits with a bang; I make a mental note to apologize later. The dramatic act has served its purpose, though: all eyes are wide and fixed on me. You'd be surprised how much time this kind of thing saves; when you take people off-guard, they tend to react without thinking and fall in line with authority.

I point. "You, glasses—c'mere. Yes, you." Without a word, the kid slides his phone into his pocket and shuffles over. He's just under a meter and a half tall and I'd wager not a day older than fifteen, but I'll give him some credit for looking me in the eye. "Kid, please tell my friend here that Action Man is not en route to join us."

"Um...sorry, yeah, that guy's not coming. Sorry."

"PERFIDIOUS FIEND! HOW HAST THIS MERE STRIPLING DETAINED THE WORLD'S MIGHTIEST DEFENDER?" Master Mystic's hovering and glowing again; the kid crumples to the ground and covers his head with his arms, crying.

"I'msorryI'msorryI'msorryI'msorryIdidn'tmeantoI'msorry"

"Whoa, buddy, hold on. Look kid, I don't know how long I can hold this guy back, so I'd suggest you come clean, tout suite. Otherwise..."

He lowers one hand from his face, peers up at me, and sniffles. "I didn't think anyone would even show up but then people started coming and then more people kept coming and things started getting out of control and do you have to tell anyone?"

I help the idiot to his feet. "Why'd you pretend to be Action Man in the first place?"

He wipes his nose and steals a glance at Mystic's impassive visage. ""I...I was just bored, you know? I didn't think anyone would take it seriously. But when I actually got a response...I couldn't resist, um..."

"Forwarding it to everyone you know?"

"I guess. Then next thing it's on Readit and Facespace and Pinbox and Turnover and then just fucking everywhere. It's like...crazy shit."

"So why'd you even come out here then?"

"Well...I had to see." He shrugs. "You know. Pics or it didn't happen. B-besides, how would anyone even know it was me?"

I gently turn him around, to face eleven pairs of eyes staring agog. "Look around, genius. Notice anything? All these other assholes came dressed for a pop culture convention or a photo shoot. Conversely, you look like you just got cut from the high school badminton team."

"Oh. Yeah."

"Yeah. So, look, how about you go and stand over there for a minute while I try and talk Master Mystic out of turning you into a dung beetle. In the meantime, try not to fuck anything else up, yeah?"

"Y-yeah."

"Thanks." I duck back inside, motion for Mystic to follow, and shut the door behind us. "So, you got that, right? Kudos on your timing cranking up the bad cop routine, by the way."

"What police officer do you speak of, Jack Quick?"

"Never mind. But you understand what happened here, right?"

"The youth transmitted an intentionally deceptive communication, compromising the integrity of our endeavor."

"That's pretty much the sum of it, yeah."

"Then if we are in agreement, the only decision remaining is to settle on what form his punishment should take—corporal dissolution?

Astral death? Or perhaps leniency is called for, such as a mere blinding or mild dismemberment?"

"I don't know, Mystic. How about your punishment for giving out our secret location to an unverified, unknown human?"

"You heard the youth's words, Jack Quick. His actions were those of a liar and a villain. My mission on this plane is explicit as to proper treatment of such individuals."

"Uh huh. Can I see the email?"

"Cast your gaze upon yonder display, and let the craven scoundrel be condemned by his own words."

FROM: actioman@cmail.biz
RE: ESTABLISHED SUPERTEAM RECRUITING 4 HI-STAKES MISSION - GR8 OPPORTUNITY
YO dawg this the Action man. I herd yr call and answr in tha name of JUSTICE AND TRUTH lol. Mos def I got mad power and the need for speed, all that. Sorry no time 4 links, gotta rush off 2 save Argentina from tsunami but just serch "Action Man" and yeah there ya go.
NEway yeah so hit me up an we can go tear it up old skoool
-ACTION MAN

My eyes roll. "Come on, man."

"By what means was I to know this electronic communication was deceptive, Jack Quick?"

"Uh, everything about it? Yes, the kid was trolling you, but this is at least half your fault. Maybe more." Before Mystic can protest, a loud knocking on the front door interrupts us. I grit my teeth and hiss, "Look, just wait here a minute. You put the fear into that kid one more time and someone is going to need to hose off your doorstep."

I'm just about to open the door when the knocking starts up again, even louder than before. My face flushes red, adrenaline surges through my body, and I kick the door open again, striking my best arms-akimbo pose and intoning, "HOW DARE you...interrupt, um..."

I trail off after a few seconds. Glasses is still standing exactly where I told him to, pointing at a dark-suited man on Mystic's doorstep.

"I told him not to, sir! I did!"

"It's true, Mr. Quick. Be comforted this young man performed to the best of his ability, but I'm afraid I simply won't be dissuaded. May I step inside and speak with you a few minutes?" He smiles from behind mirrored sunglasses, one foot already inside the doorway.

"Sorry, we're not currently accepting visitors. And I didn't catch your name?"

As he removes his sunglasses, I realize he waited until this moment to do so in order to punctuate the moment as dramatically as possible. I hate him instantly.

"No, you didn't. And no, you don't have to let me in. But you will, because otherwise I'm going to shut this whole thing down immediately."

He shoves a badge in front of my face. My heart sinks as I read: "Doko, Ric. Senior Field Agent, Department of Extrahuman Abilities & Powers."

He smirks. "Satisfied?"

I nod; he replaces the badge in his pocket. "Good. Now why don't we go inside, sit down, and discuss this thing like rational adults. It's just possible that no one needs go to jail today."

Fuuuuck. "Fine," I say, stepping aside and waving him in. "After you."

"Much appreciated." Doko steps across the threshold, then stops short, turns, and beckons to the terrified kid standing nearby. "Let's go, short stuff. You're coming too."

"M-me? Why?"

"Kid, don't waste my time with stupid questions. Your chances of going home tonight are directly related to how effectively you do exactly what the fuck you're told from here on out."

Glasses hustles through the doorway with Doko tight on his heels, grimacing almost imperceptibly as he passes. I hustle to pull the door shut before any other potential applicants start getting ideas; at the back of the crowd I spot even more would-be heroes arriving by the carload. Too many more and we're going to have to hire a parking attendant—or at least a bouncer.

* * *

Agent Jerkwad marches Glasses in, sits him down at the table, and parks himself in Mystic's favored chair. The tone of surprise in Mystic's voice almost makes it worth it.

"Jack Quick, be these mortals foolhardy—or tired of living?"

Glasses coughs and points: "Hey man, this guy dragged me in here."

Doko tents his fingers before him. "Master Mystic, Mr. Quick: if you'd be kind enough to allow me a few minutes, I believe I can sort this out in a way that will work out far better for everyone. Please, have a seat."

For a second, I think Mystic's going to flip out. Fortunately he sits instead, though not without muttering "We shall see," under his breath. I take the seat next to Mystic; Doko places his badge identification on the table and clears his throat.

"Thank you, gentlemen. To properly introduce myself, my name is Ric Doko, and I am the designated Department of Extrahuman Abilities & Powers officer for this half of the state. Unfortunately for all of us, that makes me ultimately responsible for whatever is going down here today, both in the eyes of the federal government and—most relevant to me and the vacation I've had planned and scheduled for eight full months—my immediate supervisor.

"Just after tucking into my lunch today—a generous helping of leftover enchiladas packed for me by my lovely wife, thanks for asking—I received a priority override message from said aforementioned supervisor, asking whether I was aware of what was going on out here and what, if anything, I was doing to ensure the situation was under control. Naturally, I was surprised to hear about this, but I've been doing this job too long to get fucked now—so I feigned a choking fit and hung up the phone, buying myself time to do a little quick research. Do you know what I found?" He looks around the table. "Nobody? Fine, I'll just show you."

He pulls a piece of paper from his pocket and tosses it beside his badge. I lean up to read it; no one else moves.

WANT 2B A HERO? OPEN AUDITIONS TODAY ONLY - ALL APPLICANTS WELCOMED

Hey! Did you always want to be a hero with one of the world's greatest hero groups? Well NOW'S YOUR OPPORTUNITY!

We NEED people who want to be heroes and don't have time to waste. NO PREVIOUS EXPERIENCE NECESSARY! The only requirement is: you MUST show up today! All applicants who can come to 668 Neighbortree Road (off Rural Route 9) between 1 and 7 TODAY ONLY will be given a shot!

Qualified applicants will be offered salaried positions complete with substantial benefits packages including health insurance featuring extranormal provisions. No age limits, no power too small! Hope to see you TODAY!

I hold my head. "Oh. Fuuuuuuck."

"Yes, Mr. Quick. That is what I said as well. Now, because I'm good at my job, I recognized that address as the location of the fortress where we now sit. So, I call my boss back to tell her I'm on top of the situation, then I place another call and get the number of the phone used to place this ad. As it turns out, that phone is registered to a Christine Ghazini, a forty-three year-old, divorced loan officer from Mishawaka with sole custody of her son Edwin."

Glasses sinks lower in his chair.

"Now that we're all caught up, I'm going to do you boys a huge favor: I'm going to give you all the benefit of the doubt and assume you're exactly as dumb as you seem, which is the best case scenario by far. Because otherwise you'd be making a real asshole out of me here, and no one wants that, right? So, Edwin, please save us all a lot of time and tell us what you did."

"No one calls me Edwin, it's just E."

Doko rolls his eyes and sighs deeply. "No one cares, Edwin. Please just provide the answers I asked for. Now."

"I-I put the ad up."

"After…"

"After he sent the address to me thinking I was Action Man."

"Now we're getting somewhere. So…"

"Look, Mr. Doko, I appreciate your help, really I do. But now that the troublemaker has been identified, I think we can handle it from here."

"See, Mr. Quick, that's where you're wrong. I don't think you can, and here's why: while young Mr. Ghazini here did cause me some annoyance by interrupting my lunch, he also did me a favor by alerting me to the fact that a couple of guys who really, really ought to know better are trying to form a new superteam in my district, on my watch, practically under my nose, without me knowing about it."

"What do you mean?"

"What do I mean? Come on, Quick, let's not drag this out any longer than necessary. Do you really think you can just gather a bunch of highly powered individuals together out here in the boonies with no oversight? Never mind the fact that there haven't been any successful new groups in the last fifteen years; before you can even pick out team colors or make up a battle cry you need to be approved to operate on local, state, and federal levels."

"There have too been new groups in the last fifteen years! The Kinetix, for one, and the, uh, the Savior Squad! And I know there were at least one or two others."

Doko shakes his head. "I can't imagine it will shock you too deeply to learn that those are all government-created teams. They make more appearances at schools and malls than they do actual crimefighting. For the kids, you know? It's show business. Bread and circuses."

"Well…that's not the way it was in our day."

"Exactly, Mr. Quick, exactly. Finally you recognize the problem: we're no longer in your day."

"ENOUGH!" Mystic slams a gauntleted fist onto the table; E flinches so hard I think he's going to hit the ceiling. "WHILE YOU MORTALS BLATHER, UNFATHOMABLE DOOM APPROACHES ALL!"

Doko isn't fazed. I get the feeling he's seen this kind of thing before, more than once.

"I'm sure it is, Master Mystic, but that doesn't fix our problem. Now, the simplest thing for me by far would be to shut this whole thing down, go home, and cross off another day on the calendar until I'm basking in sweet, sunny San Diego. But let's say you're right, hm? It doesn't look good if the planet ends on my watch. True, the proper thing for you to do would have been to register this gathering at least thirty days in advance, but as you well know, that didn't happen. And now, well, here we all are."

"Look, Mr. Doko, I'm sorry about that. We really weren't trying to put one over on you or get away with anything, we just didn't know anything about any of these rules. From this point forward, though, we'll do our best to comply."

Doko smiles. "Oh, I know. Because I'm going to do you guys a huge, huge favor."

"What's that?"

"I'm going to sit right here and help select your team members. And after that, I'm going to sit in on every meeting, check every report you turn in, and generally make sure you follow the law of the land to the letter. And even when I finally do manage to go on vacation, my buddy Edwin here is going to sit right here and stream the meetings to me."

"Wait, I can't—"

"Before you object, Sparky, let me explain something: either you have a new part-time job or you have pending charges of electronic harassment. Now, in the former case it's your call how and whether to break the news to your mother, but in the latter? Well, I'm afraid I don't have any choice."

"Fine," E grumbles.

"I knew you wouldn't let me down. What about you two?"

Mystic doesn't look any happier than the kid. "This is not the assemblage I had envisioned, Jack Quick."

"Yeah, I've got to say this isn't really how I pictured this going down either."

"Look, if it helps you guys, that was never going to happen anyway. You were already on our radar thanks to your little ad; this little shit just managed to speed the process up about a thousand percent."

"All right, Doko. I guess we'll do it your way."

"Oh, don't look so downcast. Because now that we're all officially signed off, I can quit with the preliminaries and tell you all exactly how this is going to go." Doko smirks as E groans. "Save that 'til later. Trust me—this is going to get a lot worse before it gets any better."

* * *

"Alright, the first thing is that as long as you operate as a team of powered heroes, consider yourselves employees of the federal government."

"Um, what if we..."

"Mr. Quick, we have a lot of ground to cover, not much time to do it in, and you'll just end up asking the same questions everyone does. If you will please let me continue, I guarantee your queries will be answered by the time I'm finished. Deal?"

"Well, I—"

"Fantastic. Anyway, to answer the question you were undoubtedly about to ask, any team of powered individuals lacking official sanction is legally classified as a 'villain gang,' and all law enforcement assets for controlling organized crime will be brought to bear on said individuals. In fact, even if you two take nothing else away from this little talk, you need to understand this: the federal government takes unregulated use of extranormal powers very, very seriously. Maybe back in your day, any random asshole who got bitten by a radioactive mongoose could pick a name and a costume and run around punching punks and commies with impunity, but it doesn't work that way anymore."

"It didn't work that way back then, either."

"I'm sure you're right, Quick. But just so we're clear, let me ask you this: can you honestly say you don't think regulation of powers is necessary and justified?"

"That's not what I'm saying."

"Good, because for a minute there I thought you might have been advocating the overthrow of the federal government through violent means, and if I ever thought that I'd definitely have to report such a thing to my superiors, who would then be forced to take immediate and appropriate action to ensure the continued security of the republic. You see what I'm getting at?"

"Yeah, I get it. We play by your rules or not at all."

"Wrong. First, they're not my rules: they're the people's rules—or the people's government's rules, depending on your particular political bias. Either way, you don't have to respect me, but if you don't respect one of those two things we're going to have a problem sooner or later.

"And second, you don't play, period. This is work. Government work, yes, but work nonetheless. All members will be—must be—compensated for their time in accordance with federal guidelines, as well as provided with medical coverage, retirement programs, and other benefits. Now, the less time I have to spend spoon-feeding you, the happier we'll all be, so I'd recommend the team leaders—that's you two—bone up on basic business law, group dynamics, and project management. Once we get the rest of the new Fighters picked out, I'll have some reference materials sent over."

I clear my throat. "Actually, I'm not sure I really want to be a team leader. I figured that everyone would vote once the membership was settled, to keep it fair. And to tell the truth, I'm not entirely comfortable using the Fighters name, either. I mean, it's just the two of us from the old gang."

Doko sighs, rubbing the bridge of his nose. "See, this is why this would go so much faster if you'd just be quiet and let me talk. When not impractical, your ideas are outdated. When not outdated, your ideas are illegal."

"What the hell's that supposed to mean?"

"All right, look; cards on the table, okay? All appearances aside, I'm on your side here. And I'm sorry to speak bluntly, but it's obvious to anyone with eyes to see that you two don't have a fucking clue what you're doing. I'm pulling for you, I really am, but there's only one way this has even a prayer of working, and that means you need to listen carefully and follow my directives to the letter."

"We never—"

"I get it. This isn't how you did things back in the day. But since you put that costume away, a metric shit-ton of laws have passed covering use of extranormal powers for any purpose whatsoever. Fortunately for you, the one thing all those laws have in common is that they're subject to a grandfather clause built into the original Extranormal Powers Regulation Act, the wording of which specifies that any powered group pre-existing the Act's passage may continue to operate relatively unmolested. Legacy heroes don't count—the Incorporated Sons of Justice wasted their inheritances challenging that one—but it seems to me that with two original founders sitting here, you have an arguably valid claim to reactivating the Fighters."

Doko jerks a thumb towards the front door. "Why do you think all those hopeless cases flocked here so quickly? They've got nowhere else to go. Hell, I recognize half of them from my case files—a bunch of desperate wannabes and no-hopers who hassle the Department relentlessly for even the smallest opportunities to get into the hero game. Never mind their utter lack of either power or suitability."

"Great. So let's go out there, you can point them out and send them home, and we can get on with it."

"Oh, no no no no. Some of these assholes have been waiting years for their big break. They all saw me come in here, and if they don't get their fair shot at making the team you can bet they'll be waiting outside my office first thing tomorrow. Trust me, they know better than anyone how tight the rules regarding this kind of thing are—some of them have been looking for a loophole for years."

"So what do you want us to do about it?"

"Well...if I was in your place, I'd step outside, apologize for the delay, and ask everyone to line up. A lot of these shmucks are hardwired for the 'outsider who plays by his own rules' archetype, so that'll probably trim a few right away. Whoever's left, we bring them in for interviews one by one, ask a few questions and let them run through their spiels—trust me, they'll all have one—and they'll go home happy."

Doko catches my eye and glances over at Mystic, who's been sitting silently long enough to make us both nervous. I cough and try to pull him into the discussion: "Well Mystic, how's this all sitting with you?"

"All of this nonsense is meaningless. When all is wiped clean from the slate of existence, petty regulations will not stave off the darkness."

"Right, okay." I give Doko my best 'Help me out here, bro' shrug, hoping he's sitting on some strategy for handling recalcitrant immortal entities.

"Master Mystic, if I'm reading this correctly, you're the one who initiated this reactivation of the Fighters. While I understand this may not be the way you pictured it getting done, I promise you it's the fastest possible route to you getting what you want. Go ahead and use some sort of truth detection spell on me if you need reassurance."

"Why do you suppose I haven't already, mortal?"

"Fair enough. But is this upcoming crisis you're worried about going to hit within the next thirty-six hours?"

"Death may come at any moment. None truly knows the hour of his fate until it is upon him—and perhaps not even then."

"Right. But assuming that hour isn't in the next day and half, we can get a properly sanctioned, one hundred percent legal team of powers in place to help you handle it when it does come. You get what you want, I get what I want, everyone's happy except this dumbshit kid who thought it was a good idea to punk a wizard who can see through time. Is that acceptable to you?"

E squirms in his chair for a full fifteen seconds before Mystic finally intones, "It is acceptable."

"Great. Now that we're all on the same page, let's get this circus rolling." Doko pulls his chair over to the far side of the table. "I'll oversee the proceedings from here, where I'm clearly not involved in the decision-making process. E, you take notes. Jack..."

"Yeah, yeah, I'll run the interrogations. Anything particular you need me to ask?"

"Interviews, not interrogations. And you only need to ask them one thing: 'Tell me about your power.' Anything else and you're doing more work than necessary, which is counter to the spirit of a government job. Frankly, given the questions you've asked so far, I think we'll be just as well off if you keep any others that spring to mind to yourself, but I'll leave that in your hands. Just steer clear of religion and sexual orientation, yeah?"

As I get up to open the front door, I swear I hear Mystic sigh. It might just have been the wind, though.

* * *

Of course, the kid with the haircut is first in line. "First up, we have, uh...Edge, right? Oh, I'm sorry—one at a time, please, miss."

"S'okay, she's with me. Here, babe—hold this for me?" Edge passes his trenchcoat to the dark-haired girl by his side, revealing a sleeveless Union Jack t-shirt and a studded belt beneath. I'm surprised he didn't spring for leather pants to complete the ensemble, but perhaps the cost proved prohibitive.

"Is this a team act?"

"Nah, we just do everything together. Wouldn't want my girl to miss out on a moment like this!"

Doko stares down at his phone, interest gone. E steals a sideways glance at Edge's girlfriend's chest, to her visible annoyance. Edge proffers a handshake towards Mystic's unmoving, unresponsive form; after he holds his hand in the air for five seconds, I take pity on the kid, reach over, shake his hand once and release it.

"Well, Edge, thanks for coming in. And, um..."

"Christine."

"...Christine, please have a seat over there. So, Edge, what've you got for us today?"

"All right!" He strides to the center of the room and strikes a dramatic pose I recognize from a popular dorm room poster of the Gentleman Detective. "Before I get started, I want to thank you for this opportunity to show you what I was born to do." He takes a stance as if a wrestling match is imminent, raising both arms above his head. "Because what I was born to do...is kick ass!"

Edge claps his hands together with a bang, blue plasma discharge glows between his fingers, and the smell of ozone fills the room. He raises one crackling fist above his head and points with the other; E and I both crane our necks to see what he's pointing at before realizing he's just striking another pose.

Edge nods. Out of the corner of my eye, I see an apple come flying past my head, and E flinches. A burst of cobalt electricity from Edge's palm engulfs the airborne fruit, which falls sizzling at his feet. Edge leans down to pick it up, smiles, and takes a bite: "Just like Grandma used to make."

I lean forward, drumming my fingers. "Okay, Edge, the power blasts are a definite plus, and we can always use someone with a distance attack. But what kind of control do you have over voltage and amperage? Do you need a refractory period after using the power?"

"A...what?"

"Do you have to...take a break and wait a bit before you can go again?"

Christine giggles; Edge seems to get the idea.

"Oh. Nah, dude. I get charged up, I go for a while. Check this!" Tossing the still-steaming apple onto the table, Edge passes chain lightning back and forth between his hands, crackling like a Tesla coil in an old Frankenstein movie.

"Very impressive. Any combat skills?"

"Me and my girl took some karate classes down at the Y together, and I beat down a cowboy dude hassling me outside a bar one time, no powers involved...so, you know."

"All right, Edge. I guess I don't have any other questions. Bear in mind that you are the very first person we've seen today, but I have to say you seem like a pretty strong candidate."

Edge pumps his fist and exclaims, "Badass!" His girlfriend claps her hands together and smiles.

"A-hem." Doko looks up from his phone for the first time since Edge stepped into the room. "I have one request: can your girlfriend step outside?"

Edge scowls. "Man, if you got a problem with her, you got a problem with me."

"I don't have a problem with her, but I might have a problem with you. Members of this team must, of course, be prepared to follow orders without question. So I'll ask just once more: can your girlfriend leave the room?"

"I have a right to be here too!"

Doko smirks. "Are you auditioning for this team? If not, then actually, no, you don't."

She tears up, her face contorted in anger. "F-fuck you, you jerk. You don't know what you're doing!"

"I have a feeling I do." Doko picks the apple off the table and gestures toward the door with it. "Either way, I'm afraid I must ask you to take your leave of us now."

Edge looks like he's about to flip out, but Christine strokes his arm reassuringly. "It's okay, baby, I'll just be right on the other side of the door. Right on the other side."

Doko watches as she strides to the door, Edge's trenchcoat clutched to her chest. The second the latch clicks behind her, Doko wheels around on Edge.

"Okay. Think fast!"

Like a major-league pitcher, Doko whips the apple directly at Edge's head. Edge shields himself with his arm, the apple caroms off Edge's bony elbow, rolls off the table, and settles at Doko's feet.

"What's the matter, son? Batteries running low?" He picks up the apple.

"No, I just...I just wasn't ready."

"Oh, okay. One more then?" He winds up as if he's going to throw again, and Edge flinches. When he turns back, his face is downcast with humiliation, while Doko's is suffused with triumph.

"That's what I thought. Go join your girlfriend, kid."

"What's...what is this, Doko?"

"Seen this kind of thing before, especially with teenage couples: one's got powers, the other wants to be a hero. Put them together and they make one ultralame combo." Doko's tone is that of a burned out kindergarten teacher explaining arithmetic to a pack of collies. "Most often, guys try to search out young powergirls online, convince them they're in love, then figure out a way to steal their powers and drop them cold. That what you got going on here, Johnny Rancid? A nice little scam?"

"Screw you, asshole. We're in love."

"I bet you are. Until she stops using those powers to help you, right? Either way, thank you, don't come again."

Edge's face twists in fury, and for a second I think he's going to leap at Doko. Instead, he turns and stomps out, his shoulders slumping with each step.

As the door slams, Doko meets my astonished gaze.

"What?"

"I don't get it. Why would they even try to lie to get in? They'd die the minute we got in a fight."

"It's not about that. People are desperate for power however they can find it, and social connection with a superteam is the most common factor in non-inherited origin stories. Think about it: didn't a bunch of teams back in your day used to have a mascot or some other regular dude hanging around for no good reason? And how many of those dudes didn't end up getting powers?"

"Point."

"Anyway, a lot of wannabes think if they manage to get in with a superteam and stick it out long enough, they're bound to get their turn. Circular logic, but 'fake it 'til you make it' isn't the worst advice anyone ever followed."

I see a light go on in E's eyes as something clicks in his head. "Wait, what? I don't want to get powers!"

"Have no fear, I'm here to prevent that from happening. And hopefully even God wouldn't be so cruel as to inflict that upon this poor world. Besides, you should really be focusing on the present place and time rather than worrying about things you have no control over."

"H-how?"

Doko rolls his eyes. "Just admit the next applicant before we all die waiting."

* * *

Unsurprisingly, even after seeing all the applicants, we still have a problem.

"This is utterly unacceptable, Jack Quick. It is improper that all of the selected candidates be females."

I rub my temples. "Look, Mystic, you saw the same crop of candidates we did. What penis-endowed candidate would you prefer above the names on this list?"

"Any endowed candidate would be preferable."

Doko's head whips around. "Whoa, there. This group is coming to a quick end before it even starts if you maintain that line of thought. I can hear heads exploding at the Department of Labor already."

"Regardless, the point is indisputable. In combat situations, females are disadvantaged." I'm incredulous Mystic was able to come up with a euphemism that's almost not insulting.

Regardless, Doko isn't buying what he's selling. "No, in any group of powers our primary qualifying criterion is powerset. And among today's applicants, the most viable, legitimate powers just happened to belong to women. Electrikid has years of verifiable sidekick experience, a stint with the Last Losers, and over a dozen documented team-ups under her belt, while Tekno Knight..."

"That one lacks any inborn power or abilities. Moreover, her very name is erroneous, as no females were permitted among the ranks of knights."

"Yes, and thanks so much for blurting that out first thing during her interview. For a second I thought we'd lost her right there."

"That outcome would have been preferable."

"Not if you want this thing to work. And speaking to her abilities, she built that suit in her garage during her spare time, using consumer-grade equipment. At the very least, that's evidence of preeminent skill placing her in the upper percentile of human ability—possibly even a low-level mutation. Either way, she absolutely qualifies."

"This is not the group of Fighters I had envisioned."

"Tough cookies, Merlin. As long as your tower here is located in this country, it's this group of Fighters or none. Unless you have any ideas for superior candidates?"

"As I have repeatedly reiterated, the tower exists everywhere and nowhere, and it is only its physical aspect that..."

"Yes, fine; not the point. Either way, without a viable roster to send up the flagpole, this ends here and now. My superiors aren't going to rubber-stamp any random gaggle of halfwits, especially if it was selected based on prejudicial attitudes that went out with men's hats. Frankly, the names I wrote down here are the only ones likely to pass inspection. What about you, Quick—you got any problems with this list?"

"Not really, but isn't it a little short? I mean, basically what we're looking at here isn't much more than the two of us, Electrikid, and Tekno Knight. This last one wasn't even an applicant."

Doko isn't fazed for a second. "You let me worry about that."

I shake my head. "I'm just worried we won't have a group if these people decide against joining."

"What, do you think they took their time to come out here on a weekday because they didn't want to join up? Please."

"No, but…I guess I'm not sure we're really offering what they think they're after."

Doko waves his hand. "Who gives a shit? If they have a problem they can take a walk."

"That shall be acceptable."

"Shocker, Magic Dick takes the hard line. But seriously, Quick, try to remember who's in charge here. If worse comes to worst, I'll put E here down as a mascot or sidekick-in-training to get the body count up to a respectable level."

"I…I'm not sure I'm comfortable with that."

"No one asked you, Edwin."

"What about out in the field? There are entire ranges of power we haven't any means of addressing: psychic assaults? Weather manipulation? Sonic attack?" My head is hurting thinking of all the ways people have to kill us. "Maybe we should go back through the reject pile one more time, make sure we didn't miss anyone with potential."

"Jack, Jack…it's good that you're thinking about these things, really it is. But ultimately, very little of this is up to any of us. You already know everyone we put in the reject pile is there for a very good reason. If someone has what it takes, they'll make it through one way or another, and if they don't have it, they'll never make it no matter what we or anyone else does to help them. It's just the way it is. But look, don't stress too much: all we're really looking for today is a starting point. I mean, even if E here actually had been the Action Man, you still wouldn't have all the bases covered."

"We'd be a damn sight closer. What happens if something comes up we're not prepared to handle?"

"Same as the last couple of decades, Quick: someone else takes care of it."

"People could be dying out there while you're dicking around with red tape!"

"I'll be damned if I'm going to let you take unqualified powered individuals into the field without proper guidance."

"You may be damned in any case, mortal."

"I can't say I'd be at all surprised, Mystic. Regardless, I'm not having another Levittown happening on my watch, so no one gets to go around calling themselves the New Fighters without my approval—end of story."

My cheeks flush; I can't believe this prick has the balls to talk like that, right to my face. "That's hitting below the belt, Doko. You know I wouldn't let anything like Levittown happen."

"No, I don't know. You seem like a good guy, Jack, and I think you mean well, but this is my job and I take it seriously. That makes it my responsibility to make sure everything goes according to plan, so if that doesn't work for you, tell me right here and now and we can just shut this whole thing down before it goes any further."

The moment yawns. I'm backed into a corner and Doko knows it; my only option is to save face as best as possible. "Fine," I sputter. "Go ahead and do what you want, but don't bother asking my opinion in the future if it's just to pay lip service."

"It's not what I want, Jack. It's what the law wants."

"The law doesn't 'want' anything, you arrogant jackass," I mutter just loudly enough to be heard. The argument decisively lost, I choose to stalk out rather than suffer Doko's smug expression of triumph.

I slam the door behind me. It hits with a satisfying thud and I brace for a barrage of questions from Ken, but fortunately his tongue remains still. Counting my blessings, I plant my butt on the stoop and release something between a groan, a yawn, and a sigh.

"Rough day, huh?"

I nearly jump into the next county. "Oh, shit—you startled me."

Leaning up against the wall behind me is a scrawny, unkempt kid of about twenty, wearing an unseasonable—and filthy—ski hat.

I take a shot in the dark and ask, "Say, you don't happen to smoke?" Frankly, he looks the type.

He shakes his head. "Sorry. My dad used to. Turned me right off the habit."

"Eh, it's for the best. I quit years—er, decades ago myself. Every so often I just get the urge in stressful situations. So...yeah, I guess you could say it's been a rough day."

"I feel you. Okay if I sit?"

"Have at it."

He plops down next to me. We stare at the treeline in silence, the leaves blowing with the wind as the sun descends and the air begins to chill. The quiet helps to salve my jangling nerves, overstimulated from hours of interviews, discussion, and arguing, and after a few minutes I begin to feel like myself again. It's a good thing he didn't have any smokes, or I'd be regretting it right about now.

As the sun sinks behind the trees, I clear my throat and turn toward the kid. "So what's your story, son? I didn't see you auditioning in there. Still might be time for one more if you want to give it a shot."

"Nah, s'ok. I just wanted to come out and see the commotion. I'm not really the joining type."

"You want to know something, kid? Not many really are. I just fell into this thing after I got my powers, and more or less everyone I know has basically the same story—we didn't aim for this, we ended up here. People who get obsessed with this racket—the chosen ones, the ones who train from birth—they mostly either crack up from the pressure or smarten up and move on to something else."

"Or they die."

"Yeah. That happens. That's one reason people move on, a real good one. Still, a lot of the time I think my problem is I was never clever enough to figure out how to beat the game, but not dumb enough to be a villain."

"You think villains are dumb?"

"Eh...maybe 'dumb' isn't the right word for all of them. Some are just crazy—and sure, some are what I'd call truly evil, whatever that is.

But yeah, for the most part the average villain is just a person who's a little too dense to consider the consequences of their actions. It isn't inferior ethics that makes someone a villain so much as lack of aptitude for socialization."

"But what about cases where someone is right and the law is wrong? After all, slavery was legal not all that long ago."

"Why does everyone keep bringing slavery up today?"

"Sorry. Didn't realize it was a touchy subject."

"It's not. Well, it is, but not like…oh, never mind. Anyway, sure, the law is wrong sometimes, but that's mostly a byproduct of society changing over time. Very rarely does any culture produce an individual who is so far ahead of the curve they can properly envision and enact social change within that framework—that's why we have holidays named after most of the people who were good at it. And anyway, for the most part those aren't the kind of problems that get solved by hitting things."

"I guess not. But some of those guys think they're justified, right?"

"Well, yeah. And those are the tough ones. A dude trying to steal money, that's easy to understand, or someone with a political beef against the country for whatever reason. And crazy people, well, they're just sick. But I won't lie; the fanatics can really get inside your head sometimes, the smart ones at least. They're the ones whose words come back to haunt you late at night, when you're staring at the ceiling, wondering if you made the right choices."

By now, the sun has dipped beneath the horizon; the air seems dramatically colder in the deepening darkness. I feel faintly ridiculous. "Sorry, kid—didn't mean to get off on such a downer tangent."

"Nah, don't worry. I been thinking about that kind of stuff a lot myself lately. Strange times. But it's starting to get chilly, and I gotta get moving."

"Yeah, I've got to run too. Good talking to you." I stand and stretch my back with a pop. "I didn't catch your name? I guess the costume is kind of a giveaway, but I'm Jack Quick."

He extends his hand toward me with a grin. "Yeah, I figured. Actually, my name's Jack too."

Returning his handshake, I'm pleased to find my new friend isn't one of those assholes who seem to think any handshake that doesn't result in crushed fingers is a failure. "Really? Always glad to meet another Jack."

"Yeah, I was named after my dad. Maybe you remember him: Jack Frost?"

A blast of intense cold travels up my arm, and I try to yank my hand back, but too late: I literally can't move a muscle. My eyes begin to fog over and as my senses recede, Jack Frost Junior smirks, yanking his knit hat off to reveal pointed, elfin ears like his father's. His lips are moving, although I can't make out what he's saying any longer.

It doesn't matter, though. I know well enough why he's here, and as darkness envelops me I curse myself for at least the thousandth time.

EPISODE TWO: HEROES ASSEMBLED

Doko clicked the starter on his keychain and replaced it in his pocket as his blandly anonymous government-issue sedan rumbled to life.

"You good to get home on your own, E? Easy enough to toss that bike in the back."

"N-no, thanks. If you want me back here tomorrow like you said, my mom doesn't need to be seeing any government agents bringing me home."

"Suit yourself. We'll have to come up with a plausible cover story soon enough anyway. Let me know if you need help—if she isn't the type to buy the standard 'All good young people of today, ask not what you can do' line of bullshit, I can get creative—file some papers, call in some favors, and make it look good for you."

"Th-thanks. I'll, uh, I'll let you know."

Doko stepped into the car. "Last chance on that ride? Okay, kid—see you tomorrow." As he slammed the door behind him, the vehicle's onboard system chimed and a synthesized female voice cooed, "Welcome back, Agent Doko. How may I s—"

"Command," Doko interrupted. "D.E.A.P. database query, electric slash all. Female. First name, Christine. Include all diminutives, hyphenates, and variants. Cross reference against OJS records, age seventeen and under. Locale limit, this county plus twenty kilometer radius."

"Results: null set."

"Yeah, I thought that would've been too easy. Delete first name and gender parameters, widen age range to...nineteen and under. Also, add all state juvenile screening results to scope and widen geomap radius another twenty k."

"Results: null set."

Doko scratched his temple. "Well, there's no way those two came from further than that. Not without a speed power, not in that time. What am I missing?" Easing the transmission into gear, he accelerated smoothly onto the road back toward town as annoyance creased his brow. "Call home."

The phone rang four times before the line opened and another, significantly more human-sounding female voice filled the car's interior: "Hey, baby."

"Hey there. I'm running late but I'm on my way home. Long day, I'll tell you about it later."

"Aww, poor baby. Did you need anything special waiting for you when you get here?"

"Just you, baby. Just you."

"You're so corny."

"You bring it out in me. Anyway, I'm heading north on the one-oh-five now, so I shouldn't be too long."

"Okay, baby. See you soon."

As soon as the line closed, Doko resumed: "Command. D.E.A.P. database query: female, powerset categories: all. Cross reference OJS and state records, age nineteen and under, locale county geomap plus twenty k."

"Result set: three hundred twenty six."

"Create spreadsheet, fields: name, age, location, power rating, power categorization. Sort by power rating, output to tablet."

He pulled the car to the side of the road and extracted a black tablet from a concealed side pocket in the vehicle's door. "Should have figured I'd have to do this the hard way," Doko muttered as he scrolled through the list, briefly scrutinizing each entry before proceeding to the next. "No...no...haha, no...no...hmm."

After seven minutes, a triumphant grin spread across his face. "Gotcha," he murmured.

Doko double-clicked the location field on the tablet; in response, the car's onboard navigation system lit up. "Estimated arrival: eleven minutes."

"Perfect. Oh, and text home. Standard dinner delay message, time field forty minutes."

* * *

To Doko's eye, the squat, boxy house looked virtually identical to the one beside it, and the one beside that. It continued on that way all the way down the street, as far as the eye could or would want to see.

Doko leaned against his car, inhaling chemical vapor while gathering what intel he could from the silhouettes dancing across shut curtains and the muffled sounds of life within. The nicotine delivery system he'd been using for a year still satisfied little but his wife's anxiety over his old habit, but he consoled himself that at least it didn't set neighboring dogs to barking the way real smoke would have.

His nicotine capsule exhausted, Doko packed his vaporizer away in the vehicle's glovebox and deliberately slammed his car door louder than necessary as advance notice of his pending arrival. He was gratified to see a curtain pull back from the front window as he paced up the gravel driveway; strangers tended to be met with suspicious glares that far out in the boonies, if not the business end of a weapon—and he knew all too well that people are rarely at their best when cornered or surprised.

As Doko stepped onto the front porch he heard a series of locks being disengaged. The door opened inward until stopped short by a privacy chain.

A single eye peered through the narrow gap. "Yes...?"

"Good evening, ma'am. I'm sorry for bothering you at this hour. My name is Ric Doko, and I'm an officer of the Department of Extrahuman Abilities & Powers."

"Oh god, what did she do? I always knew this day would come!"

"It's nothing serious, ma'am. But if you don't mind, I'd like to come in and speak with you and your family for a few minutes."

"Y-yes, of course. Just a moment." As she dislodged the chain, a sudden gust of wind caught the door, blowing it back against the wall and causing the woman to leap with a start. "Oh, I'm sorry! Uh, Henry?"

A gravelly voice called out, "The hell is going on in there?"

"There's a policeman at the door, Henry. Put that videogame down and get in here!"

"Ma'am, I'm not a police officer, I—"

"Hey, that's not a cop."

"No, as I was just saying, I—"

"Henry, don't antagonize the man! He's from the government!"

"It's okay, Ange, I hear you. You here for Ellie, Mister?"

"Ellie being your…"

"Her daughter." Henry looked at Doko sideways, like a crafty spaniel. "You're with the Extranormal Powers Department, aren't you?"

"Yes—my identification."

"Nice badge."

"Thank you." Doko tucked it back into his pocket. "Now, is Ellie home?"

"Yeah, sure. C'mon in. Sorry about Angie, she gets a little jumpy answering the door after dark. Gonna take her a couple hours to get her head right." Henry held the door open and turned back to address the woman cowering by the hallway as Doko stepped inside. "Ange, I got it, don't worry. You go lie on the bed and take some calmdown medicine, yeah?"

"Okay, baby. I-I will." She scuttled away sideways, not taking her eyes off Doko until she rounded the corner and disappeared.

Henry shut the door behind Doko. "Alright, buddy, how about you come on out to the back patio with me for a few minutes and you can tell me what this is all about."

"I'm sorry, sir, but if you don't mind, I don't really have a lot of time to spare, and I really just need to speak with Ellie."

"Ah, okay. Yeah, I gotcha." Henry led Doko though the living room into a small kitchen, reached into the refrigerator and extracted two longneck beers. "Now, that being said, how about you come on out to the patio with me for a few minutes and tell me what this is all about."

"Uh...okay. But no beer for me, thanks. Still on duty."

"Who said this was for you? Just saving myself a trip." Henry nudged the kitchen's backdoor open with his foot, stepped outside, and parked himself in a battered lawnchair. Snatching up an opener from an end table fashioned from a chunk of tree stump, he opened both bottles and gestured towards a second lawnchair nearby. "Have a seat."

Doko followed him to the backyard but remained standing, arms crossed. "Does Ellie have a boyfriend?"

"Don't think you're exactly her type. And you're kind of old for her, even if you weren't sporting that ring."

"Funny stuff. Please just answer the question, sir."

Henry finished a third of his bottle in one swig, fired up a cigarette, sat back and stared up at him. "Look—Doko, right? Doko, if you haven't figured yet, Ellie ain't here right now, her mother ain't the responsible adult of this house, and this high-handed govvie spook act of yours don't impress me much. So here's how this is gonna go: either you accept my hospitality, sit down, and we have a conversation like reasonable adults, or you can keep it up and I'll tell you jack fucking squat. Either way, for the next few minutes I'm planning on sitting right here, drinking my beer and smoking my cigarette—so the way I see it, the ball's in your court, chief."

Doko gritted his teeth. "Henry, I really am here with Ellie's best interest in mind."

"Why don't you just tell me what you're here about? I'll decide whether it's in Ellie's best interest."

Doko sat.

"There you go," Henry said. "Last chance on that tallboy?"

"No, but, ah...if you're offering, I will take one of those smokes."

* * *

"Honey? You awake?" Henry tapped the bedroom door so quietly

Doko doubted anything human could hear, but after a few seconds the door creaked open just enough for an eye to peep out.

"Is...is he gone, Henry?"

"No, Ange, Mister Doko's right here. He and I just need to ask you something."

Her eye widened as she saw Doko standing behind Henry. "Ah...hello, sir. I'm sorry, I just get a little confused sometimes."

Doko shook his head. "It's all right, ma'am, don't worry about it. I appreciate any help you're able to provide."

Henry cleared his throat and enunciated, "Okay, Ange, I need you to focus. You know that boy Edge that Ellie's been seeing lately? What's his real name?"

"Daryl, I think? Something like that. Derek? No, Darin. With an 'i'."

"That does help, ma'am, but I'm afraid it's his last name that I really need."

"Ah." Her gaze drifted to the floor and remained there. "Well...I want to say Fuller but I think that's just because he reminds me of a boy I used to know from high school. He lived on Fuller Drive."

"Is that where Edge—Darin—lives?"

"No, he just looks like that boy did. He was a baseball player."

"Do you know where he does live?"

"With his parents."

"Right, but..."

"Doko." Henry put his hand on Doko's shoulder. "Enough. She doesn't have what you're looking for. You'll have to come back when Ellie is here."

Doko opened his mouth to protest before Ellie's mother interrupted, "Don't worry, Mr. Doko, it's okay. In any case, I don't know where Ellie is right now either, but I have a feeling she'll be coming back soon."

"I appreciate that, ma'am, but I have a wife waiting at home for me who's going to be getting annoyed that dinner is getting cold, and..."

Outside, a car door slammed shut and gravel crunched underfoot. Angie clapped her hands together with glee.

"Oh, here she is now! Yay, it all worked out just fine in the end. I love when that happens."

Henry smiled. "Thanks, Ange. Now, you go rest while Agent Doko has a word with Ellie. And don't forget to take your medicine."

"I never do, Henry. Don't worry."

Henry shut the door gently. "Well, you got what you wanted, Doko—happy?"

Doko cocked an ear as the car roared off and the front door slammed. "I will be."

"Mother, I swear to——" The girl who had been introduced as Christine that afternoon stopped dead as she spotted Henry and Doko. "Oh my god, Hank. What is this—this prick doing here?"

"Ellie, he—"

"Never mind, I don't care. I already know where he's going." As the girl's eyes closed the hallway exploded into flame around Doko, the aged wallpaper peeling away from its paste backing, crumpling upon itself and disintegrating into ash. One by one, every lightbulb in the hall exploded, showering Doko's head with fragments of superheated glass, while rivulets of fire raced along the floorboards, ignited the carpet, and encircled Doko's feet.

"Baby, don't do this!"

She glared back at Henry through narrowed eyes. "Don't try to stop me. This jerk needs to be taught a lesson, and I'm the girl to do it."

She shut her eyes tightly and the flames tripled in size, blasting Doko with intense, dry heat and forcing him to his knees. Blinking back tears and gasping for breath, he pulled his sleeve across his face in panic—but when he looked up, all he could see was fire.

***

"Ellie! You gotta stop this right now!"

"No! You should have heard how he talked to me! He deserves it!"

"I get this guy can be a prick, baby girl, but this isn't how you treat people. I know your mama taught you better than that."

"Oooooooo...fine!" She blinked, and the flames vanished in an instant. Coughing into his fist, Doko brushed himself off as he climbed to his feet, somewhat less surprised than one might have thought as he noted the hallway was exactly as it had been.

"Very...very impressive, Miss Carre. I thought researching your abilities ahead of time might give me a leg up on your illusion-casting, but you really have all the little details nailed down so convincingly that it's impressively difficult to shake off, despite my specialized training."

"Well...thanks. I've lived in this house as long as I can remember, so I've had a lot of time to refine that one." Her nose crinkled with annoyance. "And they're not 'illusions'."

"I apologize for my lack of a better term. And while I have the opportunity, please let me also apologize for the way I acted this afternoon. You didn't deserve to be treated like that."

"You ought to know better than to act that way. It's rude."

"It was rude, and I'm sorry for my behavior, Miss Carre. Now, this afternoon you were introduced to me as..."

"Yeah, yeah, Edge just calls me that sometimes. It's his little joke, you know?" She bit her lip. "Also, I didn't necessarily want them—you—to have my name. I guess it didn't make much difference, seeing as you're standing in my living room anyway, but it's a thousand times easier to do what I do when people don't realize their senses are being fucked with."

Henry raised a finger. "Ellie..."

"All right, all right. When their senses are being...manipulated."

"Well, Miss Carre, you have a real talent—which makes me wonder why you were willing to hide that light under a basket just to try and scam your boyfriend into the Fighters."

"Ew, don't call him that. Gross."

"Fine, to get Edge into the Fighters."

"Look, we were bored, okay? It was just supposed to be a laugh. But..." Tears welled in her eyes. "Now he's all mad at me, and you're here, and everything's falling apart..."

"Hey, hey, no, don't do that." Doko pulled a handkerchief from his jacket pocket and thrust it into Ellie's hand; she recoiled from the object.

"Ew, do you actually blow your nose with this? Nasty."

"No, I think it's supposed to be decorative."

"Never mind, here—take this thing back." Ellie went into the bathroom, blew her nose with a loud FNORRRRK, and returned sniffling. "So what are you here for anyway? I mean, other than ruining my life."

"Come on Ellie, be nice. Mr. Doko has something to ask you."

"That's right, Miss Carre. But before I get to that, I need you to tell me the absolute truth about what you did in that audition, in your own words."

Her brow wrinkling, she looked to Henry. "Henry, you know I hate talking about this..."

"Ellie, it's gonna be okay. I promise. Please, just tell the man what he wants to know."

She stared at the floor. After fifty seconds, she raised her eyes and looked Doko in the face, unblinking. "Fine. But then you owe me, right?"

"Uh...right."

"No, say it. Say you'll owe me if I tell you."

He glanced at Henry, who nodded affirmatively. Doko sighed. "I have the distinct and familiar feeling that I'm going to end up regretting this. But all right—you tell me the complete truth about Edge's Fighters audition, and I will officially owe you one. Good enough?"

"I suppose." She shuffled her feet. "So...what I do isn't exactly projecting illusions. That's the way it appears to people though, so it's usually easier to go with the two-bit explanation when necessary and move on. It's actually a lot more complicated than that though."

She bit her lip and looked down the hall. Henry smiled reassuringly. "Go ahead, baby. It's okay."

"I am, I am. So, basically, you know, when people see and hear and smell stuff, that's their brain interpreting information transmitted through their senses, right? My power lets me mess around with those sense transmissions and add my own in there. Like, when you were in the hall there, I was transmitting the flame imagery, the smell of smoke and burning plastic, the crackling sound of fire, and the feel of the heat."

"And at the audition?"

"The apple was real; everything else was me. It's a routine we worked up last month. We made a couple hundred bucks doing it for passer-bys. I can 'cast that one to about ten people at a time before the feed starts to break up, but as long as the sense of smell holds people are generally too locked in to notice anything. My transmissions don't really have to be all that detailed most of the time, actually. People's minds are naturally pretty good at filling in the gaps when they believe something's real, or want to."

"Passers-by," Doko interjected.

"What?"

"Passers-by is the plural of passer-by. Not passer-bys."

Ellie rolled her eyes. "Fine, passers-by. Now that you got what you wanted, can you go away forever and leave us alone?"

"Ellie, be nice."

"It's okay, Henry—if that what she wants, I'll leave. But before I go, Miss Carre, I'd like to offer you a job with the Fighters."

"A job?" Her eyes widened in alarm. "I don't want to work for you!"

"Now, baby, hold on a minute," Henry cut in. "This could be great for college applications, not to mention help out with tuition."

"I don't know if I even want to go to college, but I know I don't want to work with this guy. Please don't make me."

"Sweetie, I can't make you do anything you don't want to. But before you say no, please think about it. I honestly believe this could be a really good thing for you, honey."

"Miss Carre, I appreciate your concern, but please understand I don't make this offer lightly. You saw that line of people today—any one of those people would be over the moon at what I'm offering you. Both starting salary and benefits are significantly above average, especially for your age. We also offer 401K matching, so you could also get a good jumpstart on retirement, along with..."

"Retirement?! Henry..."

"Doko, just back off a minute. Let me talk to her." Doko shrugged, stepped back out to the porch, and popped a fresh nicotine capsule onto his vaporizer, while Henry leaned in next to Ellie and spoke under his breath. "Look, baby, I know retirement isn't exactly something you're thinking about right now—but trust me when I say that all this and everything that comes with it will come in handy down the line for you. Real handy." He looked over his shoulder at the screen door, lowering his voice to a whisper. "And even more than that, having a friend in the Department of Powers is never a bad thing for people like you and your mom."

"Henry..." Ellie's shoulders slumped.

"I'm sorry, kiddo, but you know that's how it is. I wish you didn't have to grow up and be responsible and all that so fast, but that's just how the cards were dealt. We've got no choice but to play them how they lie."

"Yeah, I know. Just—ugh! That guy."

"I know. Something about him gets up my back a little too, but in his favor I've got to say Doko seems like the kind of guy who stands by his word. And the second he doesn't? You let me know, and me and your mom will yank you out of there so fast he won't know what happened."

She smiled. "Thanks, Henry." Feeling faintly ridiculous, she stepped over to the screen door and cleared her throat to attract Doko's attention. He turned and looked at the girl's face, his expression as neutral as if he hadn't been listening to every word.

"All right, Mr. Doko. I'll join your gang."

He re-entered the house, the screen door shutting behind him with a bang that caused Ellie to jump. "That's fantastic, Miss Carre, absolutely fantastic. You won't regret it."

"I do have one condition, though: I don't drive, and I don't want to learn. So whenever your little group has one of its meetings or whatever, you have to pick me up and drive me home."

"Well, I'm afraid our budget doesn't cover town car service in most cases, save for visiting dignitaries and the like."

"No, not a town car, or a taxi or a rideshare or a school bus or anything else. If you want me in your weird little club, you personally have to pick me up and drop me off. Otherwise, forget it."

"Miss Carre..."

"Non-negotiable. And this doesn't count as the favor you owe me."

Doko's fingers rubbed circular waves into his temples as his brow knitted in frustration. "All right, Miss Carre, you win. But be ready to go on time, every time. And you have to explain this arrangement to my wife."

"I can do those things," she purred.

"Well then, Miss Carre, welcome to the Fighters. Our first official meeting is tomorrow at ten AM. I'll be here at nine forty-five, so be ready at nine thirty. Bring your dri—er, social security card and a picture identification of some sort."

Returning Doko's handshake with overexaggerated enthusiasm, Ellie beamed a wide, plastic smile. "Great, see you then! Now will you please get out of my mom's house so I can eat cheese crackers and watch period dramas in peace?"

Henry groaned, but as he turned and walked back through the front door without another word, Doko only smiled.

* * *

I'm securely bound when I awake, head throbbing like the aftermath of the worst bender imaginable. Between training exercises and fieldwork, I've been tied up probably a hundred times, so I've picked up enough to know sometimes you've got to have it gamed from the beginning, and in this case, I can tell right away that there's no point wasting time or effort trying to escape.

I can't see anything at all, not even darkness or shadows. Feels like a blindfold has been wrapped around my head and duct-taped in place. My limbs are ziptied to the chair I've been placed in at three-inch intervals, leaving me absolutely no wiggle room. Even my fingers have been individually restrained—someone's done their homework.

Here's something else I've picked up along the way: revenge plots are the fucking worst. There are a lot of reasons for that, but the primary one is that because they're personal, they always take your powers and skillset into account. That's where being part of a group helps; I can think of half-a-dozen occasions when one of the other Fighters pulled my hindquarters out of the fire in a pinch. Of course, back then it was a given that I had teammates sufficiently motivated to rescue me and capable of tracking me down. Whereas now? Not so much.

So goofy as he may sound, that's why I'd still be taking Jack Frost Junior seriously even if he hadn't already coldcocked me. The fact that he's gotten this far already means he's smarter than the average evildoer: based on my state of total immobilization, he must have researched experimental techniques for confining speed-enhanced humans or gotten help from someone who did.

My heart leaps as I realize that although my ears are covered with what feel like shooting earmuffs, my mouth hasn't been gagged. I immediately start yelling for help; you'd be surprised how often this works, but it's weird shouting when you can't hear anything. I can't judge how much force to put behind my words, so I just scream at the top of my lungs.

Suddenly, something hits the side of my head, sending the earmuffs flying. "God damn, you are one annoying piece of shit. Jesus, all I wanted was to keep the creepy abandoned warehouse vibe going for a bit. But no, five goddamn minutes and you start yelling all over the place."

Okay, that's definitely Frosty Junior. Can't hear much else, but it's a big room. Echoey. Warehouse is always a good guess, assuming that wasn't misdirection on Junior's part. Hopefully it was a genuine slipup and I already got him rattled enough, because one thing never changes about bad guys: once you get them talking, it's all downhill.

"Sorry, kid. I'm sure all this would freak a civilian out good and proper, but as you might have heard, I've been in situations like this once or twice before. And as a matter of fact, this hasn't even really gone too far yet, as such things go. What do you say—how about you let me go now and we'll call it even?" Now, this never, ever works, but it's a good way to wedge that all-important sliver of doubt in. The fact that I don't hear a response is encouraging; that generally happens only when they're actually thinking about it. Very rare in a blood feud.

Seeing an opportunity, I redirect the conversation: "So Frosty had a kid, huh? Didn't know he had it in him."

"Shut up, Quick. You don't get to say his name."

"Sorry, no disrespect intended. I just never saw that side of him. And you've got to be what, at least nineteen or twenty, yeah? So you definitely weren't around back before the old Fighters split, but I know I fought your dad more recently than that."

"Don't act like you know anything about me."

"I just think it's weird, that's all. I mean, your dad and me, we must've had a dozen run-ins during that time. I'll never forget this one time when one of his traps backfired, and we ended up stuck together under a literal mountain of ice with nothing to do for like ten hours before Fireblast could work his way through to us. Of course we fought for the first hour or so, but after that ran its course we ended up talking about old sitcoms pretty much the rest of the time. I still think about it whenever I flip past a Bar Wars episode of *Cheers*."

"Shut the fuck up, Quick. I'm serious."

"Look, kid, all I'm trying to say is the way I look at it, it was my job to stop your dad and his job to try not to be stopped. So yeah, we fought a lot, but in between fights there were moments when we could talk like normal people. And even when things got bad there at the end, I never, ever hated the dude."

Frost Junior doesn't answer. Hopefully that means my words are getting to him. I swallow hard and plunge ahead: "I'm not claiming we were best friends or anything, because that wasn't the case—circumstances dictated otherwise, obviously. All I'm trying to say is that over the years, we built up a certain understanding and respect between us. And never, ever did he say one word about having a son."

My skull explodes in pain. Feels like Junior whacked me upside the head with an ice fist—one of his dad's classic moves, forming spheres of ice around his hands. Hits with the impact of a bowling ball when done right, and painful as all get out. Nevertheless, the experience takes me back, and I smile despite myself.

Frost Junior doesn't like that one bit. "I'll wipe that smile off your face, you piece of shit! You don't get to say that!"

I brace myself for another blow, but instead an unfamiliar, low voice intones, "Frost. Do not undermine your performance by letting your less sociable tendencies dominate."

I hadn't even realized anyone else was in the room. Sounds like a male voice coming from several yards away, as calm and collected as imaginable—so at least it's probably not another Frost kid out of nowhere.

"You know what Quick did!"

"Yes, Mr. Frost, I do remember. However, I also recall that your

mission parameters included well-defined behavioral boundaries, which I am here to oversee. Far better for everyone if I'm able to report full compliance, no?"

"But this prick…"

"I see you are struggling with some internal dilemma. Come closer, please—the effort required to project my voice at this distance is becoming tiresome. I would also prefer not to hand Mr. Quick any more information than he has already garnered due to your demonstrated unwillingness or inability to control yourself."

"Fine!" Frosty stalks off into the background and they mutter back and forth in hushed, clipped tones. No matter how I strain my ears, I'm only able to make out a single word from their conversation—'Alliance'—but at the sound of it, my blood freezes.

After a few minutes, Frost Junior stomps back towards me, mumbling under his breath all the way. I feel the earmuffs being replaced over my head, then nothing happens for long enough that I become unsure how much time is passing.

Now, I'm worried.

* * *

Doko pulled his car up to the treeline and extinguished the engine. "Let's go, we're already ten minutes late."

"Not my fault. I was ready."

"I didn't say it was your fault. I just asked you to hurry up."

"Asking and ordering are two different things."

Doko leaped from the car and dashed up to the tower, with Ellie begrudgingly trailing behind him. He was briefly taken aback at the sight of the propped-open doorway, exactly as it had been the night before when they'd left—had Mystic never bothered to close it?—but he tried to put it out of his mind, shaking his head as he burst into the Fighters' meeting room to find Mystic sitting exactly as he had been the night before.

Bored faces lounged in the chairs bracketing Mystic's impassive form: E on one side, Electrikid and Tekno Knight to the other. Spotting Doko, Electrikid tossed her phone to the table. "Fucking finally. I thought this was supposed to be a serious outfit."

"Where's Quick?" Doko asked.

Electrikid shrugged. "Search me. Tekla?"

Tekno Knight's visor slid up with a whir. "What?" Her helmet's heads-up display reflected against her steel-gray eyes; Doko saw she had been watching old *Simpsons* episodes in there while she waited.

"He's asking about Jack Quick."

"How should I know? You were here when I got here, Electrikid. Why are you asking me?"

"Don't you have, like, tracking systems or something in that suit?"

"No…"

"Oh, my mistake. What exactly do you do again?"

"Well, give me just a second and I can pull the newsfeeds up and check to see if there's been any mention of Quick."

"Awesome. Your amazing suit gives you all the power of literally any phone on the market. That'll really come in handy when we get into a trivia-quiz battle to save the world."

"Ladies…"

"Hey, watch it with that 'ladies' crap, buddy. This isn't the fifties," Electrikid spat.

Doko rubbed his temples vigorously. "Well, this morning is certainly going swimmingly. So no one here's seen or heard from Jack at all? Master Mystic, how about you?"

"I told you this was not the group I had envisioned," Mystic intoned.

"Not now, Mystic, we have bigger problems."

"I doubt the veracity of your assertion."

Electrikid squinted at Mystic. "What the shit is this guy on about?"

"Good lord, would you mind toning the language down just a bit? There are children here, after all."

"Oh please, Tekla," Electrikid retorted. "Maybe you're a little priss, but most people start swearing on the playground."

"Stop calling me that."

"What, Tekla? It's your name, isn't it?"

"I'm here as Tekno Knight, so call me Tekno Knight."

"But that name is just so…stupid."

Tekla's cheeks flushed. "Oh, like yours is so great? What sense does it make to keep calling yourself a kid when you're well past old enough to have your own?"

"It's called brand recognition, Blondie. You might know something about it if you ever did anything worth recognizing."

"People! Come on!" Doko bellowed, redfaced with frustration. "Look, I hate to say it, but we need at least two original members for this to qualify as a Fighters reactivation. If Jack had second thoughts and decided to pass, well…"

Tekno Knight moaned. "So we can't call ourselves the Fighters?"

"No, I'm sorry, it's worse than that. Without Jack, there's no team. E, I guess you're off the hook after all."

"Are you shitting me?" Electrikid was already half out of her seat. "I should have known this wasn't going to work out. I'm gone."

"Wait!" E shouted; Doko was shocked to hear the boy speak above a whisper for the first time. "Look, here. I checked the response email in case Jack sent in sick notice, and this was—"

"Oh, I get it," said Tekno Knight. "You're some sort of super hacker, right? I wondered what you kids were doing here."

"Um, no. I found the password right here on this sticky note. Th-that's okay, right?"

Doko glanced at Mystic, who evinced no signs of perturbation. "Guess so. What did you find, E?"

"It's a—well, I guess it's—well here, just look yourself." E turned his tablet around to display an image of Jack Quick bound and strapped to a chair, a copy of that morning's *New York Times* resting on his lap.

"Oh. Oh, fuck."

"Language, Ellie. E, when did this come in?"

"A couple of hours ago, but—"

Snatching the tablet from E's hand, Tekno Knight scrutinized the photo. "The guy in this picture has his eyes covered and he's masked. Who's to say this is even Jack?"

Electrikid's eyes rolled. "Of course it's him. Do you ever hear yourself?"

"Quiet, dear. Grownups are talking. But seriously, anyone can buy a costume—where's the proof?"

Ellie peered over Tekno Knight's shoulder. "Look, do you see that little rip there in his sleeve? I noticed that when I was here yesterday, he'd tried to close it up with staples. So jank."

Tekno Knight brightened. "Hey, I think you're right—uh, Ellie, was it? Give me a minute and I can compare with my onboard video log from yesterday."

Doko coughed. "I'm glad to see some enthusiasm out of the lot of you, but we need to approach this in an organized fashion if we're ever going to get anywhere."

Ellie looked toward the ceiling. "So what do you suggest?"

"Before we can do anything, we have to determine whether Jack Quick has been kidnapped. Does everyone present agree that appears to be the case based on the evidence we have?"

"Uh, duh, boss."

"Don't call me boss, please, Ellie. All I'm trying to establish here is that because Jack Quick appears to have been forcefully prevented from attending this meeting, I have no choice but to assume his intentions remain the same regarding the reformation of the Fighters. Therefore, by the authority vested in me by the Department of Extrahuman Abilities & Powers, I formally pronounce the membership of the New Fighters—comprising all parties present along with absented founding member Jack Quick—to be official functionary operatives of D.E.A.P."

"Wooo!" Tekla's face turned crimson as she realized she was the only person in the room standing. Silently lowering her arm, she reseated herself with as much dignity as she could muster while avoiding Electrikid's scornful stare.

"Er, thanks, Tekno Knight. And now that the group is properly constituted, I'd like to properly open the New Fighters' first official case: locating and retrieving missing founder Jack Quick. E, if you could hand me that tablet?"

"Sure, but I was going to..."

"Look at the metadata to see if there's a location or other useful information embedded? Yeah, we have a tool or two for that kind of thing." Doko typed an address into the tablet followed by a couple of commands, then set it in the center of the table, facing up. "And there we have it: a nondescript warehouse in an industrial area. Property ownership attributed to a company name that doesn't connect with any known quantities, which in this case means it's almost certainly a shell company designed to obscure the actual owners. Current satellite imagery is consistent with the building's filed architectural floorplan, but under that roof pretty much anything could be happening. Who's the best here at long range reconnaissance?"

Silence and averted glances answered Doko's question. "Well, that's probably why they grabbed the guy we'd use for recon. Nevertheless, the more we know about what's inside that building, the better chance everyone here has of coming back alive."

"Um, I have a question."

"Go, E."

"Well, I mean…someone sent this picture, right? And pretty much everyone knows a phone pic has location data embedded—"

"Uh, I didn't know that," Electrikid cut in.

"I'm sure what you don't know could fill an arena," Tekno Knight said.

"Jealous," Electrikid shot back.

"Anyway," E continued, "If that's the case, wouldn't this be what they want? What if it's a trap?"

"Oh, for fuck's sake." Electrikid buried her face in her hands.

"Electrikid, please remember we're all on the same team here," Doko admonished.

"I know that. Why do you think I groaned so loud?" She turned to E, barely managing to contain her disdain. "It's definitely a trap. It's always a trap. It will always be a trap."

His cheeks reddening, E shrank back in his chair. "O-oh."

"I might not have put it quite so glibly, but statistics do bear out the truth in Electrikid's words. That said, I think our best tactic in this situation is to hope we can play the game better than they hope we can. Fortunately for us, there's no way they have any idea what we're capable of."

Tekla cleared her throat. "Uh, well…"

"Tekno Knight, you have something to add?"

"We don't really know that, do we? After all, we don't know who kidnapped Jack, what their motivations are, or anything about them, really. Conversely, we know for certain that they know our location—"

"Along with everyone else in the world with internet access," Electrikid snorted.

"That's true," Tekno Knight conceded. "And anyone with the resources to take Jack probably wouldn't balk at keeping this location under surveillance, so…"

"What are you getting at?" Doko asked.

"Well, look, don't get me wrong, I'm all about this Fighters thing. I've been working towards this for longer than I care to think about," Tekno Knight answered, nodding towards E and Ellie. "But these… these two are kids, and you couldn't call the rest of us a team by any stretch of the imagination. We don't know each other and we haven't trained together—I mean, for God's sake, Doko, I don't even know what this girl's power is! And I'm sorry, but to me what you're proposing basically sounds like you want us to stick our heads into a noose and hope a better idea pops up before the floor drops out. Is that about the size of it?"

Doko furrowed his brow. "I wouldn't phrase it exactly like that, but…"

Tekno Knight shook her head. "I'm sorry, Doko, but I thought this was going to be something different."

"I hate to admit it, but Blondie has a point," Electrikid concurred. "I met this guy once and now you want to me to risk my life for him?"

Doko sighed. "What did you two think you were signing up for here, a book club? This is the job. Helping people is what we're here for, and in this case it happens to be one of our own. And if your response to that is that you're not sure? All I have to say is: maybe you're right. Maybe this isn't for you."

Chagrined, Electrikid and Tekno Knight looked down at the table.

"Alright, what the hell. I'm in," Electrikid declared.

"We're here to help, Doko," Tekno Knight added, though her voice carried noticeably less conviction. "Just please tell me you have a plan."

"Oh, I do," Doko affirmed, smirking. "I can almost guarantee that you're not going to like it, but it's a plan."

* * *

The chair beneath me abruptly tilts backwards and I'm jerked awake, only now realizing I'd fallen asleep. I brace myself for impact as the chair plummets earthwards, but at a forty-five degree angle to the floor the chair stops short and I'm dragged backwards for around fifty yards until the chair is righted.

Through the soles of my boots, I feel an impact nearby, like a large door closing. I tug at my restraints hopefully, but my bonds don't feel any looser; if anything, they've been retightened while I was out. Whoever is behind this either knows their stuff or simply isn't taking any chances—by leaving me no room to operate, my bag of tricks is considerably limited. Without knowing precisely where I am, I can't pull any big stunts for fear of injuring innocent bystanders—moving blind at superspeed is crazy risky.

The worst part is that I have no real idea what's even going on here. This definitely isn't a simple revenge plot; otherwise, I would've gotten a lot worse than a couple of whacks upside the head by now. But if Frost isn't calling the shots, who is? I just don't have that many old enemies running around out there anymore, and I can't imagine anyone paying a ransom on me that'd make it worth taking a risk this big.

At this point, my sense of time is pretty shot. Even under the best of circumstances, it's a struggle for me to keep my internal clock synchronized with the rest of the world, but I can still hold it together enough to count to three hundred at something approaching a normal rate, breathing as slowly as I can.

You might be surprised what you can learn from five minutes of inactivity, if you're really paying attention. Based on the relative lack of air movement across my skin and the speed with which it acquires that slightly stale quality, I'm about ninety percent certain I've been locked within a small, unventilated room—most likely a closet, walk-in refrigerator or freezer. The stillness and rate of deoxygenation also makes it unlikely anyone else has been locked in here with me—at least no one breathing, anyway.

Assuming I'm right, this allows me a tiny bit of latitude. While I'm almost certainly being monitored via camera, if any guards have been posted they're probably outside this specific room. And fortunately for me, on the wrong side of the law, reliable hired help is notoriously difficult to come by—people don't become henchmen because they're good at following directions, after all—so hopefully the underling assigned to watch me is as half-assed about his job as most. Either way, this is the best opportunity I've had since getting konked by Frost back at Mystic's tower, so I don't have much choice but to take the risk and pray for a lucky break.

First, I fill my lungs with oxygen, then whip my head around in a circle as fast as I can. It's absolute murder on the neck, and I'm definitely going to be sore for a week afterwards, but once I build up to the speed of sound there isn't a pair of headphones in the world that will stay on my head, duct-taped or no.

Sure enough, after a few seconds the earmuffs loosen and fly off, smacking into something behind me with a loud bang. My first instinct is to begin wearing at my bonds, but instead I rein myself in, sit stock still, and count off another hundred and twenty seconds. It's a risk, gambling away time I could potentially spend working to free myself, but hard-won experience has taught me that I stand to gain a lot more from whatever information I'm able to glean.

By the time I hit a hundred I haven't heard much at all, which supports the fridge theory. Of course, if you get spirited away to a villain's specially constructed lair all bets are off, but in typical commercial construction, walk-in freezers are the only rooms robust enough to contain a super-powered abductee or sufficiently insulated to muffle the type of loud noises that tend to arise in kidnap situations. Plus, there's rarely a shortage of failed restaurants or shuttered distributorships to pick from, so they tend to be the kidnapper's go-to.

Best of all, when I hit one-twenty I haven't heard the door open or any human movement nearby, so shedding my headphones may have gone unnoticed—dare I hope to have avoided even video surveillance? Heartened by the silence, I begin repeatedly straining against my bonds in a pattern taught to me by the Gentleman Detective. Trade secret: even when the bonds restraining you are too durable to break or erode quickly, the fasteners and sealants used to construct commercial furniture never are.

After only fifteen seconds, the chair crumbles into kindling beneath me and I gulp for air, aching for oxygen after the exertion. Whipping my blindfold off, I find myself within a mid-sized industrial freezer, as expected. Can't see out—the window's been painted over with reflective paint—but based on the looks of the interior it's been sitting empty for some time. At least it seems to have been professionally cleaned beforehand, thank god, and it isn't completely airtight or I'd definitely be getting lightheaded after that last stunt.

Not much to work with, unfortunately. The entire freezer inventory comprises me, a pile of wood that used to be a chair, and a battery-powered security camera mounted high in one corner. I examine the door; someone's installed a modified custom lock without an emergency release, and after pushing against it I'd lay odds some sort of deadbolt or brace is holding the door shut from the other side. Without some give in the mechanism or hardened metal tools, it'd take me days to wear this thing down enough to have even a chance of escape—time I don't have to spare.

At this point, I estimate I've been free of the chair for ten seconds. I need to learn as much as possible about what I'm dealing with if I'm to have any hope of getting out of this with my skin intact. I got lucky with the earmuffs, but even the laziest monitor-watcher is bound to eventually notice me walking around the smashed chair. I'd like to think I could get away with the old 'pretend the prisoner's vanished from the cell then run out when they open the door' bit, but the skill and preparation that's gone into this tells me it'd be a waste of time and effort.

Finally I spot something: the freezer window is way too small to squeeze through, but it's been painted over from inside. Praying they didn't double-check for exterior coverage, I pluck a metal nail from the broken chair and carefully scrape away at a lower corner of the window. As light streams through, I feel like shouting hallelujah for half-assed hired help—one thing you can always count on in this world.

Pressing my eye to the makeshift peephole, I discover my time is running even shorter than hoped. About fifteen yards from the door Frost Junior stands with his back to me, gesturing heatedly. I can't see who he's talking to, but from his body language I'd venture it's the same person I overheard admonishing him earlier, or possibly some other superior figure.

All of a sudden, Frost wheels around and abruptly stalks away from the conversation, his face contorted into a grotesquerie of humiliation and resentment—must've gotten some orders he found hard to swallow. I don't let that distract me, though, as their disagreement affords me my first lucky glimpse of his presumed overseer: male, white, tall—over two meters, easy—and as bald as a bowling ball. Face doesn't ring any bells, and it won't win any beauty contests either. He's built like a pro athlete and sports a double-breasted black suit—an expensive indulgence in this line of work, or at least expensive-looking. It's almost certainly custom tailored, given his size, but unfortunately bears no visible crests, monograms or emblems. It's always easier to keep track when you know what team everyone plays for.

Doesn't look like he's using any powers, at least not that I can see from my vantage point. His right arm cradles a longhaired Siamese cat against his body while his left gesticulates wildly, presumably relaying directions to the dozen or so armed underlings scurrying around the warehouse.

As Frost nears the freezer he blocks my view of his boss once more and I inhale sharply, bracing myself against the floor. I'm praying he's either mad enough or dumb enough to come in here and try to take his frustration out on me, and I ready myself to dash through the gap the second the door opens.

Instead, Frost stops short a few yards shy of the door, holds his arms out towards me and closes his eyes. Moments later, ice is all I can see. It only takes me a few more seconds to scrape the remaining paint from the window, but it makes no difference. There could be three, four feet of ice blocking the door, easy; even on his worst day Frost's dad was capable of producing that kind of mass, and from what I've seen the rotten apple hasn't fallen too far from the tree. For all I know, the entire freezer could be sealed in one massive block—let's hope the air I'm breathing wasn't coming in from the front. And come to think of it, how is anyone or anything supposed to get in or out now?

My eyes widen, adrenalin floods my body, and I smack myself upside the head as it dawns on me too late what I'm dealing with, and I curse myself for not figuring it out faster. They're not asking me any questions, they're not letting Frosty live out his revenge torture fantasy on me—at least not yet—and they don't even care that I got out of the chair, as long as they can keep me safely contained. But with this freezer encased in so much ice, there's no way to get food, waste, or anything else in or out, so their plan doesn't include keeping me here long. And let's be honest: since no one in the world would pay ransom for me, all I am is bait.

For all I know, the Fighters could be on their way already—I know I would be if I was in their place. But if they find me before I can warn them what's lying in wait, the outcome will almost certainly be a slaughter.

* * *

"And that's that. If everything goes well, in a couple of hours we'll all be back here eating pizza. Any questions?"

Doko looked around the table. While Mystic's expression was inscrutable as usual, the unease displayed on the others' faces said more than enough.

Tekno Knight raised her hand tentatively. "Um…I thought you said you had a plan."

"Well, by the strictest definition of the word, it's technically a plan," Electrikid scoffed, "but it's certainly not a good one. Really, Doko—are you serious with this?"

"Oh, I'm a hundred percent serious. We have a limited set of skills to work with, we don't know what we're walking into, and we don't have the advantage of teamwork to fall back on. Knight, you're the least vulnerable to surprise attack, and that armor's loaded up with sensors, yeah? It just makes sense for you to take point. And Electrikid watched Voltaic's back for years as his sidekick, so she's used to second position."

"Right," Tekno Knight conceded, "but all the exposure is on me. You're basically asking me to put my head in a noose and count on Negative Nancy and Dr. Weirdo here to pull me out—can't you see why that idea might make me slightly dubious? Especially when your own part in the plan seems to be just...sitting in the car."

"Look," Doko sputtered, "I know how it looks, but my hands are tied. I don't have armor or powers to protect me, so until we know what we're dealing with, I have no choice but to follow the rules of engagement limiting nonpowers to support. You establish there are no powers in that warehouse and I'll be by your side, weapon drawn and ready to fight, but any more than that isn't in the cards."

Tekno Knight looked down at herself. "This armor isn't exactly subtle, you know. I'll be clanking in there like a big sitting duck. And frankly, if Quick's kidnappers do manage to spot me, I wouldn't put it past this one here to zap me and leave me for dead."

"Screw you, Blondie," Electrikid bristled. "Don't act like you know what you're talking about. I've been a professional at this since before you got your first training bra—although that could have been last year, from the looks of you."

"Oh, you're a 'professional'? That explains a lot."

"Professional enough to know that the two of us going in there blind is basically asking to be murdered."

"That's why Mystic's going to be your backup," Doko offered. "His mystic senses make him ideal for monitoring the perimeter, so he'll be able to prevent the two of you from getting overrun. It's a classic three point incursion, minimizing our exposure and maximizing our skills. I'll admit it's not ideal, but I don't know that we really have any choice. Do any of you have a better idea?"

"Well, what about these two?"

Electrikid rolled her eyes. "What about them? They're kids, Tekla."

"She's right, Knight. I can't allow anything that would put them in the line of fire and E doesn't have any powers anyway. They'll hold down the fort and let us know if Jack or his kidnappers get in contact."

"Agh, fine," Tekla groaned. "I guess this is the way it's going to be. You'd better be as professional as you claim, Electrikid."

"Just you watch and see, Blondie."

"Great. Guess we might as well get moving." Tekno Knight plodded dutifully outside with Electrikid close on her heels. Nearly through the door himself, Doko pulled his keys from his pocket before noticing Master Mystic hadn't budged a centimeter.

"Mystic? You coming?"

"No."

Doko squinted. "No?"

"No. I have informed you several times that this is not the group I had envisioned. I shall not further suffer your delusions."

* * *

Outside the tower, the sensors of Tekno Knight's suit clicked and buzzed. "Wasn't Doko right behind us? I thought this was an emergency."

"Don't be in such a rush to get your head blown off," Electrikid muttered.

Tekno Knight wheeled around. "Listen, do you have a problem with me? What did I ever do to you?"

"Aw, what's the matter, tin girl? Did the heart the wizard gave you come with too many feelings?"

"No, but you've been giving me shit nonstop and I'm getting a little sick of it. Yesterday, okay, I get it, it's a competition thing—but we both made the team, yeah? Maybe you should act like it."

Electrikid snorted. "Life is a competition, bitch, and you're not in my league. You think you know what's up just because you slapped this janky suit together?"

"Yeah, as a matter of fact I do. You don't know anything about me."

"I know you don't have any real powers, Tekla. You're just a tryhard wannabe and I have to back you up? Fucking bullshit."

"That wasn't my decision."

"Yeah, well, I didn't hear you protesting too loudly. Besides, it's always the norms who want it too much that end up turning. They dream and dream of being one of the powers and they when they finally get here it never lives up to their stupid expectations, because nothing ever could, and then they end up hating the world because their only dream is gone and they don't know what else to do. I've seen it a million times. People like you want it too much and it always comes around to bite you in the ass."

"You think I want to do this? I don't even want to be here."

"If that's really true, you should go home right now. Believe me, the last thing I need out in the field is some amateur tripping me up. Shit, this situation would already be handled if Voltaic was here."

"Well he's not, is he? I am. Deal with it or don't, I don't give a shit. But that's not going to change."

"Yeah? We'll see," Electrikid sneered. "I have a feeling that once you see what fieldwork is really like, you'll go crying home to your mommy in no time."

* * *

Back inside, Doko swallowed hard, struggling to keep his voice calm.

"Mystic, whatever your objections to the lineup, Jack is at the mercy of someone or something who may be planning to injure or kill him, if they haven't already. Are you going to leave it all in our hands?"

"That is not within the purview of my mission on this plane. I must remain within my place of highest power and continue monitoring for the incursion's beginning."

"So what about Jack? You know, your friend?"

"Jack Quick is but one mortal. The events of which I speak will affect all from the mightiest of gods to the lowliest of bugs. And soon, you and all mortals—including you who dare to place your petty machinations above the very clockwork of the universe—shall reap nothing but scorn and bitter ashes."

E and Ellie exchanged alarmed glances in terrified silence.

"Mystic, I'm serious here," argued Doko. "We're in a hostage situation and you're actively refusing to aid a fellow Fighter? Not only is this unacceptable for any powered team member, let alone a founder, it's an egregious violation of several laws as well as the basic tenets allowing this group to exist in the first place."

"Your laws are as applicable to me as to the winds and the rain."

"I guess we'll see about that, won't we?" Doko glowered at the impassive figure, but Mystic remained silent and unmoving as a statue.

"Um, Mister Doko?" Ellie ventured. "I don't think threatening him is going to help. Even if you manage to get through to him somehow, I can't see it ending well for you."

"It's not going to end well for Jack if we don't get moving, Ellie. You don't get it; if this stubborn prick isn't helping, then the plan will never work, not to mention the fact that there isn't any team. The battle's lost before we even started."

"I don't know about the team, but as far as saving Jack goes I think I have an idea."

"Ellie…I know you mean well, but even to save Jack's life, if I allow you to walk into harm's way, I'd be no better than Mystic here."

"Just listen," Ellie assured him, before laying out the framework of her idea.

With each sentence Ellie spoke, the scowl on Doko's face faded slightly, and as she finished, he smiled wide. "I've got to admit, that might just be crazy enough to work. Do you think you can you sell it to the Knight and Electrikid?"

"Maybe," Ellie answered. "But don't you think they'd be more likely to accept the idea coming from you?"

Doko waved his hand dismissively. "Eh, you heard how thrilled they were with my first plan—don't be afraid to take your credit where it's due. Come on," he urged. "Let's run it up the flagpole and see if we can get a salute."

"All right," she agreed, biting her lip. "But if this doesn't work, I'm going to say it was your idea all along."

EPISODE THREE: THE VILLAIN REVEALED

Jack Quick was beginning to wonder whether the Fighters were coming after him at all.

He had to admit it was probably best for their own safety not to, but it certainly didn't say a lot for his chances of continued well-being. Jack knew all too well that if whoever was behind his kidnapping couldn't get what they wanted using him as bait, the only remaining option would be to let him go—and based on what he'd seen of his abductor Jack Frost Junior, the rogue didn't seem too inclined to agree to that. More likely, they'd just make an example of him, dumping his lifeless body by the side of the highway as they departed.

Jack pressed his face to the iced-over freezer door, but it was just as solidly sealed as it had been for hours. *Looks like I'm just going to have to wait for this door to open and pray it's my salvation rather than my doom,* he thought. *If only I had some idea what's going on outside this freezer, maybe I'd know which was more likely.*

* * *

Outside the makeshift containment cell, Jack's captors were not as sanguine as he might have expected.

"Frost," said the mysterious figure in charge, "I am beginning to regret allowing your participation in this endeavor."

"What the hell do you mean?"

"All we have to show for the last several hours' effort is a massive pile of slowly melting ice."

"How is that my fault? I've done everything you told me to. I got Quick, I sent the picture to the address you gave me, and I sat on my hands and didn't do anything to him even though he fucking deserves it. It was your plan from beginning to end, so if the result isn't what you thought then I'd say that's on you."

"As you know, Frost, the parameters of your mission were dictated by the Alliance, but our operatives are expected to allow for a certain amount of flexibility in order to maximize results. In my estimation, it seems you've simply done the minimum—and I am disinclined to wait much longer."

"Well, what do you suggest?"

"Interrogation might have proved useful, had someone not placed several thousand pounds of ice in my way."

"Is that all? Give me a sec." Frost stood before the immense mound of ice blocking the freezer door, placed his hands on it, and concentrated momentarily. "Okay, it'll take a few minutes to get going, but I accelerated the heatsoak rate. Five minutes, ten at the most, and you'll be able to get in there, get Frost out, whatever you want."

"Five minutes? Not good enough. Trog, phone. Dial A6 and hold it to my ear. All right, it's ringing...Heatbreak, it's me. Do you see anything at all out there? Yes, that's what I expected. Yes, I know, but there's nothing we can do right now but wait. In the meantime, I'd like your help with something, if you'd come in here a moment. Trog, hang up."

Jack Frost Junior cocked his head. "Uh, how many powers do you have out there just waiting for you to make the call?"

"Don't presume yourself more valuable than you are, Frost. Wheels are in motion on levels far above your comprehension. You'll be told just what you need to know in order to handle your small part of the operation and no more. And let's note that while your primary qualification is making ice appear and disappear, we've already discovered you're not so great at the second."

"It's not my fault! It's basic thermodynamics: there's a limit to how quickly water can change state. Heatbreak won't be able to move the ice any faster than I can."

"Maybe not, but at least he's smart enough not to argue with me about it. I understand my appearance may not seem as imposing or threatening as some, Frost, but very few get the chance to underestimate me twice. Do you follow?"

"Y-yes, sir."

"Good. Now get with Heatbreak and let's see if we can't get in there while we have the chance. At this rate, the wolf will be at the door by the time we're able to pry any tidbits from Quick's mind."

* * *

Outside, unbeknownst to the shadowy villain, the fledgling Fighters were actually approaching the remote warehouse where Quick was being held—but unfortunately, they were still nowhere near rescuing their distressed colleague.

"This is such a bad fucking idea," muttered Electrikid.

"It really, really is," agreed Tekno Knight. "I can't believe you approved this madness, Doko. You were the one all yelling about professionalism and regulations and yet here we are about to walk naked into a hurricane. What happened to the letter of the law?"

"We don't have that luxury right now," Doko countered. "The second Jack got snatched war was declared on the Fighters. We just didn't know it yet."

"Right, but we still don't even know who snatched him. Also, we're not really the Fighters."

"Yes, you are."

"There's no one in this car anyone would recognize as a member of the Fighters, and the only guy they might know refuses to accept us as members. That seems pretty cut and dried to me."

"Look, once we get Jack…"

"If we get Jack…"

"When we get Jack, he'll affirm you as Fighters members. And either Mystic will fall in line or he won't, but we'll have to worry about that later. Right now lives are at stake and regardless of what anyone has to say about it or whether this team continues past today, today you are the Fighters. Now I don't want to hear any more about it, because we're getting close and we need to stay focused."

"Okay, boss, point taken. I still don't think there's a chance in hell of this working, but nice locker room speech nonetheless."

"Objection noted, Electrikid. Tekno Knight, are we close enough for your scanners to pick up the location?"

"Yeah. But like I told you, this is just an interpolation of satellite data with unsecured surveillance cameras, motion detection, air movement, and thermal readings. It's nothing special."

"It's all we have, so it'll have to be enough. What are you getting inside the warehouse?"

"Not too much. Four human forms. One small animal, probably a stray. Here, Ellie, I'll send this feed to your phone. That enough for you to work with?"

"Let me see: this cluster here is our villains, I guess. Where's the—oh, I see, he's holding it. And this one over here is probably Quick? Seems straightforward enough; signal's a little weak, though."

"Oh, right. Everyone log on to the car's onboard wireless; coverage out here can get spotty, and we're dead if we don't stay linked up."

"So what you mean to say is: we're dead."

"No, but we're definitely in serious trouble if this thing starts going south on us. Ellie, you set?"

"I suppose."

"Okay, then. I guess it's time for you to get in the trunk."

* * *

Inside the warehouse, Jack Frost Junior smirked triumphantly.

"See? I told you."

"Yeah. Sorry, chief, but he's right. It'll go a little faster with both of us working it, but five minutes is still pretty good."

"It's been five minutes already."

"Okay, ten minutes. But look, this is a lot of ice, yeah? The kid's a born pro."

"Results are all that count. While the two of you struggle to achieve them, I will amuse myself otherwise."

Frost breathed a sigh of relief as the hulking figure stepped away. "Whew. Hey, Heatbreak, thanks for backing me up."

"No problem. You know, your dad and me ran around together a few times back in the day. The team-up was a little on-the-nose to go long with, but we had some kicks."

"Yeah, I knew that. Still, I appreciate the kind words. That little fucker's been riding me nonstop."

"Hey, whoa, whoa. Keep your voice down. You shouldn't be saying that stuff. Sure, it's super easy to let your guard down, but underestimating him will get you killed."

"Oh, come on."

"No, kid, I'm serious. He has absolutely no pity or empathy. I don't think he's even capable of it. Trust me, I've seen what happens to people who get on his bad side." Heatbreak shuddered.

"Okay, okay. Message received. I'll watch my mouth."

"Good kid. Looks like this ice is about clear. How do you want to handle Quick?"

"Uh...well, what do you think?"

"Usually blocking the path works pretty well. He can't work up much speed in an enclosed space, so as long as he doesn't have a straight shot it's not a major problem. Been in there a long time, too. Can't imagine he's feeling in top form." Heatbreak shook his head. "You were really able to just walk right up and give him the old icy palm, huh? Damn. Quick must've really let himself go. Can't imagine that working back in the day. Kind of sad, really."

"Sad? Fuck that. You know what that fucker did to my dad."

Heatbreak looked at Frost Junior, his eyes lidded and watery. "Oh, kid. Don't tell me you're all on that revenge kick. That never gets you anywhere, trust me on that. You've got to look at this as a job if you want to get anything out of it. I mean, look at me, still working shit gigs like this at my age—that ain't what you want. And your dad wouldn't have wanted that for you either."

"Gentlemen, I hear a lot of discussion over here. Is there some issue the two of you need me to clarify?"

"Uh…no, sir. But we're just about ready to melt the last of this ice and get inside."

"Good. Let's see what we can shake loose."

* * *

Outside, the Fighters were also beginning to near their target—and Tekno Knight's unease was running commensurately high.

"Electrikid? Are you there, 'Kid?"

"Quiet down, damn it. Yes, I'm here. Do you want to the entire world to know? Just keep moving forward."

"Sorry. This is super disorienting for me."

"Fuck, you have all those sensors and crap, don't you? Shouldn't this just be like when pilots fly a plane with the instruments?"

"It's not that simple."

"Fine, then just hold up your end and trust me to handle mine. Okay? I'm busy enough trying to watch your back, so quit distracting me."

"All right, jeez. We're just about to the warehouse. I'm going to suction a mini-cam to the window and add visual to the feed."

"Uh, I'm not watching the feed. I'm using my eyes."

Tekno Knight sighed. "I know that, Electrikid—that was for the others' benefit. Here we go…are you getting anything?"

Doko's voice crackled in Tekno Knight's ear. "I got you. I have visual confirmation of our recon assessment, and it looks like they're just about to open that freezer. The two of you, proceed toward the open doorway while I confirm whether Quick's in there."

"Okay, boss. We're just about to the door now. Is Ellie projecting to the interior?"

"Give me a second. The visual's still coming up…okay, you should be good. Do try and keep the noise down, though."

"Will do." Tekno Knight gingerly stepped into the warehouse, half-expecting the floor to drop away beneath her. "We're inside. All three hostiles are facing away, looks like they're still concentrated on that freezer. Tall one has a cat riding across his shoulders. Funny, I used to have a cat that rode my shoulders that way."

Electrikid backed in behind Tekno Knight, eyes swiveling as she scanned the area. "Wow, lonely single woman likes cats. Shocking news."

"I didn't take you for the type for cheap puns. And I don't like cats, anymore."

"Field team, let's keep it down. Ellie's already straining to keep you both covered, let's not push it. Ellie, you holding up all right back there?"

"F...fine. Starting to break a sweat though. Can't you do anything about the heat back here?"

"Sorry. The trunk is far and away the safest place for you right now, but that double layer of armor doesn't let the AC reach."

"Ugh. And you had to go for the dark paint job?"

"Sorry, kid. Just hold tight, you're doing great. Field team, where are we?"

"About halfway. No sign of anyone noticing us. Still looking at the freezer door, but without Ellie masking our presence they'd definitely hear us by now."

"You, maybe," Electrikid sneered. "I could sneak up and they'd never know it."

"Sure, sure. And then they'd knock you out and throw you in with Quick. Anyway, hon, you might want to get charged up or switched on, or whatever it is you do to get your powers ready. That door's going to be open anytime, and..."

Tekno Knight stopped midsentence as the large figure before them raised one meaty hand and a chilling voice rang out.

"A moment, Heatbreak. I sense we have visitors—a familiar presence to boot."

"Ah, what are you talking about, chief? I don't see anything."

"No, you wouldn't, would you? But nevertheless, I'd appreciate some assistance if you and Mr. Frost would leave the freezer where it is. You see, the company we've been awaiting is right over there, beneath the large lighting fixture; evidently, some unknown force is presently blocking your senses from detecting them. Fortunately, they thought it unnecessary to do the same for me—so the upper hand is once again ours."

"Uh, guys, I'm getting a lot of resistance back here all of a sudden." Ellie's voice was panicky and desperate. "I can't hold it!"

"Let it go, Ellie. Their cover's blown," Doko replied. "Save your energy. I've got a feeling we're going to be going to plan B sooner than later."

Tekno Knight stared agog, her mind awhirl with confusion as the menacing powered thugs bracketed her and Electrikid. The massive figure stepped methodically towards the two, the cat perched proudly on his shoulders as the pair emerged into the spotlight of illumination at the center of the room.

"Two yards forward, Trog. That's good. Now lower me to her level." The hulking, black-suited figure held his arms out before him; the cat ran down them, smugly reseated itself on the man's folded forearms and sneered into Tekla's faceplate.

"Well, this is certainly an unexpected treat. So the resuscitated Fighters were desperate enough to accept you, eh? I'd have bet against it, but I suppose congratulations are in order."

Finally locating her voice, Tekno Knight croaked out words she never dreamed she'd speak. "Oh my C-Christ. Mister Fluffy, is that you?"

The cat's ears folded back in obvious displeasure. "I'll thank you never to soil my ears with that demeaning appellation ever again, woman."

"Ah, what the fuck! Blondie, is that fucking cat talking?"

Over the comlink, Doko was panicking. "Tekno Knight, what's going on? I need your status. Electrikid, do you need help?"

"It's the cat, Doko, the cat's in charge here. And I think it knows Tekla!"

"He...he was my pet. I called him Mister Fluffy.

The cat's back arched. "I told you never to say that name again!"

"You named your cat Fluffy? That's imaginative."

"It was short for Mister Fluffypants Q. Snugglebottom."

"Oh my god. You are such a dork."

The cat's tail flipped from side to side in agitation. "Ladies, if I could have your undivided attention?" The cat looked from Heatbreak to Frost; each took one menacing step toward the women. "Thank you. Now then, Tekla, I would highly appreciate you not using my former pet name. I do not recognize it and I shall not respond to it. When necessary, you may refer to me by my chosen sobriquet: Professor Scratchclaw."

"Fluffy..."

"Professor Scratchclaw! I have the upper paw here, woman. Do not force me to unveil my wrath! Now then, we know you're here as members of the Fighters, searching for your missing founding member Jack Quick. Based on what I overheard of your pathetic attempt to infiltrate this warehouse, you two are merely the first wave, or advance team. I assume your colleagues are somewhere nearby?"

"You tell us, smart cat," Electrikid defiantly muttered.

"Oh, I shall. I was merely giving you the opportunity to potentially curry my favor. For you see, though I admit having the woman who once dared to call herself my 'owner' blunder unsuspecting into my claws is a delightful windfall, neither of you figure into our primary intent this fine morning. Therefore, I am allowed some latitude as to your...handling, let's call it."

"Handling?" Tekno Knight didn't like the sound of that.

"Why, yes, dear. For instance, as newly inducted rookie members of a long-defunct superteam, few would find it surprising were you to meet up with a violent demise—especially after overconfident leadership sent you into a dangerous environment without so much as a faint notion what you were up against. Disheartening, really, but such tragedies are sometimes necessary to highlight deficiencies in stagnant bureaucracies. Should this eventuality bear itself out, you should be comforted your sacrifice will be for the greater good."

"Wow, that is so comforting!" Electrikid scoffed. "Just tell us what you want, cat."

Scratchclaw shook his head sadly from side to side. "So predictable. No recognition for the slow building of anticipation, the tension increasing as the seconds tick by. I suppose what they say is true: in times such as these, conversation truly is a dead art."

Electrikid rolled her eyes. More than anything, she hated villains in love with the sound of their own voices. "This isn't a conversation, it's a monologue."

"True. I'm glad you recognize that much, anyway, even if you seem to lack an appreciation of the form. But perhaps you two are simply holding out hope? Deluding yourself that these feeble attempts at what you call repartee will delay us in our agenda long enough to allow time for the rhetorical cavalry to ride to your rescue? Perhaps I should pull the curtain back a bit more and illuminate the true hopelessness of the situation in which you find yourselves. B team?"

In each corner of the warehouse, large boxes of blinding yellow plasma energy suddenly flashed before them. When the spots in their eyes cleared, Tekla and Electrikid found themselves surrounded by over a dozen costumed men and women, all facing the two menacingly. Electrikid swore the cat was grinning at her as he intoned, "I'll spare you lengthy introductions, save only the human responsible for this latest coup: Quanta, take a bow."

"My pleasure, Professor S." A largish woman wearing a green trenchcoat over a purple jumpsuit stepped forward and curtseyed exaggeratedly. "You ready for part two?"

"Please. If you would, Quanta?"

"You got it, fuzzy. All right, people—stand back!"

Quanta closed her eyes and concentrated for a moment. As she opened her eyes, the air flashed yellow and suddenly, standing where she had been was Doko's car. Inside the sedan, Doko looked around and found himself surrounded by over a dozen threatening, powered rogues.

"Ah, shit..."

"Yes, shit indeed," smiled the cat. "Mr. Doko, I presume? Kindly step out of your vehicle, if you please, and do me the courtesy of opening the trunk latch, yes? Trust me; it'll go much better for whomever you've ensconced within. Whatever armor plating you've installed would surely prove insufficient against the force assembled here, and our methods of forcibly opening a reinforced trunk, though effective, can be quite messy."

"Rrrgh." Doko reluctantly depressed the release switch and

stepped from the car as the trunk popped open. "It's okay, Ellie. Just come stand by me."

"Yes, girl, you do that thing. Government man, place your weapons and identification on the floor. Frost?"

As Frost Junior stepped forward and retrieved Doko's items, Ellie pointed at him. "Hey, this guy was hanging around the auditions yesterday!"

"He was indeed, young lady," confirmed the cat. "You are quite observant for a human of your age. I am similarly observant myself, however, and it appears a crucial member of your little club remains to be located."

Tekla, Electrikid, Ellie, and Doko exchanged glances. None spoke.

"Come, people, surely you aren't harboring any delusions about your ability to prevail in open melee? You are outnumbered by more than four to one, surrounded by powers more than capable of countering your own. Even should the well-protected members of your group survive, I can't see it going well for the lesser among you—you normal humans simply aren't built for it."

He looked past them to the open warehouse doors as Quanta walked back into the building. "Anything?"

"I looked everywhere within my range, Professor S. Not a peep."

"He must have come. Without Mystic, this would have been a suicide mission. You, girl, tell me now and you can go free: where is Master Mystic lurking?"

Tekno Knight interjected, "No matter what, he's not going to let you free, Ellie."

"Quiet, woman. You are not qualified to be making any being's decisions for them. The kitten will make up her own mind."

Doko coughed and spoke quietly to the terrified girl by his side. "Go ahead, Ellie, it's okay. Just tell them the truth. There's nothing they can do about it either way."

Ellie swallowed hard, her throat aching. Her mouth was bone dry after her confinement in the steaming hot car trunk. "He's—he's not here. He didn't come with us. He's back at his place."

"Don't lie to me, girl. He must be here. We have his only remaining trusted fellow teammate at our mercy.'

"I don't know what to tell you, kitty," Electrikid smirked. "Maybe Mystic's not as attached to Quick as you thought."

"Don't be ridiculous—you disgusting, soft creatures ooze empathy. How could he abandon the only human connection he has left in the world? *Sssss*....put me down, Trog."

The black-suited man knelt, allowing the cat to alight his paws on the warehouse floor. An orange-suited man wearing an antennae-covered helmet stepped forward. "Uh, I told you this wasn't going to work."

"Quiet, Manstro, I am still in charge of this operation. Mystic could be getting away as we speak; I won't waste another second entertaining these ridiculous lies. Frost, Heatbreak, escort our new guests to rejoin their teammate. The rest of you, spread out and search every square inch of space within five miles. Go now!"

* * *

The sound of cracking sheaves of ice being pulled away from the freezer door woke Jack Quick with a start. Instinctively, he backed against the far wall, praying silently that the door would open wide enough to give him a straight shot.

Jack watched intently as the door cracked open just wide enough for Heatbreak to shout inside: "Right, speedboy, you up? Company comin' in. You going to behave? Trust me, this's far and away the safest place for you right now."

Jack sighed, feeling his chances of escape dwindle. "I'll take your word on that. But sure, I'll behave."

Quick's calves twitched with anticipation. He breathed deeply as Heatbreak eased the door open, the stale freezer air slowly reoxygenating. Heatbreak peered through the narrow gap, gesturing at Jack.

"Alright, speedboy, take a quick peep through here for me, if you would." Quick could just make out a forearm gripped tightly in Heatbreak's left hand. "This is your little group's girl member. Well, her arm anyway. Notice how it's still healthy, attached to her body, and all the other stuff you generally want from an arm? You stay where you are and maybe it'll stay that way."

"Okay, I get you," Quick muttered, while simultaneously thinking, *girl member? Which girl member?*

Heatbreak wasn't satisfied. "I'm serious here, Quick. I know we've gone back and forth on that whole friend versus foe continuum a time or two, but this isn't my call. I'm just following orders."

"Famous last words," Quick shot back.

"Cute," Heatbreak answered. "But for real, Quick, you don't want to make me prove how much I'm not bluffing. Clear?"

"As ice." Jack Quick turned his back to the door and placed his hands on his head, assuming the position. Though it wasn't much of an impediment to Quick's powers, he'd found that its familiarity tended to put criminals at ease. Heatbreak eyed Quick suspiciously as he stepped away from the door, allowing Frost Junior room to herd Doko, Electrikid, Tekno Knight, and Ellie single file through the narrow opening.

The second Tekno Knight's armor was clear of the doorway, Heatbreak shoved Ellie through and slammed the door shut behind her. The unmistakable crackling of Jack Frost Junior's ice sealing the exit over followed rapidly after.

Jack lowered his arms and turned around, his eyes scanning each of the freezer's new inhabitants. "So. The New Fighters, I presume?"

Doko brushed off his pant legs. "Yeah, I had to take a couple of liberties after you didn't show up this morning."

"What's she doing here?" Jack asked, indicating the girl he thought of as Edge's girlfriend.

Ellie crossed her arms, looking skyward. "Uh, trying to rescue you? You're welcome, by the way."

"Welcome for what, bringing me company during my imprisonment? Doko, what possible justification could you have for bringing this little girl along?"

"We didn't exactly have a plethora of choices, Quick. That little show Ellie put on for her boyfriend's benefit was impressive enough for me to recruit her."

Ellie pouted, "I told you, he's not my boyfriend."

Quick wasn't convinced. "Be that as it may, do you really think a superpowered group is the best environment for an underaged goth chick?"

"I'm seventeen. And don't call me goth!"

"Sorry. I see black hair and you cast spells, right? That spells goth to me."

"My hair is naturally black! I'm not goth!"

Doko stepped between the two. "She doesn't cast spells, either, Quick. She's a sensory projector."

Jack backed down in the face of Doko and Ellie's twin assault. "Okay, okay. I didn't mean anything by it. But, look around us, yeah? This isn't exactly a Department of Education-certified afterschool program."

Doko hung his head. "I know. It's my fault. Mystic backed out on us at the last minute and we were caught shorthanded. I didn't expect to be walking into a damn Alliance convention."

Jack cocked his head. "Frost Junior and Heatbreak reviving his dad's old double act doesn't necessarily make this Alliance business."

"Think you're missing a few puzzle pieces there, Jack. Whatever this is, it's a lot bigger than some musty old blood feud. Trust me, we did have a plan to get you out of here, but it all went pear-shaped the moment Professor Scratchclaw called in Alliance reinforcements. I didn't get a full head count, but I confirmed Ed Rattle, Quanta, Lefthacker, Fire-Eater, Manstro, Sashimi, and Faction, plus at least seven or eight more I didn't even recognize. With those numbers and Scratchclaw calling the shots, we have more than enough evidence to call this an Alliance gig for sure."

Jack scratched his head. "So that's Professor Scratchclaw? Huh. Somehow I expected him to be bigger. So if this isn't about Frosty's daddy issues, do we have any clue what the kitty's after?"

Doko shrugged. "So far, all we know is they were super disappointed Master Mystic wasn't with us."

Jack nodded. "Yeah, I know how they feel. Why didn't he come?"

"You know, too busy ranting about his mission and things not living up to his expectations. That sort of thing."

Jack grimaced. "Not too thrilled about you inducting Ellie here?"

"To say the least," Doko answered, rubbing the back of his head. "I mean, I figured he wouldn't be thrilled, but it's not like he had any alternatives. I wasn't expecting him to just sulk it out."

"Uh, hey, if you girls need your gossip time that's cool, but while you were jabbering I think I figured out how we can get the fuck out of here."

"That's great, Electrikid," Doko said. "But before we do anything we need to figure out a plan to put into action once we escape. Quick, I think that pretty much brings you up to date. Have you managed to pick up anything useful while you've been stuck in captivity?"

"Not much." Jack shrugged. "That security camera doesn't seem to have a microphone, but up until now there wasn't anyone in here for me to talk to. They probably weren't expecting to have multiple prisoners."

Interjecting, Tekno Knight cleared her throat. "Yeah, there's no way they're counting on keeping the five of us in here very long. They didn't even bother trying to get my armor off."

"They probably thought it looked too ghetto to bother with," Electrikid smirked. "You wouldn't bother taking a toy gun from a child, would you?"

"Come on, Electrikid. Heads in the game," Doko admonished. "Anything else?"

"Well, this all started when Jack Frost's son ambushed me outside Mystic's place," Jack said. "I suppose they must've heard about the ad like everyone else and sent him on over to grab me."

Doko nodded in agreement. "They probably picked him because he doesn't have a record yet, so he wouldn't be recognized, and he went along because of his grudge—but Frost is obviously being played just like we are. Still, you're right about the makeshift nature of this cell; the Alliance couldn't have too much prepared beyond what we've already seen. Even a mastermind like Scratchclaw can only have so many trump cards up his sleeve, especially if they just slapped this whole job together yesterday."

Tekno Knight leaned forward keenly. "Yeah, this whole operation definitely has a makeshift feel about it. I mean, right now they're all just running around out there like headless chickens trying to find Mystic. I honestly don't think they even split into organized search parties or anything. Granted, cats aren't notoriously great at organization, but I'd have thought he'd direct a hunting effort with a little more zeal."

Doko agreed, "I couldn't detect any particular patterns of powers either, so their army is probably just whoever they could get to show up. Maybe we can make that work to our advantage. As long as we're confined in here we should be fine—at least until they figure out Mystic isn't out there—so while we have a few minutes, Tekno Knight, why don't you tell us what you can about Professor Scratchclaw."

"Oh, geez. I don't know. He's a cat, you know?"

"Oh my god, Blondie, that is some stunning insight. Bra-vo."

"Electrikid, seriously, the snark isn't helping...but I can't deny I was hoping for a little more insight, Tekla."

"Sorry. But when Fluffy lived with me, he was a normal cat. He liked sitting on my lap, having his chin scratched, and yelling at birds through the window—you know, cat stuff. It wasn't until after that he started hiring big dudes to carry him around, hooking up with the Alliance, and, well...the talking. I mean, I don't really know Professor Scratchclaw at all; I really just knew Fluffy, you know? Honestly, just seeing him freaks me out."

Ellie smiled sadly. "You're not alone there."

Doko clapped his hands together with determination. "All right, people, so here's where we stand: Electrikid thinks she can get us out of here, but we've got over a dozen powered adversaries walking around out there under the guidance of Professor Scratchclaw, each ready to pounce on his command. We know they're looking for Master Mystic, but we don't know why. We don't know what their ultimate goal is, but we know they're willing to commit kidnapping in order to reach it. Anything else?"

Silence.

"Okay. Does anybody have any ideas how we can avoid immediately being overrun the second we escape this freezer?"

Silence.

"Okay," Doko sighed.

* * *

Outside, Professor Scratchclaw scowled as his underlings filtered back into the warehouse, each as empty-handed as the next. He had to concede that it was starting to look like Master Mystic had indeed bowed out of the rescue effort for his old friend.

Scratchclaw shook his head, narrowing his eyes in irritation. *Stupid humans, the minute you count on their apelike attachments to each other they let you down just like they always do. It must be built into the species.*

"Is that everyone, Heatbreak?"

"Uh, I think Dropkick and Striker are still out there, Professor."

"Oh, for fuck's sake. They probably took the opportunity to go play grab-ass with each other. Frost, go find those two idiots and get them back here as soon as you do. Anyone else missing?"

"No, I'm pretty sure everyone else has reported back in. Not a sign of Mystic anywhere."

"And you're sure he isn't just hiding? You know what that…thing is capable of. He could disguise himself as a bush, or a fly, and none of these morons would have a clue."

Heatbreak shrugged. "I guess so. But he doesn't really seem the type, does he? I mean, from the briefing yesterday, I thought the scorched-Earth approach seemed more like his thing. I was expecting him to come blasting in here and turning us into frogs and uh, bushes and whatnot. Big entrances, grand gestures, ironic punishments, that kind of stuff."

"Mmm. You may have a point; subtlety doesn't generally go hand in hand with such power. Still, let's not forget: Mystic's playing the long game on a scale beyond anything any of us can even comprehend. In this case, considering what's at stake, he might even be willing to humble himself."

"I don't know, chief. In my experience? Guys like that, they'll cut off their nose, ears, lips and more to spite their face. I never yet heard a hero admit he was wrong."

"Ugh. That's certainly true. Still, I suppose I wanted to give the New Fighters the benefit of the doubt and assume such a blundering attempt at a rescue was an effort at distraction rather than accept they could really be that incompetent. But you're right, it all makes sense:

bullheaded, self-assured, and thoroughly ineffectual. That certainly fits my previous experience with the blonde one."

"Yep, that's a hero all around, chief." Heatbreak breathed a sigh of relief. While everything he'd said regarding heroes was accurate in his view, he had also learned a thing or two about other villains in his time, especially the types that aspired to leadership positions. He'd half-expected Scratchclaw to petulantly demand they go back out to search fruitlessly for hours, but at least now there was a faint outside possibility that this half-assed operation the cat had dragged them into might even be wrapped up before the sun went down.

Scratchclaw licked his paw, preened his ears, and stretched himself to his full height. "Well, Heatbreak, before we go changing course midstream, we'd better be damn sure he's not out there. Because right now, we're left with no choice but the unthinkable. Trog?"

The cat's hulking helper raised his right hand high in the air. Around the warehouse, the chatter of idle conversations trailed off as all eyes turned towards the cat perched on Trog's muscular shoulder.

"All right, people. Everyone but Dropkick and Striker has reported in, and I've sent Frost to retrieve them. I'm sorry to report that Mystic doesn't seem to have taken the bait, so we're a go for plan Z; take your positions and be ready for anything. Remember what's at stake here: if we don't pull this off, it could mean the end of everything."

* * *

Outside, neither Dropkick nor Striker was remotely concerned about Scratchclaw's apocalyptic predictions.

"Shit, dude. I don't see anything either."

"Come on Dropkick. Don't let me down. It's been like, ten minutes since we saw any of the others. You know I didn't have a chance to grab all my stuff before heading out here."

"Yeah, because you went back to sleep while I stayed up getting prepared."

"Fine, you're the industrious grasshopper and I'm the lazy ant. Just keep looking."

"More like clumsy ant. Look, I'm tired of this. It probably fell down a hole. We're going to get bitten by a rattlesnake or something if we keep poking around under bushes searching for crap that isn't there."

"Man, you know that piece is special to me. Marsha brought that back from Arizona for me."

"All your pieces are special to you. Just get over it, just tell her the truth for once. It's not a big deal. Look, I got a soda can."

Striker recoiled. "Forget that. Don't you know that stuff gives you Alzheimer's?"

"Ah, that's not true. That's an old wives' tale. Besides, it's all we have."

"Fine, whatever. Hand it here. Ah shit, never mind—here comes that tool Frost."

"You think he'll be cool? Stop snickering, you know what I mean."

"Nah. He's all Little Mister Tryhard, living up to his father's legacy and that crap. He wants in the Alliance so bad you can taste it from here."

"Ouch. Like I always say, leave the daddy issues to the strippers."

"No, I said that. Last week, when we were watching cartoons."

"You sure? I don't remember that."

"Sure I'm sure. Marsha shot me a shitty look over it and I haven't gotten it wet since then, that's how sure I am. Anyway, keep it together; put that shit away for now."

Jack Frost Junior crossed his arms as he approached the two snickering rogues sitting on the ground, backs leaned against a huge boulder. "There you two are. Did you find him?"

"Master Mystic? Oh yeah, yeah, we did. It was tough, but Striker got him in a headlock and I gave him the old kangaroo kick. Sent the magic man flying over that dune right yonder; go take a look if you don't believe me."

"Yeah," Striker nodded. "He's totally right over behind that boulder."

Frost glanced briefly at the dune behind them; Dropkick and Striker broke up giggling. Frost pressed his lips together tightly, his nostrils flaring. "Jesus, you two chucklefucks are useless. If we weren't so shorthanded, you wouldn't even be here."

"Who's this 'we', snowman? Last I checked, we're the card-carrying Alliance members here. You're just a scrub pledge."

"Yeah, sure, a scrub pledge entrusted with a crucial part of the plan."

Striker rolled his eyes. "'Crucial part of the plan'? You only got sent to do that because no one else wanted to. Anyone with half a brain would've figured on getting turned into a rat or worse."

"Well, I pulled it off, didn't I? That should say something for my future in the Alliance."

"Oh yes. Kudos, young Frost." Striker chortled as Dropkick clapped three times slowly, each stinging slap of his hands echoing across the barren field. "Congratulations, your certificate for outstanding achievement in the field of cannon fodder should be showing up any time."

Frost's lips were a thin line as he looked through narrowed eyes between the two tittering rogues. "Look, if you clowns are about done with your little comedy routine, Scratchclaw wants everyone back at the warehouse tout suite."

"Hey, come on dude. Stay cool."

"Yeah, it's isssolated enough out here," Dropkick added, emphasizing and elongating the first syllable of 'isolated' until Frost's brow creased in annoyance. "C'mon, take a seat. Let's chill out before heading back."

Frost flushed red, stomping off in the direction of the warehouse. Dropkick and Striker burst out laughing.

"Haha, oh shit dude. That was priceless."

"'Iceless', you mean?"

"Hah...that's a stretch, but I'll give it to you—points."

"Damn, that dude is wound tight. What a shmuck. What's the point of being a villain if you can't have a little fun?"

"Ah, he's probably okay. I bet you were nervous as shit on your first Alliance mission too."

"Yeah, maybe. But I was never such a buttsniffer. You should have seen him kissing up to that moron Heatbreak, just because his dad used to pal around with the guy. Heatbreak was eating it right up too.

It's probably been ten years since anyone even pretended to take him seriously."

"Yeah, well, there's a reason for that. Smoke 'em while you got 'em."

"Got that right, 'Kick. And, uh, speaking of which—this is cashed." Striker yawned, poking at the soda can and stretching his back. "Guess we ought to get heading. Don't want to catch the cat's claws, after all."

"All right, all right. Sun's starting to get a little warm out here anyway. Maybe Frosty can whip us up some snowcones." Dropkick struggled to his feet, looked down, and let out a burst of laughter. "Oh shit, here's your piece! I was totally sitting on it, dude."

"Oh, awesome—toss it here. I wasn't looking forward to explaining that one to Marsha."

"You're so fucking whipped, Striker."

"Striker? That's no way to treat a lady!"

The two friends' raucous laughter echoed across the plain as Jack Frost Junior's ears burned with resentment.

* * *

Jack Quick jolted into readiness as the freezer door suddenly flew open, slamming against the wall with a loud bang. *They must not have piled as much ice in front this time*, he thought, leaping to his feet. Electrikid, Tekno Knight, and Doko also assumed defensive stances, their reflexes only slightly behind Quick's, though no attack seemed forthcoming.

The second the door was clear, Doko stepped in front of Jack, furiously waving his arms to disperse the haze of steam. *I'll give Doko this much credit*, Jack thought: *for a government employee, he sure isn't shy about putting himself out there*. Knowing his powers would serve a little more effectively, Quick spun his wrists speedily, whipping up a pair of small vortices that rapidly thinned the thick cloud of water vapor obscuring the freezer door. As the sickly mist concealing the far corners of the warehouse dissipated, Jack saw an array of threatening figures standing in a semicircle, all facing them with arms crossed. At the apex of the semicircle, directly in front of the doorway, the black-suited goliath cradled his feline master in his arms, the cat busily grooming his ears with one damp paw.

As the last of the steam cleared, the cat lifted his head, looking past Quick to Doko. "Well, government man—or Mister Doko, I should say—my associates have verified the information provided by your kitten here." He nodded at Ellie. "I applaud your truthfulness, young human. Would that all members of your species spoke with such credibility."

Behind him, Jack heard Tekno Knight mutter inaudibly under her breath. Scratchclaw stopped brushing his fur back, narrowing his eyes in annoyance. "What was that, Tekla? Please speak up and enunciate if you have something to add to the discussion."

Tekno Knight looked away, wincing. "No—nothing."

"Hm. All right, then." Completing his grooming, the cat straightened his spine and looked Doko directly in the eye, his tail slowly swishing from side to side as he spoke. "If I may continue, I was about to say that because this one has established a level of honesty I am unaccustomed to from typical humans, I shall give you the benefit of the doubt and address you as if you were members of a more rational species."

Doko set his jaw. Knowing the villain had the upper hand, he had little choice but to ride it out, hoping and praying the road led someplace more pleasant. "All right then, kitty. We're honored you've lowered yourselves to speak with us mere humans. Go on then, say what you have to say."

Scratchclaw stuck his tongue out and looked to Ellie. "You see? Such manners, and here I am trying my best to communicate on your level. Still, I forewarn you, some among your group will find what I am about to tell you difficult to accept. Typically I would consider this approach futile, but the fact of the matter is, we are left with few options. I pray you will accept my words in the spirit they are delivered: a last, desperate bid for survival."

Doko pursed his lips skeptically. "Whose survival? Yours? Why should I trust you?"

"The survival I speak of is mine, yes—but also yours, along with that of everyone you have ever known. And as far as trust, I thought

I'd already adequately addressed that issue, but perhaps you require additional perspective. You see, unlike most of those you laughably call 'heroes', I freely admit to being motivated entirely by self-interest, enlightened or otherwise. Therefore, when my goals coincide with your goals, you can be assured there is no duplicity in my words, because I openly admit disinterest in helping anyone or anything other than myself."

"I'm not sure I find that particularly reassuring, but go ahead."

"Fine. Our mission this day had one and only one goal: to lure Master Mystic from his tower, ambush him, and hopefully utterly destroy him."

Doko cocked his head. "And you'd admit this to a federal law enforcement officer why?"

"Because, human, if you don't assist us in wiping the entity you know as Master Mystic from the face of the Earth, soon this entire universe and everything in it will itself be wiped from existence."

Suddenly Jack Quick shot ahead of Doko, his finger jutting at the sneering cat. "What the shit are you talking about, you little fucker?"

Scratchclaw looked at Ellie. "Kitten, please inform this old tom that in polite circles, pointing is generally considered rude."

"I don't care about your politeness, kitty. That's my friend you're talking about killing there."

"Really?" Scratchclaw raised one eyebrow at Quick. "Your 'friend,' you say. All right then, so you'll be taking responsibility for enabling him when all of creation is deconstructed? I suppose some might find that comforting, but me, not so much. When I go to bed at night, I like to be assured the world will be there in the morning."

Jack bared his teeth. "Cat, you'd better start making a damn sight more sense really fucking soon, or the next time you blink you're going to find yourself in the next county."

Unimpressed, Scratchclaw looked to his underlings. Each stepped forward one pace, tightening the semicircle around the confining freezer. "I would remind you which party has the upper hand here, and advise you to take my words in the spirit in which they are offered."

Turning dismissively from Quick to Doko, the cat continued, "Anyway, before this one so rudely interrupted, I was trying to warn you: for some time now, the Alliance has been tracking an approaching threat of cataclysmic proportions. All our soothsayers and future scientists have been working the problem in partnership with some of the top organizations in the world, all donating their resources to help discern the nature of this threat."

"You mean top criminal organizations," Doko interjected.

The cat shot him a withering look. "Top organizations, full stop. Anyway, last week Futura had a vision of Master Mystic—your 'friend'—presiding over the unraveling of this universe, cackling with sheer joy as the very fabric of reality tore asunder beneath his cruel heel."

Jack Quick sneered. "Futura? She's half crazy and all bad. We can't go on her word."

"On that, human, you and I agree. I pride myself on being a rational feline, and at that point the Master had been out of the public eye for much longer than I've been alive. And yes, I concede Futura can be a little…let's say dramatic for my taste. But then, when out of nowhere the long-concealed location of Master Mystic's hidden fortress was suddenly revealed to all and it was discovered that Mystic was attempting to reactivate the Fighters, well, suddenly, Futura's predictions didn't seem quite so unhinged."

"That's not the case at all. Mystic called me to help fight this threat you're talking about!" Pleading, Quick turned to the other Fighters. "Fabric of reality unraveling, cataclysmic threat to the universe—those were practically the same words he used on the signalphone. If he was trying to destroy everything, why would he call and tell me beforehand?"

"I know not, human. Who can ponder the motivations of an ancient, immortal entity like that which inhabits the form you call Master Mystic? I can't say I find it at all surprising you favor your fellow human above me, but I do find it disheartening that even in the face of overwhelming evidence to the contrary you stick so transparently to your quaint notions of brotherhood."

Doko shook his head. "So what would you have us do, cat?"

"Isn't it obvious, government man? You join with us, we march together back to Mystic's fortress, and you lure him out so we can destroy him once and for all."

"And if we don't?"

"If you don't?" Scratchclaw sighed. "I'm puzzled that you still seem to feel this is a negotiation. I assure you, that is not the case. It's we who have the upper hand, and for once our motives coincide with you who call yourselves heroes. We are simply trying to do what's necessary to ensure we all have a world to wake up in tomorrow, and next week, and the week after that. What better definition of a hero could there be?"

Doko shot Quick a look; Jack shut his mouth. Doko looked around at each of the Fighters' faces, trying to get a sense of their feelings. He hadn't known any of them long, but already he'd come to trust them. And in trusting them, he found a strength he'd never known on his own.

Turning back to face Professor Scratchclaw, Doko stuck his chin out and cleared his throat.

"All right, kitty. You win."

EPISODE FOUR: THE CIRCLE TIGHTENS

"Come now," Professor Scratchclaw purred. "Surely you don't want to begin such an auspicious undertaking as this with a defeatist attitude. After all, underexposed as the New Fighters may be, one would think the first ever official team-up of a government-sanctioned team of superheroes with our own humble organization to be an occasion meriting a certain amount of pomp and circumstance."

Jack Quick was incredulous at the cat's words. "That's the first time I've ever heard the Alliance of Evil described as a 'humble organization.'"

Scratchclaw smiled. The effect was startlingly sinister on his feline countenance. "Mr. Quick, I realize you've been out of the hero game for a bit, but surely you're aware we rebranded ourselves as simply 'the Alliance' quite some time ago? I know I personally always found labeling one's actions and intentions as 'evil' out of the gate more than a bit limiting. And under circumstances such as these, when we find ourselves taking action for the benefit of all, well…it would simply have been incorrect." He turned back to address Doko. "I suppose one can't blame your uninformed speedster here for holding the nature of our scheme against us, but I'll admit I'm surprised to find you so pleasantly rational about this matter, government man."

Doko shrugged. "I can't say I like the way you went about it, but as a fully-operational superteam, we're compelled to investigate the legitimacy of potential world-shattering threats regardless of the source of the information—even if that source is a manipulative feline supervillain, and even if that threat may stem from one of our own members. So if what you say is true, we don't really have any choice in the matter. Mystic is more powerful than the rest of us put together—"

"Hey!"

"Sorry, Electrikid, but you know it's true."

"That doesn't mean it feels good to hear it put that way."

"Sorry, 'Kid, but we have to be realistic about our chances. If the kitty here is right and Mystic is looking to bring the universe to an end, it'll take the combined efforts of everyone here to have even a fighting chance at subduing him. And if Mystic goes full-on great annihilator, subduing him is our best case scenario. I don't want anyone flying off the handle half-cocked—and that goes for you and your forces as well, Scratchclaw—but we need to prepare ourselves to do whatever might be necessary to solve the problem."

Jack Quick sputtered. "Surely you're not talking about..."

Doko stuck his chin out defiantly. "Don't be obstinate, Quick. You're smart enough to know exactly what I'm talking about."

Scratchclaw purred. "It appears there is some dissention among your ranks, government man. I can understand why that old tom might require additional persuasion; accustomed as he is to thinking of himself as the hero, it must be difficult for Mr. Quick to accept that his role in this little drama has merely been that of a pawn."

Quick lurched forward, but Doko held up a hand, stopping him where he stood. "Yes, I think a few minutes might be necessary for me to convince the more recalcitrant members of my team of the wisdom of your words. But if you'll allow me that time, I'm certain I can bring everyone around to what needs to be done."

"Excellent. I'm sure you'll understand if I request you remain confined within your makeshift cell until we have full assurance of your cooperation, of course."

"Of course. Say, ten minutes?"

"You have three." Scratchclaw signaled with his paw; the semicircle tightened as the Fighters retreated once more into the dank confines of the cramped freezer.

Heatbreak stepped forward and shut the door. To Jack Quick, the click of the lock sounded like the final period at the end of the story that once was the original Fighters' legacy.

* * *

The moment the freezer door locked behind them, Quick exploded at the stonefaced government operative. "Doko, I don't care what you say. There's no way I'm taking the Alliance's side against my only friend in the world!"

"Shh, keep your voice down," Doko admonished. "Of course you're not. None of us are. Even if what they said was true, that's not the way to go about addressing a problem like that—but Scratchclaw and the others will never be able to see it that way."

Ellie exhaled a sigh of relief. "Oh, wow. I really thought we were going to have to go up against him for a minute there."

Tekno Knight looked quizzically at the young girl. "Which one? Master Mystic or Fluf—the cat?"

Electrikid interrupted, "Either way, we're still stuck between a rock and a hard place. Creepy the Cat and his loser brigade out there have at least three times our raw firepower. I say our best option is a strategic retreat."

Tekno Knight frowned. "Like it's that simple? Even if we were somehow able to slip past all of them and make it outside, we already know at least one of them can teleport. I somehow doubt Doko's sedan can get us away faster than Quanta's energy fields."

"Well then, what's your big idea, Blondie? You go right ahead and take on that mob out there if you feel up to it, but having actually been in a fight or two in my life, I think I'll pass, thank you very much. We shouldn't be taking on an army like that with anything less than eight or nine offensive powers, let alone this random gaggle of nitwits."

"Come on, Electrikid," Doko reproached. "Let's not belittle ourselves in the course of figuring out what to do."

"Sorry, but you know I'm right. Without reinforcements, this is a total no-go. Don't you have some way to call for backup?"

"I did, but even if I could get a signal through this metal box I doubt any signals are coming in or out without Scratchclaw's say-so. It's not just a question of our escape, after all: let's not forget that outside this freezer are over a dozen wanted felons, several of whom we know to be directly involved in Quick's kidnapping. If we could get out there long enough to send an SOS, then somehow hold our own long enough for assistance to arrive, not only could we possibly get out of here with our hides intact, but also bring them to justice."

Quick shook his head. "You're fooling yourself, Doko. Even with my speed, we'd be dead long before help arrived."

Tekno Knight grimaced. "So what do you recommend, Quick? You're the real pro here, after all." Electrikid glared at Tekla, but kept her lips pressed tightly together as Jack replied.

"Honestly? I say the second they crack that door open again, we make a break for it and don't look back until we're miles away."

Electrikid broke into a wide grin. "See? Quick agrees with me. Ellie, what do you think?"

Ellie looked surprised. "Me?"

"Sure," Electrikid affirmed. "You're stuck in this situation just like the rest of us, right? And you don't even have a janky metal suit to protect you like Blondie here."

"Well..." Ellie thought back, mentally retracing the circumstances that had brought them to the isolated warehouse. "What I keep thinking is: what if he's right?"

"Who, Doko?"

"No, Scratchclaw. Tekla, do you think he's telling the truth?"

Tekno Knight shuddered, holding her hands out in front of her. "I don't know. I don't even want to think about it. Just seeing him makes me queasy."

Electrikid groaned at Tekla's unease. "The one thing you might actually be able to help with, and it's too much for you to handle. You should have just stayed at home, girl."

Tekno Knight shook her head. "I should probably get myself checked for early onset dementia, because I'm actually starting to find myself agreeing with you. But, Ellie, if I had to guess, I don't feel like Fluff—Scratchclaw is lying, necessarily, though I seriously doubt he's telling us the complete truth. He's obviously trying to somehow manipulate circumstances in his favor; it's what he does. But regardless, that's a question for another time."

Doko frowned. "She's right. Even if there might be a tiny kernel of truth at the heart of Scratchclaw's plan—and I'm not saying there is, Quick, I'm saying *if*—we need to focus on the problem at hand. And as far as our mission goes, right now that means getting out there and capturing as many Alliance members as possible."

Electrikid threw her hands up. "So that brings us back to square one. If we can't all run away, and we can't call for backup, what other choice do we have?"

Doko looked at each of the four people trapped within the small freezer with him, wheels turning inside his head as he mentally recombined their strengths and abilities in as many configurations as he could conceive, trying to hit on the magic combination that might enable them to both maintain their honor and fulfill their purpose.

Finally, after a full minute and a half of silence, he smiled. "I've got it. Haven't any of you ever seen a cowboy movie? There's only one thing to do in this situation: call in the cavalry."

* * *

Outside the warehouse doors, Jack Frost Junior rattled the locked handles to no avail. "Hey, I'm out here, you guys!" Repeatedly and incessantly he kept banging the doors, finally managing to elicit a response as Heatbreak swung one wide.

"Sorry, kid. Scratchclaw had us holding formation. The door was locked to keep the heroes confined, but they're stuck back in the freezer for now. You coming in?"

"Fuck yeah, I'm coming in. There's not a damn thing out there, I'd bet my life on it. Well, other than those two morons Dropkick and Striker, of course."

"Oh, right. Where are they?"

Frost Junior shrugged. "Search me. They said they'd be right behind me, but who knows with those two. I told them Scratchclaw wanted them back ASAP though, so it's on them."

"Alright, get in here then." He hustled Frost inside and locked the door. "Right about now shit's starting to get real, so we need to keep the perimeter tight. You didn't see anything out there?"

Frost shook his head.

"Okay, take a place over there at the end of the semicircle. The Fighters' time is just about up, so be ready to go if it looks like they're going to make a break for it—but wait for Scratchclaw to give the command before you so much as make an ice cube. If you go after Quick before it's time, the cat'll have you strung up and hung out to dry before you know what's happening."

"Fine, fine," Frost muttered, trudging to the far end of the warehouse. He wondered if Dropkick and Striker were really following along. If not, he hoped Scratchclaw wouldn't hold their tardiness and irresponsibility against him as well.

Taking his place in line and crossing his arms, he sighed. *This gig is getting worse all the time*, he thought, watching Heatbreak make his way back to the freezer door and open it just wide enough for Doko to step through, the remaining Fighters lined up dutifully behind him in single file.

"Ah, Doko," Scratchclaw purred. "I trust your negotiations went as expected?"

"They did," Doko intoned. "My team is comprised of professionals, after all. Once I convinced them of the veracity of the threat posed by Master Mystic, each of us quickly realized what we'd have to do in order to save humanity."

"Yes, of course, humanity—along with every other species that exists within the known universe," Scratchclaw sighed. "Still, despite the dismayingly anthropocentric tone of your words, I'm always pleased to see reason prevail. Now, if you'll come with me, we can—"

"NOT SO FAST, EVILDOERS!" A deep, resonant voice rang out from the far end of the warehouse. All eyes turned toward its source, only to see the corrugated metal warehouse doors crumple inward upon themselves as if crushed by some irresistible force, tumbling to the floor in a heap of twisted metal.

As the huge cloud of dust thrown up by the doors' collapse began to clear, four powerful figures stepped through the massive hole where the doors had been, each so recognizable they were known worldwide —and beyond—merely by their silhouettes. All along the onlooking line of rogues and villains, eyes filled with terror and jaws dropped.

"Is that Action Man? And the Gentleman Detective? Shit, it's all of them!"

"Oh, no. Sister Sensation took me in last time!"

Scratchclaw groaned, covering his face with one paw. "Fantastic. Just when one group of would-be do-gooders had finally begun to listen to reason, in barge the Alpha Guns to fuck it all up."

"THAT'S RIGHT," intoned the Action Man. "SURRENDER IMMEDIATELY, FOUL VILLAINS!"

Scratchclaw hissed defiantly. "Never, human, not even if we were fighting solely for ourselves. And today, we fight to save all of reality. Join us, Alpha Guns, if only for your own sakes—for otherwise you will surely perish!"

"NEVER, FIENDISH FELINE!" The Action Man turned to his compatriots, raising his fist in a rallying salute the same way children everywhere did when imitating him. "NOW, ALPHAS—ATTACK!"

* * *

As the Alpha Guns leaped at them, it occurred to Scratchclaw that something was awry. No, Jack Frost Junior wasn't the sharpest of tools, but even that one should have noticed the most famous superheroes in the world gathering outside only moments before he'd returned to the warehouse. Yes, Action Man and Sister Sensation could have moved fast enough to avoid his gaze—but the Detective? Or Space Patrolman?

Scratchclaw surveyed his poorly-disciplined underlings, rushing into battle with the looks of defeated men already plastered on their faces. True, few who faced the Alpha Guns escaped to tell the tale, as many in attendance could personally attest from prior experience. Yet as a master strategist, Scratchclaw knew only too well how much of any battle's outcome depended on motivation and perspective, and he couldn't deny the Alpha Guns' sudden appearance had taken much of the fight out of his forces.

The cat sighed. *If only there had been time to properly brief everyone so we'd all be on the same page*, he told himself, knowing even then the humans would probably still have found some way to ruin his plans. Despite his fearsome reputation, there was only so much one could do with the size and appearance of an average housecat. *Forever to be underestimated: that's the lot of the small mammal*, Scratchclaw mused, watching Manstro leap into battle toward the Gentleman Detective. The Detective swung widely at Manstro, connecting with his temple and sending him tumbling to the floor. Mere seconds later, Sashimi collapsed in similar fashion just a few yards away—though to Scratchclaw's keen feline eyes, the Detective's punch had seemed to fall slightly short of her jaw.

Wait...small mammal, underestimated...

Suddenly, the realization hit Scratchclaw like a bolt from the blue. He yowled as loud as he could, trying to recapture the frenzied villains' attention: "It's not them! Stop, stop! It's not them! It's the girl, it's a sensory projection; the Alpha Guns aren't even here!"

Standing in the freezer doorway, Tekno Knight grinned, cranking her white noise generator up another notch to drown Scratchclaw's words of warning beneath a blanket of sonic chaff. Bad enough she'd had to endure the cat's weird low voice as he crowed and berated them; when Scratchclaw got agitated his tone reminded her how he'd sounded on the night the two had parted ways for the last time as pet and owner. Tekla shuddered as she watched his tiny jaw open and shut silently on her heads-up display, recalling the events of that fateful night. If only she could have drowned him out this way from the beginning.

She turned and shouted over her shoulder, outside the range of the noise generator, "You holding up okay back there, Ellie?"

Crouching behind Tekno Knight, Ellie peered through the older woman's armored legs, directing her projections of the world's most famous superheroes. "F-fine," she whimpered, though Tekla noted with alarm a thin red line of blood trickling below Ellie's left nostril.

"Just a little bit longer, hon, you're doing great. Quick and the 'Kid have taken out four or five already, and the rest are scattering quickly."

Gritting her teeth, Ellie strained to maintain her concentration. She'd never maintained so many moving elements in one of her projections for so long before—but then, her life had never been on the line in quite the same way either. It was lucky for Doko she'd been such a big Alpha Guns fan when she was a kid: even now, she found it easier to maintain the illusion they were actually there in the warehouse subduing the panicking rogues by reverting to the costumes they'd worn years before. Fortunately, only the ornamental details had changed; the essential designs always remained basically the same for trademark and marketing purposes—and their surprise had hit with enough impact that few of the rogues seemed to have the presence of mind to check the shape of the Action Man's belt-buckle for continuity errors.

"I-I'm okay, Tekno Knight. But please, tell me they're almost done."

"Just a sec, hon," Tekla answered. "Even my instruments are having a hard time keeping up with Quick." She engaged her suit's auto-tracking sensors, gasping as the screen snapped back and forth faster than her eyes could follow, her high-def cameras barely managing to track Jack Quick as he rocketed unseen around the warehouse, carrying Electrikid on his back as Ellie's projections of the Alpha Guns appeared to connect with each villain in turn and then letting Electrikid shock them into unconsciousness before invisibly speeding off to repeat the process in another area of the chaotic melee. "Jesus, he must be going just under the speed of sound."

A light flashed on Tekla's display and she jerked her head rightwards. The still-intact warehouse door cracked open, but distracted as they were, none of the still-conscious Alliance members appeared to notice the discontinuity with Ellie's projection, and she turned her attention back to the Fighters as the door silently shut once more.

* * *

On the other side of the warehouse door, Striker looked quizzically at his friend. "Hey, why'd you close it? Isn't the cat going to be ticked?"

"I, uh...think it's too late for that," Dropkick replied. He wasn't sure what exactly was going on inside, but the sight of his fellow Alliance members swinging wildly at the air and running around like chickens with their heads cut off was enough to convince him that whatever it was, was something he wanted no part of.

Striker's eyes narrowed in annoyance. "Why?"

"Dude, just trust me. Leave that door shut and you'll sleep a lot better tonight. Me, I'm heading back the way we came as fast as I can; I highly suggest you do the same."

Striker shrugged. "Okay, fuck it. If you say so, I'll go with it."

The pair dashed off back towards Striker's battered Nissan, concealed behind some bushes a half-mile away from the warehouse. Striker didn't even bother looking back once before idly checking his phone. "Hey, Marsha isn't expecting me back for another few hours. Let's just go to your place, get baked and play games."

Dropkick rolled his eyes. "Could we maybe wait until we're a hundred percent sure we're not being followed before discussing future plans? Christ."

"Oh please, don't fool yourself. If Scratchclaw gets out of this one he'll be able to find us no matter what. And if any heroes are around, we're screwed anyway. So what's the diff?"

"I guess you're right." He scratched his head, looking around as they crested the top of a hill and the Nissan appeared before them. "I don't see anyone coming after us anyway, unless they're invisible or a ghost or whatever."

"Great." Striker unlocked the car and popped the trunk, frantically throwing the identifiable pieces of his costume into the vehicle as he disrobed. "Here—get your street clothes back on. Let's go hit the weed shop and then get some burgers."

The classic rock of Foghat replaced the sounds of battle ringing in the villains' ears as they cruised away from the battleground, Dropkick already far more occupied with figuring out his lunch order and deciding which strain of marijuana he wanted to buy than he had ever been with Scratchclaw's plan.

* * *

Back inside the warehouse, Faction fell unconscious to the floor a few yards in front of Tekno Knight as Jack Quick came screeching to a halt, gasping for breath. Electrikid dislodged herself from his back, looking slightly askance at him as she regained her wobbly footing.

"You're breathing awful hard there, speedboy. You trying to tell me to cut down on the chocolates?"

"Been...been a long time since I...r-ran that fast trying to carry someone," Quick panted, smiling up at her. "And don't call me 'speedboy', thanks."

"Ah, I don't know. I think it has a certain ring to it; Heatbreak's a real poet. I guess he wasn't sharp enough to see this one coming, though." She kicked at Heatbreak's unconscious form lying prone beside the freezer. "I figured he might have had half a clue, since you fought him back in the day and all."

"He was never exactly a mastermind back then. And based on the fact that he's still doing this kind of thing, I doubt he spent the past couple of decades in night school. Plus, I never had your ability to shock someone into unconsciousness in a fraction of a second. That sure would've come in handy a time or two."

Electrikid looked pleased. "Yeah, I've got to admit, it's nice not to have to fight it out mano-a-mano for once. Zap them, run away, zap them again—a girl could get used to this."

"Well, it never would have worked without such an awesome distraction. We'd better not count on this working the next time we face the Alliance, if there is one. Speaking of which: hey, Ellie? You're good to cut the feed."

"Oh, thank god." Ellie collapsed to the floor, exhausted. Tekno Knight shut down her white noise generator and reached out to her, helping the young woman to her feet.

Across the warehouse, Lefthacker sputtered with confusion as Space Patrolman and the other Alpha Guns vanished from his view. "Wh-what the...?" Surveying the warehouse, suddenly all he could see was the crumpled forms of Alliance members littering the floor and the grinning, victorious Fighters regrouping outside the freezer that had served as their prison until moments before—and like Dropkick and Striker, Lefthacker too decided to slip quietly away while he had the chance.

Doko stepped out of the freezer. Before even looking around at the fallen villains, he walked directly to Ellie, clinging to Tekno Knight's armor for support, holding a tissue to her nose: "I'm fine, I'm fine! That just took it out of me a little more than I expected. Trust me, I'm okay!"

"I'm sure you are, Ellie, but I promised Henry and your mom I'd watch out for you, and all this has already gone way farther than any of us ever expected when I asked you to join the Fighters in the first place," Doko rebutted. "Those losers that Electrikid and Quick zapped aren't going to be going anywhere in the time it takes me to check your vitals, so sit down."

"Ugh, fine," Ellie relented. "I don't see the kitty, though."

"Ah shit. You're right." Tekla's head spun side to side as both her eyes and her suit's instruments scanned for Scratchclaw's diminutive form. "I don't see his big friend, either."

"That's okay, guys. Considering we're all in one piece and we managed to capture more than half the Alliance members holding us hostage, I think we can safely call this one a win." Doko finished checking Ellie's pulse and breathing, and helped her back to her feet. "Like I said, once you guys really learn how to use your powers together as a team you'll be unstoppable. Just remember: strike fast, take advantage of the confusion, and take the win before they even know what's happening."

Electrikid snorted. "Oh, sure. You're first in line to take the credit for this one, but let's not forget who came up with the 'sneak into the warehouse' plan that got us captured in the first place."

Doko nodded. "No, you're right, 'Kid. We all have a lot of work to do before we get there, me included. But you guys did great, all of you —especially you, Ellie. I'll admit I was worried about your ability to hold such a complex illu—projection for so long, but you handled it like a champ."

Ellie blushed, smiling. "I'm a lot better on offense than defense."

"Noted for future reference." Doko placed his hands on his lower back and arched his spine. "Ahh, it's so good not to be crammed into that stinky freezer. I don't know how you tolerated the smell in there for so long, Quick."

"I didn't really notice, to tell you the truth. Too busy thinking about other things, I suppose. It's been noted that I tend to hyper-focus just on whatever's right in front of me, often to the exclusion of all else. I used to think of it as a strength, myself, but others have occasionally felt differently in the past." He coughed.

"Mm. Or maybe I'm just overly sensitive to smells." Shaking his head, Doko surveyed the aftermath of the melee. "Not to toot my own horn too loudly, but wow, did this work or did it work? Even if the ringleader got away, you guys must have knocked out at least fifteen of these guys."

"Fifteen? Oh come on, we zapped at least twenty of these losers. I tell you, if I could figure out a way to get around unseen like this guy, well, I'd be an A-lister myself." Electrikid beamed and slapped Quick on the back.

Quick jumped with surprise at her affection, but smiled back at the young woman. "We did make a pretty good team out there, huh? Hope your stomach's okay, I couldn't slow down too much to take some of those tight turns or someone might have spotted us."

Electrikid waved her hand dismissively. "Nah, I've had worse. At any rate, within a minute or so it was all over but the shouting anyway."

"Speaking of the shouting, we'd better get these perps cuffed and ziptied before any of them start stirring," Doko said, popping the trunk of his car and extracting the necessary supplies. "Here, Tekla, hand these around while I call in for a couple of wagons to come pick up the garbage."

Extracting his phone from his pocket, Doko was relieved to see the signal indicator at full strength. He hated to admit it even to himself, but seeing zero bars on the display while inside the freezer had panicked him nearly as much as the confinement.

Smoothing his clothes down, he dialed the home office while the members of the Fighters busied themselves immobilizing their unconscious foes. "Francine? Doko here. Listen, I—"

"Doko?!" Francine's voice was full of anxiety. "Where the hell have you been? Don't you know—"

"Whoa, whoa! I'm sorry, Frannie, but I was locked in a freezer with no cell reception until just a few minutes ago."

"Don't you mean to say *we* were locked in a freezer? As in you and the actual members of the Fighters, with whom you're not even supposed to be going into the field?"

"How do you—look, Frannie, I'm sorry about that, really I am. But there were extenuating circumstances in this situation that I couldn't get around any other way."

"Oh, really? And what, pray tell, was your rationale for bringing an untrained minor into the line of fire? I told you yesterday that was a bad idea."

"You mean Ellie? Without her, there's no way we would have…wait, look, never mind. I'll explain all this later in my official report. Right now, I just need you to send some wagons out to cart away the nearly two dozen known Alliance members we managed to apprehend, dubious methods or not. When I file my report, we can go over the details then. And at that time, feel free to ream me out to your heart's content, but right now, I'd really just like to make sure we have some mobile confinement on the way before one of these pricks wakes up. I'm texting you the coordinates now."

"Fine," Francine seethed through gritted teeth. "They're on the way. But Doko, don't think you can sweep this under the rug. You know this isn't the way I like to do things."

"Uh, Doko?" Behind him, Tekno Knight tapped him on the shoulder. He held up a finger to signal that he'd be with her in a moment, but she wouldn't be dissuaded. "I really think you might want to take a look at this."

"Tekla," Doko hissed. "Can't you see I'm on the phone with my supervisor? And in case you're not so good at picking up on social cues, she's super pissed at me for some reason, so I kind of need to…"

"Yeah," Tekno Knight muttered. "I know." She held her phone out in front of Doko's face and his jaw immediately dropped. Onscreen was a photo, partially blurry, but easily recognizable as Jack Quick, bearing down on the unseen photographer with Electrikid perched atop his back, her hands crackling with power. Behind them, Tekno Knight could be seen blocking the freezer door while Ellie crouched beneath her, her nose bleeding but her jaw set in defiance as she held her hands out protectively in front of herself.

"Oh. Oh, shit. Where the...where did this come from?"

"It just started popping up only a few minutes ago, but it's already the top trending topic on all social media platforms. Every broadcast news service broke into regular programming already to announce that there's a new superteam out there on the front lines."

She punched a few words into her phone and held it back out for Doko to read the headlines: "*Fighters Back In Action? Jack Quick + Electrikid = ? Is This The First Photo Of The New Fighters? Where Is Master Mystic?* Oh, geez. Frannie, I'm, um...I'm going to have to call you back."

"Getting caught up on world news, I assume?"

"Look, Francine, I'm sorry, I really am. But look, when you see my report, I'm sure you'll agree I didn't have any choice."

"I'm sure I will. But you know how this works: right now, your little...your little experiment isn't just blowing up in my face, it's blowing up in everyone's faces, all over the world. You know this isn't how they like these things to be handled. Every minute that picture is floating around out there uncontrolled without a story attached to it, the more damage your little escapade causes. And any second now, someone far enough above my pay grade that they don't have to give the slightest shit about my opinion is going to be calling me, demanding to know exactly what the hell I'm doing to get a lid on this thing. And do you know what I have to tell them right now? Nothing. Not a goddamn thing."

Doko exhaled, long and slow. "Fine. You're right. I'm sorry. What do you want me to do?"

"I don't know, Doko. You're there, I'm not. Use your judgment. Do your job, for Christ's sake. But whatever you do, get out in front of this disaster and do it now." Francine's voice disappeared with an angry beep as Doko replaced his phone in his pocket, entranced by the scroll of headlines continuing to fill Tekla's screen. "They just keep coming. That one's in French!"

"Must be a slow news day, I guess," Electrikid snorted. "Oh well, what's done is done. Can't put the cat back in the bag now, so to speak."

"But how?"

Tekla replaced her phone in her pocket. "I already ran a few traces. Looks like it first appeared on Manstro's Instaphoto stream, then got picked up by the fan groups who follow every detail of this crap obsessively. My guess? Manstro might've figured out we were pulling some sort of sense trickery and tried to take a picture to see if it showed something his eyes weren't seeing. Just our luck, he snapped it at just the right moment as Quick and Electrikid were bearing down on him—and that it got posted as he hit the floor, whether he meant to or not." She nodded towards Manstro's prone, ziptied form lying out cold beside a pile of his comrades. "Maybe he's just one of those attention whores who autoshares every single picture they ever take."

"Fucking loser," Electrikid snorted. "No wonder he's a C-lister, even on a good day. "

Outside, the rumble of trucks pulling up to the warehouse alerted Doko to the arrival of their backup and the captured villains' transport. "Alright, people, let's wrap it up here. Quick, you running on your own or piling into the car with the rest of us?"

Quick winced. "After being whacked on the head, tied up, and held captive for hours, my caloric load is running a little low for long sprints. That last stunt pretty well burned up the last of my reserves."

"Suit yourself. But—"

"Not riding bitch!" Electrikid dashed for the vehicle and jumped into the front passenger seat; Tekla rolled her eyes.

"I was about to say, fight it out among yourselves for seating."

Ellie sighed. "As long as I don't have to get back in the trunk, I don't care. I'll sit in the middle, Jack, you're taller anyway."

"Thanks, Ellie, I appreciate it. But uh, mind if we swing through a drive-through on the way back?"

"Sure, no problem. I'm sure we could all use a little something to keep us going. And I'm buying—or the government is, I should say. For some reason, I have a feeling a little discretionary use of the petty cash fund will be the least of my supervisor's concerns." Doko exhaled slowly as he started the car. *And if nothing else*, he thought, *it'll buy me a little more time to figure out what the hell I'm going to do.*

* * *

As Doko's vehicle sped off in search of sustenance, an unassuming hatchback raced in the opposite direction, its hulking driver's sunglasses and baseball hat doing little to disguise the slackjawed look of dullness on his face.

Curled in the back seat of the small car, Professor Scratchclaw cringed as the ringing phone interrupted the smooth classical stylings of his preferred public radio station.

"Philistines couldn't even allow me the luxury of calling in on my own time," he growled, to no one in particular. "Admittedly, I'm fairly certain I own this particular performance of Mahler's Fourth, but one can hardly call it civilized to interrupt the work midmovement." He sighed. "Ah well, the sooner we get this over with, the sooner I can get back to dear old Gustav."

Extending one paw, he touched a screen mounted on the back of the car seat. A dark, hooded silhouette filled the screen, and Scratchclaw covered his face with his paw. "Why must you insist on making video calls if you're only going to conceal yourself? Trust me when I say that body language is not so intrinsic to human communication that your meaning would be unclear, were you to omit the visual element."

"Don't think you can deter me with glib misdirection, Scratchclaw. As the duly elected leader of the Alliance, I have questions and I demand answers."

"Of course," Scratchclaw purred. "Simply attempting to streamline the process so we'll all get what we want that much more rapidly."

"You can save time by cutting the smarm, cat. Just explain why your supposedly foolproof plan ended with the majority of your underlings in government custody and our goals unmet."

"It's always the same with you humans. The second you personalize anything, it becomes yours and yours alone, as if the ramifications of my failure don't impact upon all of us equally. Yes, I concede my operation was a failure; there's no other way to portray it but as an unmitigated disaster. Yet I believe if you review the minutes of our last meeting, I myself characterized my plan as a long shot at best, and necessary not so much to advance Alliance ends as to ensure the universe we all share continues to exist."

"None of this directly answers the question, Scratchclaw."

"Fine. If I had to theorize, I suppose the novelty of working for the common good rather than enlightened self-interest was a disruptive factor—which reminds me, I'd like to file a formal complaint regarding Striker and Dropkick's complete lack of discipline. I would also point to my inability to share the true import of the job with all operatives equally as possibly resulting in lower motivation than would have been ideal."

"We discussed this, Scratchclaw. And as was indicated to you then, the council decreed that information was to be released on a need-to-know basis."

"Yes, but one might argue they'd have fought a bit harder knowing their failure truly meant the end of all things, rather than simply one more quickly rectified incarceration."

"Asked and answered, cat. Only a poor craftsman blames his tools for his failure."

"Tools is right," Scratchclaw muttered under his breath.

"What's that?"

"Nothing important. In any case, the operation is a failure. The mantle of Grantu remains with Master Mystic, the wheels of universal destruction remain in motion. All is as it was: thoroughly hopeless."

The tone of the silhouetted Alliance leader's reply was clear displeasure, but in Scratchclaw's view somehow fell short of recognizing the full import of the situation. "Hmm. Well, acquiring the mantle would have been a valuable asset in our future plans, admittedly. But speaking bluntly, at least the world seems not to have ended. And I suspect once our legal eagles start working their magic we'll see many of the operatives you lost back in the fold before too long. So don't beat yourself up about it too badly, kitty; now that the tower's location is public knowledge, in the future perhaps we'll have another opportunity to steal it out from under Mystic's nose anyway."

Scratchclaw goggled. "Are you mad? Mystic is in full command of enough power to end everything at any moment! If we don't remobilize as many…" He trailed off as the truth behind his superior officer's words became clear to him. "You…you don't care, do you?"

"Care about what? I hardly think conclusions arrived at by a common house pet merit a panic state." The sneer in the gloating voice's tone was palpable, though the face remained as hidden as ever.

Scratchclaw seethed. "Regardless of my species, my deductions remain sound. I didn't hear any dissent, counterclaims, or alternate approaches proposed during the planning stages of this mission."

"This failed, defunct mission, you mean? It seems to me—and all of us here on the council, in case I'm not making myself clear enough for you—that now that you've taken your shot, the matter is out of our hands."

"But—"

"What do you propose, Scratchclaw? A frontal assault on Mystic's tower? You know as well as any of us that would be suicide, or you would have proposed such a solution already. No, we tried it your way—but now, the heroes will have to sort out their own problems."

"And what? We just pray there's a world when we wake up in the morning?"

"Well, if that's the only solution you're able to come up with, I suppose you're welcome to it, Scratchclaw," the voice purred. "Myself, I think the Alliance has better things to do than pursue your personal obsessions. And frankly, I'd be amazed if the Fighters didn't as well."

"You'd better hope not," Scratchclaw retorted. "Because now that my plans lie in ruins, those idiots are the only thing standing between all of us and complete annihilation."

* * *

Back in Doko's car, while fishing around for the last of her fries, Tekla marveled at the pace at which the photo of them in action continued to spread.

"Look at this: the Japanese morning headlines are starting to hit. We're the top pop culture topic across the board over there."

"Ugh, don't remind me," Doko groaned. "Honestly, I was kind of hoping this thing would have blown over by the time we finished lunch. Haven't any other shiny objects popped up in the last couple of hours? Is it too much to ask for one well-timed celebrity blowout to knock us off the front page?"

Tekla shook her head. "Sorry, boss. For whatever reason, this one shot Manstro took is the trend of the day."

Doko rubbed his temples. "Great. Still, that's what online is for, right? The newest, the current, the latest and greatest, all that? All we have to do is make the story go away. No problem. I mean, what's so interesting about this one stupid picture anyway?"

Electrikid smirked back over the top of the seat at Tekla. "You can't see it? Come on, Quick and I couldn't have looked more totally badass in that shot if we'd planned it. You can practically feel us bearing down on that shmuck Manstro; it's just too bad your clunky metal suit is there in the background cluttering up the shot. I'm surprised more people aren't cropping you out, actually."

Tekla glared back at Electrikid, her nostrils flaring. "Well they aren't, are they? In fact, the foreign coverage seems especially curious about Ellie and me. By the time the story hit overseas, you and Quick were both positively confirmed by the experts."

Electrikid stuck out her tongue. "So what? Who cares about foreign coverage?"

"Well, uh, actually they're probably all working from the same wire story at this point," Jack interjected. "In the absence of actual facts or new developments, they're all just spinning their wheels and filling time until someone else adds to the story."

Ellie leaned over the seat to look at Electrikid's phone, now with Manstro's shot of them in the warehouse set as her home screen. "You can see why it's caught people's attention, though. I mean, whenever you see real heroes—"

"Oh, nice. Thanks for that, kid," muttered Electrikid, yanking her phone away.

"I mean, n-not real, but you know—big, famous ones like the Alpha Guns. Whenever you see them it's always set up just so, and it all feels so plastic and fake. Even when they're supposed to have just defeated an alien invasion or whatever, they all look like they just got out of the makeup chair, you know?"

Jack stared back at her. "What do you mean, 'supposed to have' defeated an invasion? Are you saying they didn't?"

"No! I-I'm not saying that at all. I just—I'm just telling you how it looks to me. But I know, uh, a lot of other kids at my school feel the same way. They never saw any of the Alpha Guns in real life, any more than they ever saw Santa Claus or Jesus."

Jack smiled. "I see. So from their perspective, they don't have any reason to believe one thing over another."

"Y-yeah. I mean, for the most part it doesn't affect most people's lives one way or another, as long as the world keeps turning."

"Right. And the way things have been handled while the Fighters have been defunct, people have gotten used to a certain tightly controlled, perfectly packaged public presentation where superheroes are concerned. Is that it?" He leaned up, directing his voice over the seat towards Doko. "That's why your superior was so upset, isn't it? You're off the reservation with all of this."

Doko squinted his eyes against the glare of the afternoon sun streaming through his windshield. "Look, I'll concede events have gotten a little off script. And yes, there's a certain way Department higher-ups like things to be handled when possible. But you guys were there; there's no way anyone could have anticipated things going down the way they did."

Jack shook his head slowly. "Doko, Doko. The one thing you should always know about these things is that they never, ever go the way you expect."

As Doko's car rounded the final corner coming up on Mystic's tower, his passengers' jaws all dropped simultaneously. Doko just sighed at the sight of the formerly obscure fortress now entirely encircled by vans bristling with satellite feeds, each vehicle emblazoned with a different logo, collectively representing every single news agency he was familiar with and some he wasn't.

On hearing the car's approach all eyes turned toward them, followed by a stampede of camera operators, on-air reporters, and supporting technical crew, each jockeying to be the first to report on any new developments.

It was Ellie who spoke first, her voice dry and cracking with shock as she peered out of the car's one-way windows at the gaping, staring faces surrounding them: "Uh, Doko? That certain way D.E.A.P. likes things to be handled—is there a protocol in place for handling unplanned press conferences? Because I think you're about to conduct one."

Doko just sighed again.

* * *

"This is Betsy Carmichael from CN News, reporting live from outside the fabled tower of Master Mystic, longtime magic-wielder for classic superteam the Fighters, long thought defunct. This morning, however, a single blurry photograph from the Instaphoto stream of known Alliance associate Manstro has ignited a frenzy of renewed interest in the decades-inactive Fighters. Shown here, the picture appears to capture longtime Fighters speedster Jack Quick in the midst of battle alongside Electrikid, former sidekick to Voltaic, and two other women whose identities remain unknown—although some internet sources have tentatively identified the armor-clad blonde woman to the left of the frame as Armorine, or possibly a new incarnation of Knightess. No theories as to the younger, dark-haired woman's identity have yet been —wait! Roger, if you're seeing this, a dark sedan with blacked-out windows has turned into the tower's driveway and is slowly progressing up to where we're standing. I'm going to attempt to get closer to the vehicle."

"Thanks, Betsy. Again, for viewers just joining us, that's CN News' own Betsy Carmichael reporting live from the previously unknown secret headquarters of the Fighters." The shellac-haired, blinding-white human smile turned back to face the camera before continuing, "Picking up on our top story, after over fifteen years of inactivity, evidence has surfaced within the last twenty-four hours indicating a revival of the classic superteam the Fighters is in the offing, or has possibly been secretly active for some time. Early reports yesterday were dismissed as the results of an internet prank gone awry, but what was mere speculation only hours ago has exploded into a firestorm of activity. For more, let's turn to our in-house expert on superhuman activity, Gordon Del Mundo. Gordon, why has this single, poorly-shot image blown up into such a hot topic for discussion?"

"It's simple, Roger. For decades now, the superhuman narrative has been so carefully shaped and controlled by the powers that be—please pardon my little joke—that few of your viewers under the drinking age will be able to recall any similar incidents during their lifetime. Even most thirtysomethings have never before borne witness to events such as this: looking on as what appears to be either a new superteam or a new iteration of a classic team emerges into the limelight for the first time."

"Mm. Yet, Gordon, haven't we seen similarly promising debuts in recent years from quickly-forgotten teams such as the Kinetix or Team 9000, to name but two? What makes this new team of Fighters so much more fascinating to the public at large?"

As the camera cut to Del Mundo, Roger yawned widely. Del Mundo looked askance at the orange-tanned anchor, but continued apace. "One word, Roger: authenticity. The teams you mentioned, along with many others, have all failed to find favor with the public for one reason or another, but I and many of my fellow enthusiasts in the superfollower community trace these teams' common failure to launch back to the nature of their origins. All were carefully coached, shaped, and managed from day one, forced to conform to a narrow cookie cutter template, and taught that the worst thing they could possibly do is go off-message. They don't connect with the public because we can sense those 'heroes' aren't there to protect them; they don't even register to most as relatably human, existing only to advance the ends of their superiors. And whether those superiors are the government or the Alliance, Roger, public confidence in institutions of authority is at an all-time low—and who can blame them, really? I mean, the Kinetix toys were in stores before they even so much as got a cat out of a tree."

"Mm. Perhaps, Gordon, but some would point to the Levittown tragedy as evidence that closely monitoring the activities of specially powered individuals—while constitutionally suspect—may be necessary. After all, we haven't had another incident of the magnitude of the Levittown event in the past two decades, have we? Isn't that evidence that the government's current policies—while somewhat draconian, as you and yours would argue—are, in fact, working?"

Del Mundo gritted his teeth. "No, Roger. No, I wouldn't say that. In fact, I'd—"

Smiling, Roger turned back toward the unblinking eye of the camera. "I'm sorry, Gordon, that's all we have time for right now. I've just been told that we're going to cut back to Master Mystic's tower, where our reporter on the scene Betsy Carmichael is waiting to bring us all the latest updates on this enthralling situation. Betsy?"

"Thanks, Roger. Five minutes ago, I—along with the assembled representatives of a dozen press agencies—bore witness as a single government-issue sedan drove up, parked outside the tower, and sat silently. We have confirmed the plates on the sedan are registered to the local division of the Department of Extrahuman Abilities and Powers, though D.E.A.P. representatives had no comment when contacted. Sixty seconds ago, all of us here—reporters, camera operators, and other technical crew alike—each simultaneously received text messages alerting us that a spokesman would be emerging from the vehicle to make a statement regarding the Fighters—predicated on the condition that all press representatives withdraw to a distance of ten yards from the tower itself as well as the sedan, conditions with which we have now complied. As such, we expect the aforementioned...yes, hold on, Roger...yes, we're being told that the driver's side car door is opening. It looks like a man is getting out, holding up a badge. Neil, can you get a close-up of that?"

The picture wobbily zoomed in, just managing to catch a fleeting few frames of Doko's D.E.A.P. identification before he withdrew it, replacing it in his jacket pocket as he slipped out of his vehicle. He shut the door firmly behind him as half a dozen camera operators jockeyed for position near the car, each desperately trying to catch a glimpse inside.

"Hey there, guys, ten yards is ten yards. You saw the ID. Don't make me prove I have the authority to back it up."

Sheepishly, the cameras turned as one to focus on Doko's face as every inch of the bustling ten-yard circle of activity around his car suddenly fell silent; a bristling tableau of microphones, lenses, and blank, open faces, all staring in his direction.

He coughed, suddenly more aware of himself than he'd ever been, and nervously cleared his throat.

"Um...hello. And thank you for joining us here today. I, er, I'm afraid this outpouring of support for the New Fighters has taken us all off guard—"

An unknown voice shouted, "Sir, if you please, what's your name?"

"Oh, um, sorry." Doko fumbled his identification back out of his jacket, opened it and turned in a three hundred and sixty degree circle, holding it out for all to see. "Doko, local representative of Department of Extrahuman Abilities and Powers."

Though no lenses or microphones could be seen to turn away, an audible "aw" of disappointment went up from the crowd of journalism professionals.

"That's right, I'm D.E.A.P., but that doesn't mean you're going to leave here empty handed today. However, as I was saying, I will concede that none of us anticipated the debut of the New Fighters would be the focus of such international interest. In fact, er, we..."

"Can you comment on the Manstro picture, Mr. Doko?"

"What about Quick and Electrikid? Can we speak to them?"

"Who's the girl, Doko? Who's the girl?"

Doko waved his hands exasperatedly. "People, people. I'm sorry, today we're not prepared to answer questions regarding the lineup of the Fighters, such as it may be."

"Is that confirmation that the new team is, in fact, a new iteration of the Fighters?"

"No, no, it's just—look, I'm sorry, no questions. That's it. Just, um, please clear away from the path leading up to the tower—that's right—and I can finish my statement. Come on, come on—the sooner you're all off the path, the sooner we can all get out of here."

A few moments of muttering and shuffling later, Doko continued, "Thank you. Now, as I was saying, this outpouring of interest in the New Fighters has taken us by surprise, so I'm only going to be making a short statement today. First of all: yes, I can confirm that a new iteration of the Fighters has been convened, and further that the picture you're all here to ask about is in fact a genuine photograph taken in the midst of the new team's first group activity. However, because this first call to action took the form of an unplanned emergency, we are unfortunately not prepared at this time to answer your questions—other than to claim responsibility for capturing over a dozen wanted Alliance members as the New Fighters' first victory."

The crowd erupted into displeased murmurs.

"Now, now. I'm sorry, but you guys know we have procedures we need to follow. None of the New Fighters have been properly debriefed, and we have to interface with the proper authorities to ensure any relevant information is delivered into their hands as soon as possible in order to ensure all parties are able to continue doing their very best to help keep America safe. But rest assured, I know you and the viewing public out there want answers. And we're prepared to give them to you—just not yet."

"When, then?"

Doko smiled. "I'm glad you asked, sir." He withdrew his phone from his pocket and clicked a button. "If you'll all return right here, exactly twenty-four hours from now, we'll be ready to introduce the New Fighters the right way—and yes, to answer any and all questions you might have." *Until the tightly-structured question-and-answer session period winds down, that is*, Doko thought to himself before continuing aloud, "Tomorrow, I'll be pleased to introduce you to the complete lineup of the New Fighters, let them answer your questions, tell you about our plans, and—who knows? We might even have some special surprise guests on hand to make it especially worth your while."

Doko's last sentence seemed to placate most of the dissatisfied rumblings among the group, but one agitated reporter bearing a thick beard and a thicker Germanic accent muscled his way to the front of the crowd and jabbed an accusatory finger at Doko. "I think you shape and manage this event like any public relations campaign, sir. Why can we not talk to your colleagues now?"

"My colleagues?" Doko feigned surprise. "Well, besides the fact that the current membership of the Fighters, whoever they may be, are not exactly my colleagues—after all, I'm merely a humble public servant—they are most likely currently occupied with far more important endeavors than answering to…who did you say you're here representing, again?"

The bearded reporter turned and whispered to his camera operator before answering Doko. "Never mind," the man muttered, "I see you are one-track man."

Before Doko could react, the man darted past him and flung Doko's side door open, sticking his microphone inside as a crush of cameras and reporters pressed in behind him. "New Fighters! Do you concur with what this man has claimed?"

Doko merely stood aside, shaking his head. "Reinhard, I'm so disappointed in you. Did you really think I've been keeping the hottest superheroes in the world baking in the back of my car while I talk to the press on their behalf? Use your head."

Reinhard backed away from the open door, which swung wide, revealing the car interior: vacant but for the discarded fast-food trash littering the floor of the back seat. The bearded man's face evinced shock, both at the fact that Doko evidently knew his name and at finding Doko's car vacant. "I—I swear there were other…"

The other journalists returned dejectedly to their previous positions, refocusing their equipment on Doko as he smirked triumphantly. "Now, if no one else wants to violate my personal space in the name of journalistic freedom, I'd like to conclude my statements for the day and invite you to return to this same spot in twenty-four hours. Yes, Reinhard, even you—but maybe tomorrow, I'll keep my doors locked."

A satisfying chuckle rolled through the crowd as Reinhard's cheeks burned with frustration. Doko casually pushed his doors closed and clicked the locks shut as he strode up to the tower's entrance, looking back over his shoulder and calling out as if he had not a care in the world, "See you tomorrow!"

* * *

As the heavy door shut behind him, Doko exhaled all the breath in his body and collapsed back against the firm wood, his head sinking to his hands as he felt the stress and pressure of the past day come collapsing onto his shoulders all at once, forcing him to the ground as he wiped tears from his eyes. His head in his hands as he tried to steady his breath, he barely noticed Jack Quick come stepping up to him, munching a large cheeseburger and seemingly oblivious to Doko's distress.

"You okay there, chief?"

"F-fine. Just wasn't expecting to have to deal with...well, any of that." Wiping his eyes before looking up, Doko cleared his throat as he addressed Quick. "You managed to get everyone inside okay without incident, I presume?"

Quick nodded. "Quick as a flash and—er, yeah, I did," he trailed off. "Some of those cameras looked high-res enough to give the devotees some freeze frames to pore over for the next day or two, but even if they were shooting in high-speed I doubt they'll be able to make out much more than a shapely blur or two."

"Good. No problems keeping your speed up?"

"Nah." He tipped the half-eaten hamburger in Doko's direction. "Really glad I went ahead and got the third sandwich, though. Thanks again for picking up the tab; it's been so long, I forgot how badly Fighters victory parties used to put a dent in my wallet."

"No problem, Quick. As long as I somehow manage to slap together a professional-quality press conference presentation in the next, oh, twenty-three hours, everything should be alright. Got any ideas?"

Quick shrugged. "Search me. We never had any of that back in the day. A nosy reporter or two poking into your secret identity or a plucky freelance photographer itching to make his career with a too-close action shot were the only journalistic problems the old Fighters ever had to deal with. But if you want my two cents, you seemed to handle it all pretty well."

"Thanks, appreciated. Mystic hook you guys up with a view portal outside or something?"

Quick shook his head, pointing back towards the other room with his thumb. "Nah, we caught the whole thing live on CN News. They broke into every channel but the game show channel and Wolf News Network."

"Ah. So, er, how is his royal Mystic highness reacting to all this? You know he refused to come with us to rescue you, right?"

"Uh, yeah. Electrikid may have mentioned that once or a dozen times while we were waiting for our food. But as far as Mystic himself goes, well, I guess you ought to come see for yourself."

Doko sank his head in his hands once more. "Okay, just…just give me a second.

* * *

Doko braced himself as he walked into the meeting hall, unconsciously covering his eyes with his hand as he pretended to brush his hair back from his forehead. But as he looked around while the Fighters finished the last of their takeout hamburgers, few seemed concerned. Beside Master Mystic, E dug hungrily into the remainder of Jack Quick's third order of fries, abandoned by the speedster in favor of yet another sandwich.

"E. How'd everything go while we were gone?"

E shrugged. "Fine, I guess. You tell me."

"What do you mean?"

E looked up at Master Mystic, sitting impassably at the table, chin lowered to his chest. "I mean he's been sitting like this since the moment you guys walked out the door. Not a word, not a movement. Nothing."

"So what have you been doing?"

E shrugged. "Not much. It's been pretty quiet. I'll admit I was sort of w-worried about being left here alone the whole time with Mystic, but honestly I sort of forgot he was there? Mostly I just played around on my phone, but even that started to get really interesting once that photo popped up." E nodded toward the untouched bag of food sitting on the table before Master Mystic. "Th-thanks for remembering to bring us something to eat, by the way. If he doesn't want his, can I get the apple pie out of here?"

Doko started to answer, but caught himself—as Master Mystic

suddenly raised his head, looked around the room, and stood, spreading his arms expansively. E withdrew his hand from Mystic's sack lunch instantly as the Master's voice filled the room.

"Ah, my colleagues! I see you have returned victorious from your first mission. Truly, savoring the glory of a task successfully accomplished is among the sweetest of nectars this world has to offer. I encourage each of you to revel in your achievements, and to allow yourself to feel the pride in your actions you have so richly earned. For on this day, you have put your own lives on the line in order to protect those who are too weak to defend themselves—and can there be any higher, nobler act? I say no."

Doko goggled at the sorcerer. "You...say quite a bit there, don't you? And I note your tone is significantly changed from the last time we spoke."

Master Mystic waved his hands dismissively, then folded them before himself. "That was a mere ruse, designed solely to allow the necessary conditions for success to come into existence."

"A ruse? Some of the things you were saying about your fellow Fighters went well beyond the limits of acceptability. And while I'm pleased to hear you change your tune, I can't say I'm any more convinced by this melody, if you catch my drift."

Master Mystic looked down at Doko, his face a mixture of pity and condescension. "Your turns of phrase only serve to conceal the truth at the heart of your words, Doko. Let the facts as they stand provide testament to the intent behind my earlier manipulation." He gestured at the other baffled figures around the table: "Have you all not just returned to this humble tower flush with the adrenaline of your first victory as members of this illustrious organization? And were I to have accompanied you on this mission, it is inarguable that you would not have accomplished these ends in the same way. Nay, had I taken the position you desired, the Fighters would inevitably have triumphed in the end, as we always have and always will—yet were those ends attained on the platform of my mystic might, none of you would have the sense of confidence and proficiency in your abilities you now enjoy."

Doko cocked his head at the magician's train of logic. "I—suppose that's true."

"Of course it is true," Master Mystic intoned. "All these events have come to pass just as I had foreseen. And now that they have, the end result is a stronger, more capable team than could have been forged outside the field of battle. I do truly regret the deceptive nature of my subterfuge, but I ask you on this occasion to accept its necessity—for the evidence of its success is within you all."

Doko shook his head. "Mystic, I'm not sure I buy any of this, but for now we have bigger problems. I see you waving your hand there, E, don't worry; I'm going to have to have a long talk with the Master here about the true impact of his comments earlier. And no matter what his story is now, it's going to take a lot more than a pat explanation to get back up to where we started."

Master Mystic seemed unshaken. "I am confident I will be able to provide whatever assurance you—and my teammates—require."

"Well, that's a step in the right direction, Mystic. Because much as I hate to admit it, having you standing onstage next to Quick tomorrow will be a real asset. So if I have your absolute guarantee that you won't pull any last minute antics like you did earlier, we can table that discussion for now."

"Consider such assurance granted."

Quick cut in, "Onstage? What kind of event are you planning for this press conference? And who are these 'special guests' you were talking about?"

"Well, Jack, that's one of the things I need to discuss with you. I apologize for bringing up what might be a touchy subject, but right now time is of the essence, so I'll cut right to the chase. Are you on terms with your ex-wife or any of the other former members of the Fighters? Or even your old sidekick—what was his name?"

Jack's jaw dropped. "Doko, I can't believe you're asking me this. What do you need with them?"

"Look—Jack, all of you—technically, yes, per government regulations we only need two original members for this to qualify as a Fighters reactivation. But our real battle tomorrow isn't going to be judged by my supervisor, or even based on the law; we're going to be thrown into the crucible of public opinion. Hell, we already have been, really. We just have this one shot to reshape the narrative into one we can live with." He punched up some figures on his phone. "It's not ideal that Manstro's picture got out there before we had a chance to set the scene, dot the tees and cross the eyes properly, but the upside is it's giving us a chance to track the tides of public opinion before we even officially debut. And based on what I'm seeing, there's a lot of resistance among older demographics to acceptance of the New Fighters."

Jack shot a look at Mystic. He thought he saw his old friend's mouth curl in a smirk in triumph, but the expression passed and returned to flat, expressionless blankness before he could be sure. "Really, Doko, I'm surprised you care so much about popular opinion."

Doko shook his head. "I don't, not really, but I'm not ignorant, either. And high approval ratings are going to have a big impact on our ability to get anything done, whether it's obtaining cooperation from other teams and agencies or getting budget approvals rammed through. Trust me: for every percentage point of approval the Fighters gain tomorrow, it'll be one less battle we'll have to fight."

"So where do Sloan and Fatty come in?"

At the mention of his former sidekick, all eyes turned toward Quick.

It was Electrikid who spoke what all save Master Mystic were likely thinking. "Fatty? Are you shitting me? You called your sidekick Fatty?"

Quick blushed. "It wasn't...I didn't make it up. I swear, it was what he said he preferred to be called."

"Sure, Quick. I'm sure he did. After all, who wouldn't love their name to be an insult, right? That's why Tekla here was super cool with it when the headline on Readout called her the Tin Woodsgirl."

"Did they really?" Tekno Knight tapped frantically at the keypad on her glove. "Aw, shit."

"Look, regardless of what Quick's buddy did or didn't like to be called, the fact is we need to put out the call to anyone who can help shore up our credibility tomorrow. If you don't feel up to it, Jack, I can make the calls, but they need to be made one way or another."

Jack rubbed his head ruefully. "No, I get it. It's long past time I talked to Fa—Morty, anyway. But I actually talked with Sloan yesterday, and she made it pretty clear there's no way American Rose is going to make a comeback, New Fighters or no."

"Okay. You call your old buddy, and leave that one to me. Anyone else from back in the day who might enjoy one last moment in the spotlight?"

Jack strained himself trying to think back. "Geez, Doko, I know you're trying to get this thing off good and positive and all that, but the Fighters—the old Fighters—didn't exactly end on the best of terms." He looked at Mystic's impassive visage. "We stopped for what seemed like good reasons at the time, reasons I don't think can be overcome by a phone call out of the blue twenty-some years after the fact."

"You'd be surprised what people are willing to do to get back into the headlines, Jack—look in the mirror sometime if you don't believe me—but I get you. And I want you to be on your best form tomorrow, so I'll be the point of contact if you don't think you're up to it. It is my job, after all. Might as well start making myself known to the relevant parties now, while I have the chance."

"No, I need to be the one to call Morton," Quick demurred. "But, uh, I'll give you Sloan's office number. Outside of that, I don't know how to get in touch with anyone else. And frankly, I would have thought they'd have showed up when Mystic summoned them if they were at all interested."

Doko smiled. "Jack, I know this might be hard for you to believe, but my powers of persuasion can be quite convincing at times, even though they aren't backed by anything special other than my own wits. Just give me what contact info you have and let me do the rest. And if you do manage to turn your buddy around on the matter, so much the better. Mystic?"

Mystic's head slowly turned to face his questioner. "Yes?"

Doko sighed. "I'm giving you the benefit of the doubt. Do you have anything worthwhile to contribute here?"

"I suspect not, Doko. As Jack Quick indicated, the Summons Sorcerous went out to all former Fighters associates simultaneously. To use my powers further with the intent of persuasion would involve erosion of their free will, and it is my understanding that this is a line you would prefer not to cross."

"Er...sure, we'll leave it at that. And for what it's worth, I appreciate you making an effort at social interaction."

Mystic smiled. The younger Fighters seemed comforted by the look, but Jack recoiled at the incongruous sight of the unfamiliar expression on his friend's face, only now realizing he'd never seen Master Mystic exhibit such emotion. "Our goals are now aligned, government man. And in such a state, comfort yourself that there is little I would not do to advance our common objectives."

"Well, that is a great comfort, Mystic. Quick, if you could provide that number for American Rose—"

"Sloan, you mean."

"Sure, Sloan, American Rose, whatever. If you give me the number I'll get rolling on my end, and you can do your thing as well."

Quick wrote a series of digits from memory on a piece of scrap paper and handed it to Doko, then breathed deeply. "I'm just going to step in the other room here, guys. If you need me."

Shutting the door behind him, the ludicrous nature of his words struck him immediately. He knew that if anything, his voice would have been a detriment to any attempt to entice Sloan to tomorrow's press event. Hell, even now, he wanted to ask her if she would bring the kids.

Shaking his head, Jack tried to focus on the task before him. But now that he was alone with his phone, he found his breath rushing in and out in short gasps as he tried to gather his composure.

It's been too long, Jack thought. *It's been way too long, and I have no one to blame but myself for that*. He looked at the picture assigned to Fatty's contact in his phone—a thirty-year old shot, if not older, and filed under 'Fatty', of course—and a flood of memories from their time together flashed before Jack's eyes.

* * *

He was my buddy back in the day, as well as my assistant and pretty much constant companion. Nothing more than that, though I'm sure there were plenty of jokes thrown our way. At least he wasn't a teenage boy; Fatty was just my friend. I hope he's still willing to be.

We haven't talked to each other in longer than I care to remember—long enough that I ought to have stopped calling him 'Fatty', even in my head. It was never meant to be a pejorative nickname, at least as far as I knew; it was just how he introduced himself to me, and I never gave it a second thought until the day decades later when his wife icily informed me 'that name' was not an acceptable way to address her husband. I guess I saw her point, but the way she delivered the news—as if I had been the one who'd coined the unflattering nickname—was still offputting. I started calling him 'Morton' when I needed to address him and even tried 'Morty' since it had a similar ring to the name I was most comfortable using, but I don't think that made anyone happy. Soon enough, it was a moot point.

My hand's shaking as I dial his number. Too late, I think I should have emailed or texted rather than called. More time to plan out my approach, figure out exactly what I want to say, avoid any embarrassing missteps. Too late now, as I hear the phone distantly ring; again I kick myself for my damned impatience.

"Jack?"

For a second I don't answer, and the second stretches into hours before I croak out "Yeah, it's me," like a teenage boy going through puberty.

Hours elapse once more before his voice comes back down the line. "Wow. Jack, it's good to hear from you. I saw the picture of you back in the costume this morning. Is everything okay?"

"I..." I want to say 'yes' so badly. I wish I had thought to call him at least two or three times over the years, just to chat and catch up. But I didn't, and now I'm that guy. I should just lie, swallow my worry and spend whatever time we have to speak with each other learning about whatever life he's built for himself, like a real friend would.

When it comes down to it, though, I'm not a real friend. If I was, I would have been at his wedding. I would know whether he and what's-her-name are still together. I'd have been there for him when he needed me.

So I don't lie. I've never been any good at it anyway; if I had been, I'd probably be a lot more successful than I am.

"Ah...well, I don't know. It's...I don't know what it is, but something's wrong. Master Mystic called, I dug the costume out, and now here I am calling you." God, I sound like a crazy person. I realize now, this is why I needed to talk to Fatty: we saw so much crazy, indescribable shit together that he's the only person who might still take me completely seriously. Certainly no one else in the world has any reason to, not anymore.

"Are you okay, Jack?"

"I think so. I mean, I don't have any reason to think I'm not. But ever since Mystic woke me up yesterday I've had this weird feeling."

"What is it?"

"I don't know. It's like being eavesdropped upon by someone you aren't even sure is really there."

"Jack..."

"I know I'm not making much sense, but damn it, just listen to me. Please."

"I...Jack, I get it. I know what you're talking about, because I feel it too. It started right after my phone rang, before I even picked it up and saw who was calling."

"Thank god! Man, I'm so glad I called you. You're the only one that might remember all the crazy stuff we saw together: the case of the crying knight, the mystery of the modern magician, the time you were a pirate..."

"Yes, Jack. Good memories, all. But honestly, you know I didn't see a tenth of the stuff you did. Yeah, I got turned into a pirate that once. But on most of our 'adventures,' I'd stumble into some problem and you'd race off to solve it while I sat killing time, just waiting for you to zip back and tell me how it ended."

"Aw, Fatty, that's...I never meant to—"

"I know, Jack. It's just the way things were. Are. I just couldn't keep up with you. And after you met the others, it was obvious to me that I didn't fit in. Sure, I tagged along on some of the early Fighters missions, but no matter what, I wasn't one of you and I never would be. So eventually, I just faded into the background, got out of the way and let you guys do your thing. I saw some stuff in my day, but most of the real out-there, hard-to-believe, honest-to-God craziness? That was all you, off on your own in other dimensions with the team or..."

"Or with Sloan? Is that what you mean?"

"Yes, Jack. With Sloan. Or any of them. And don't try to flip this around on me being jealous of you, because as God is my witness, I was never for one second anything but proud of you and our time together. Not every kid who plays ball gets to go on to the big leagues. Most of us don't."

"Well, I'm sorry it worked out that way. I didn't mean for it to. And actually, the reason I'm calling is—"

Jack heard Mort fumble with his phone. "Jack, whatever you're about to ask me...don't. I'm begging you, just don't."

"But Fa—Morty..."

"No, Jack. It's okay. I'm fine, things are fine here. You don't need to feel sorry for anything you've done where I'm concerned. It's just life, Jack. Just life."

"You're right, I know. And I'll respect your wishes, but I just...I just miss the early days. When time seemed to stretch out forever, another mystery waited around every corner, and it was just the two of us. That was the last time I really felt like I understood the world."

"I know, Jack. I miss those days too. But no matter what we do, they aren't coming back. And where the Fighters are concerned, I'd rather leave it in the past. That's where it belongs, for me."

"Yeah, okay, I know. I'm sorry."

"Shut up, Jack. Stop being sorry for things you had no control over. Just...just go do what you do and save the world. Tell Sloan hi from Fatty. And hey, don't forget to smile."

There's a muted click, and he's gone. My first instinct is to redial and tell him I'm not going to be seeing Sloan, but I think better of it.

I shouldn't have called at all. Now, I really want a drink.

* * *

As Jack returned to the other room, head hanging low, Doko stepped in front of his path. "So, how'd it go with the old sidekick?"

"Eh. Fine, I suppose."

"Great. So we can count on him to be here tomorrow? Do we need to arrange transportation?"

"Oh, um, no. He's not actually coming."

Doko frowned. "You do realize that was why you were calling in the first place, right? In what sense do you consider that a 'fine' outcome to your conversation?"

Jack shrugged. "I don't know, Doko. We chatted a bit, reconnected. He wished me—us—well, but he's moved on with his life. A long time ago, from the sound of it." He glared at Doko. "He doesn't need me haranguing him about getting back into the life for a fleeting moment in the spotlight."

"All right, Jack, all right," Doko replied, waving him off and beaming a triumphant grin. "It doesn't matter, anyway. You'll be pleased to know none other than the one, the only, the original Owlhoot will be present tomorrow to help pass the torch from the old Fighters to the new!" He coughed, considering his words. "Of course, including you as one of the new as well as one of the old; you're the bridge between the generations. You and Mystic, of course. And speaking of whom…"

Doko nodded towards Mystic, still seated in his place at the table, once again as immobile as he'd been when they'd returned with lunch. "Is this, er, normal?"

"Nothing's normal around here, Doko. You know that."

"All right, all right, but you know what I mean. Does he typically go catatonic like this for such long stretches of time? I mean, he fell silent again literally the second you left the room to make your call, and he's been like this ever since. Hello? Mystic? Are you in there?"

Jack was about to warn him off from further incitement of the silent mage, but after waving a hand before the sorcerer's inscrutable face and receiving no response, Doko simply scowled.

"You see? Nothing. I tell you, Jack, I'd feel a hell of lot better about putting all these wheels into motion if we had just a little more of a give-and-take relationship with our other founding member."

Jack couldn't help but agree. "Honestly, Doko? I would too. I was just saying a minute ago on the phone with Fa—er, Morty, that ever since Mystic called and woke me up, things have felt off somehow. Like I'm being watched all the time, or like I'm being followed."

"Well, it has been a long time since you put your running gear on, yeah? Only natural you'd feel some anxiety about getting back into the old game. Like your old buddy there; whatever they were, it sounds like had good reasons not to come back. But you? You jumped right back into it like you hadn't lost a step. And look: sure, you got bushwhacked right out of the gate, but you turned it around by the end. And now, here it is just a day later, and you're arguably as big as you ever were." He clapped Jack on the back. "Come on, it's just been a crazy couple of days. Cut yourself some slack. Anyone would be a little shaken, super-powers or no."

Jack shook his head from side to side, trying to loosen his neck and clear the cobwebs from his mind. "Okay, yeah. Maybe you're right. " He looked around the room. "Where'd everyone else go?"

"Well, right now they should all be well on their way back to their respective homes to get some much-needed rest, Jack—which is where you should be right now." He led Jack toward the tower's exit. "Go on. After I make a couple of calls, I'll be right behind you myself. Still trying to get your ex to commit for sure, but things look promising. And even if that falls through, I have a few tricks up my sleeve. Trust me, Jack: just go home, close your eyes for eight or twelve hours, and don't worry about anything other than being back here at two PM tomorrow. You'll get to see some old friends, some new ones, and maybe even make a couple of people happy while you're at it. Doesn't that sound good?"

Jack grimaced wearily. "It kind of does, yeah. So, Owlhoot, huh? I shouldn't be surprised that old cowpoke wouldn't give up a second in the spotlight, even if he wasn't feeling up to answering the call of duty; he always was a real showman. You did good, Doko. He should be a real asset, and it'll be good to touch base with him again. But don't you think…"

Doko cut him off, sensing Jack about to attempt to justify making a call to his ex-wife. "Shh, shh, Jack. This is what I do. Let me handle it, and I guarantee it'll all turn out better in the end for all of us."

"And what about…" Jack nodded toward the immobile form of Master Mystic.

Doko shrugged. "Right now, I don't think we have any other choice but to take him at his word and hope this is just the latest in a series of baffling, antisocial-but-not-technically-problematic behaviors. As long as he stands up in front of the cameras with the rest of us tomorrow like he promised, I'm willing to let a lot slide for now—and honestly, this press conference is the only thing he's shown real interest in since I got involved with this outfit. So if it helps bring Mystic back into the fold as well as getting us our rubber stamp of public approval, I'm willing to tolerate him sleeping sitting up like a goddamn bear."

Jack looked cockeyed at Doko. "A bear?"

"Sure. Don't bears sleep sitting up?"

"Eh, I think you're thinking of monks. Or protestors."

He waved his hand dismissively. "Whatever. Still, I just can't help thinking an ounce of insight into whatever's going on inside his head would go a long way towards putting the pieces together." He yawned, stretching. "Oh well. You head home, I'll wrap things up here, and who knows? Tomorrow, maybe the Master will deign to share the insights of his extra-deep meditation session with us mere humans."

* * *

Unbeknownst to Doko or Jack, within Master Mystic's seemingly placid form raged a psychological battle of Brobdingnagian proportions.

Across a featureless plain stretching to the horizon in all directions, Nelson Kendall ran. He felt as if he'd always been running, and for perhaps the thousandth time in the last twenty-four hours, he wished for even a tenth of his old friend Jack Quick's abilities. Yet his wishes remained unanswered, as he knew they would: he didn't deserve an answer to his prayers.

Without slowing his pace or missing even a single step, Kendall raised his face to the sky—only it wasn't a sky, not really. Only the sickly pale orange color distinguished it from the dusty, ersatz ground passing beneath his feet, and he knew them both to be only as real as he believed them to be. Over the decades, he'd spent a good quarter to third of his life within Mystic's soulscape. And though it had never been what he'd call a good time, he had to admit having to run flat-out at his top speed the entire time definitely took some of the enjoyment out of the experience.

Again without slowing even minutely, he bellowed his frustration to the unresponsive orange sky, a pained scream of intolerable agony that would have been audible miles away were the landscape measurable in conventional units of distance. And as his surroundings lacked material features for the soundwaves to reflect against, Kendall's shout dissipated without even the comfort of an echo to mark its passing.

He felt his strength ebbing further into the hopelessness of despair, yet continued placing one foot in front of the next, mechanically. He wished he could see what was happening outside his body; ever since Mystic had seized control the day before, he'd only gotten fleeting glimpses of the outside world. *The real world*, he reminded himself.

If only he'd been able to warn Jack, if only he'd gotten it together like he'd promised he would years ago, if only Ingrid had been around to help contain…well, he'd screwed that one up all on his own. In fact, the more he went over the events in his mind—something he'd been doing near-constantly for the duration of his containment—the more he was led to the conclusion that everything that had ever gone wrong was his own damn fault.

He dared to slow just long enough to steal a brief glance back over his shoulder, but Grantu's demons hadn't lost a single step, even after what felt like weeks of running. And why would they? He wasn't sure if they really existed outside Grantu's soulscape, after all, and he sensed that they had been brought into being to keep him running, never able to rebuild his strength. That was all they seemed to be interested in, after all; they clearly weren't interested in catching him, or they easily could have. No, as long as Kendall kept moving, they kept nipping at his heels, and as long as he stared straight ahead while he ran, he was barely aware they were still there. So Kendall ran, his legs aching, his lungs bursting, every cell in his body afire.

Still, tortured as he was, every now and again he allowed the faintest traces of a smile to crease his face, as he reveled in the simple fact that as long as he was there, Grantu—Mystic—was incapable of carrying out his fondest wishes, his world-shattering might reduced to a miniscule fraction of his true power. Excruciating as every step might be, as long as Kendall kept running, he knew the world outside—the real world—was safe.

And it always would be, Kendall thought. After all, he'd seen the results right before his own eyes, just before this latest term of confinement within Grantu's soulscape had begun: of all the other old Fighters, only Jack Quick had been fool enough to answer Mystic's call to action. And Jack wouldn't be enough, not by a long shot.

No, Kendall gloated in mute victory, there was no chance whatsoever of the old Fighters ever reconvening—after all, he'd seen to it personally. And as long as that remained so, the universe was safe.

EPISODE FIVE: NOBODY'S CHILDREN

After all the events of the past couple of days, I'm almost surprised to wake in my own bed, on my own time. It strikes me as an indulgent pleasure, if a simple one, but the moment I spot the costume draped across the chair by the bed, it brings me thudding back to reality.

Remembering my responsibilities, I sigh, rising to snatch up the uniform. I finger the hole in the sleeve, briefly regretting not stopping somewhere along the way yesterday to have it stitched up before I remember that tailors and seamstresses don't stay open late any more, the way they did back when more people relied on them.

I shake my head; I'm far from my best in the mornings, but it's okay. It'll do me good to slow down and concentrate, and I'm not so old and useless that I can't learn a new trick or two. I know I've got a needle and thread in a drawer around here somewhere; I'll just watch a few instructional videos, practice at superspeed until I have the technique mastered, and stitch it up so seamlessly not even the nitpickiest of commentators will ever be able to tell it was ripped.

The whole process takes a little longer than expected, thanks to an inconvenient internet slowdown and the fact that my costume's fabric is a little denser than most standard needles are supposed to be able to handle, but I get the knack eventually. As I finish a perfect running stitch, I hold the sleeve at arms' length and admire my work until I spot the wall clock opposite the couch and catch my breath. *That can't really be the time, can it?*

Too late, I realize the exertion of the past couple of days caught up with me with a vengeance, causing my system to demand more recuperation than usual. Fifteen hours total, in fact—I'm going to be late to Doko's press conference if I don't get moving. Thankfully, I did at least shower before collapsing into bed yesterday. Otherwise, I'd be in real trouble, assuming I'm not already—as much as I'd love to be able to shower at superspeed, I haven't ever been able to lick the water pressure problem to deliver the showerstream I'd need to do so, at least not without creating a potentially explosive hazard for anyone within half a mile.

I drop everything on the couch, dash into the bedroom for my keys, whip the costume back onto my frame, and slam the door behind me before the discarded needle even has time to come to rest. Hopefully when I come home I'll remember it's there before it ends up sticking out of my buttcheek.

* * *

Sure enough, when I arrive at the tower, the crowd of reporters, cameramen and assorted hangers-on has already reassembled, in slightly more orderly fashion than yesterday's gathering but at least half again as large. If I had more time, I'd invisibly scout out the crowd at superspeed to get a sense of their mood before this thing kicks off, but unfortunately my extended slumber hasn't left me enough leeway. The late hour of the day is likely to have many grumbling—if I'd had a chance, I could have told Doko these news types prefer their press conferences to be scheduled before lunchtime, especially this close to the weekend. It's not like anyone's getting an exclusive or winning an award for their coverage here, so half of them are probably half-checked-out already, thinking about their party plans or the list of chores awaiting at home. To them, it's just another story, and even the most interesting press conference is a tightly choreographed performance holding few surprises for those who know how the routine typically goes. Media pros with instincts that honed can gauge any room in moments, and I'd bet my shirt the minute this thing goes off-book they're going to be all over us like a pack of rabid dogs.

No time to worry about that now, though, and not my problem, fortunately. Not directly, anyway. I hope Doko knows what he's doing, but if he doesn't, well—as long as I don't end up getting whacked over the head and kidnapped again, I'll call it a win.

* * *

Inside, Doko is even more agitated than expected. Granted, I did manage to push it right up to the last second before finally appearing, but at the moment I stumble into the room I'm not technically late—not that that seems to slow Doko even a beat.

"There you are! Good lord, Jack, where have you been?"

As I have no legitimate excuse for my tardiness, I decide deflection is my best strategy. "Never mind where I've been, I'm here now and I saw what you have set up out there. Didn't you think to set out some kind of craft services or at least coffee? Reporters are like surly zoo animals who have been kept confined too long—they may not like having to be here, but they're a lot more likely to put up with it gamely if you keep them fed and drugged."

"I only had so long to slap this together, Quick. And these suggestions might have been welcome back when they might possibly have done some good, but right now unless you're volunteering to dash back out for a few hundred danishes and a dozen carafes of Skydollar's premium brew, we need to get organized, get out there, and get this over with."

"On that, at least, we agree." I look around. "Where is everybody?"

Doko hooks a thumb over his shoulder. "In the other room, reviewing the briefing I so carefully prepared," he enunciates, waving a sheaf of papers at me. "Not that you'll have time to pay proper attention to such—"

"Done," I interrupt, replacing the papers in his hands. "I have to say, holding that surprise to the end should come off as a well-choreographed piece of theater, assuming the others are on the same page."

Doko rolls his eyes. "Right, of course," he mutters. "Forgot who I was dealing with for a minute there."

"Lucky for you, I haven't," a familiar voice announces. "And I never do."

"Sloan," I blurt. "So you actually came."

"Of course," she responds, loftily. "I've been here for over an hour. It might have been nice to have the opportunity to coordinate our actions ahead of time for this circus, but I see you were going by your own playbook, as per usual."

I should know better than to try to defend myself to her, especially when I'm in the wrong, but seeing her back here in the Fighters' old headquarters for the first time in so long brings up so many emotions, it's all but impossible to keep myself from falling back into old habits and patterns of behavior.

"I was just trying to make sure I present the best possible image for our big debut," I stammer. "Don't you think that's just as important as starting on schedule? Nothing interesting ever happened on schedule."

"Bad thing to say to a woman with her own TV show, Jack," Doko counters, peering irritatingly closely at my sleeve. "And you definitely should have taken this to a professional."

"How did you know I—look, forget about that now," I sputter. "It's good enough to get through for now."

"Mmm, I suppose," Sloan concedes. "You're lucky you're a man. I guarantee every little detail of the girls' outfits will be dissected, torn apart, and talked to death on a hundred fashion blogs over the weekend. Something like that would-be sleeve repair would be enough to get them raked over the coals until the next fashion week, but if you keep that side away from the cameras, you might even get away with it."

"Speaking of outfits..." I look Sloan up and down. "Still a big no on the American Rose costume, even for the Fighters reunion they said would never happen?"

"Until you got here, I was about fifty-fifty whether it was going to happen myself, Jack. I'm not much more convinced now," Sloan retorts. "And I told you, the costumes are long gone."

Theriot walks in, shaking his head. "Oh, come on, honey—you

know listening isn't Jack's strong suit. And now that the gang's all here, it'll be over before you know it." He smirks at me and extends his hand. "Glad you finally deigned to join us, Jack. Good to see you again." I meet his grip; he squeezes my hand just a little too hard, as if I had any doubt he's just being polite.

"Um, good to see you, too, Jon." I crane my neck, trying to look past him into the other room. "Who all do you guys have sequestered back there?"

"Don't include me in this sideshow, Jack—I'm just here acting as Sloan's head of security," Theriot demurs. "Surely you didn't think she'd ever design to set one foot back in this halfway house of horrors without me thoroughly vetting the place first?"

"And to answer your question," Doko cuts in, "everyone else arrived on time, Jack: Tekno Knight, Electrikid, E, and even Owlhoot were all outside waiting when Ellie and I arrived. I hope you haven't decided to take a cue from Master Mystic's playbook and make up your own rules as you go."

"No, but..."

"What's the problem, Jack? I thought we had this all straightened away last night. When you left, you didn't seem to be harboring any lingering issues that I could tell—I'm not a mind reader, after all."

After all. After all... I shake my head to clear the persistent clouds from my mind. "Everything's fine, Doko. Let's just move on."

Sloan rolls her eyes. "I recognize that hangdog expression all too well—it's burned into my memory after God knows how many fruitless hours of couples counseling. Allow me to interpret, Mr. Doko: Jack is hoping we'll beg him to share whatever's bothering him and therefore pry it out of him, because either he hasn't faced whatever it is or hasn't fully come to terms with it himself. Perhaps he isn't even aware, but more often than not this sort of passive-aggressive behavior on Jack's part is his way of getting the people around him to conform to his wishes without him having to explicitly ask for their assistance, because that might indicate some flaw in his fragile self-image or even invite confrontation of the non-superheroic sort. Does that about cover it, Jack?"

"I guess so," I mumble. "You don't have sound so clinical about it, though."

"My apologies, Jack. I suppose it's my fault for ever believing Mr. Doko's fervent assurances this event would function in a professional, businesslike manner. If you were capable of that, well..."

Mercifully, she doesn't finish that sentence. I can't imagine any way it might have gone well for me.

"All right, I'll bite," Doko allows. "What's bugging you?"

I stare at the floor for ten seconds before responding, haltingly. "I was, uh, I was hoping Sloan might bring the kids along," I confess. "I don't get to see them that often, and I have moments of triumph to share so infrequently, it just would have been nice to have them here, today."

The look of disdainful amazement Sloan shares with Jon tells me instantly that I shouldn't have said anything. "This is business, Jack," she states flatly. "It's a promotional opportunity to me, nothing more. The fact that you'd think otherwise is, well...disappointing. But if you really want the kids to revel in your little 'moment of triumph', rest assured that they'll be far more impressed when it shows up in their social media streams than they ever would have had you asked me to drag them here. Believe me, they take anything that pops up on Turnover or Readit twice as seriously as anything their old mom tries to tell them."

"That still doesn't compare to having them here and being able to see their faces."

Jon covers his eyes with one hand and whistles low. "Should've let it drop, buddy..."

Sloan wheels around and jabs one manicured nail at my chest. "Goddamn it, Jack, what's it going to take for you to get it through your thick, stupid skull that I don't want my children anywhere near any of this ridiculous costumed bullshit? Everything involved with dressing up in those outfits is an open invitation to trouble. And you want to bring your children—our children—here, today? Where even you, with your amazing powers, were knocked out and dragged off to god-knows-where literally less than two days ago?"

"That's not going to happen again, Sloan."

"Oh, really? Can you guarantee that? Did you catch the guy who kidnapped you?"

"Well, no," I admit, scratching at the floor with my foot. "But this is a totally different situation—then, I was alone and unprepared. Now we have a whole team here, not to mention dozens of witnesses milling around outside."

"Right, there's that as well. If you don't think an attention-starved sociopath would find a gaggle of salivating media pros as tempting a target as any bank, you're fooling yourself."

"Well, if you think this is such a disaster waiting to happen, why did you come at all?"

Sloan sighs. "I told you, Jack. It's publicity, and good publicity that comes cheap is too rare to pass up, even given my personal objections to the situation. If things go as Mister Doko promised they would and we get lucky, this little event just might be the most interesting thing that happens this weekend. If so, we'll own the news cycle until Monday morning—and the type of ratings boost that could result from exposure like that could be enough for us to finally justify raising the show the show's ad rates for the first time in longer than I care to think about." She looks down her nose at Doko. "Of course, that eventuality is looking less and less likely every minute."

"She's right," Doko says, shoving an agenda into my hands. "I'm afraid we don't have any more time to indulge your hurt feelings, Jack, so assuming you're still on board..."

The implications of his comment sting more than I might have expected. I suppose I'm as vulnerable as any male of my generation to suggestions about my masculinity, or perceived lack thereof. So, predictably, I set my jaw, stick my chin out, and pull it together immediately, lest any more of my feelings evidence themselves to those around me. God knows what disasters might befall me were I to allow others to know I'm human.

I take a microsecond to scan Doko's agenda again. "This all looks pretty straightforward to me," I comment. "Anything not here I should know about?"

"Just to remember that so far, despite all the hype and hoopla, all anyone out there knows about the New Fighters is based solely on one picture and the few sentences I said yesterday. Everything else up to this very moment has been baseless speculation and theorization, all of which will be swept away and forgotten in the wake of what we're about to establish. What we do here today will define for all time the canonical secret origin of the New Fighters in the eyes of the public. So let's not screw it up too badly, okay?"

I raise one eyebrow. "What do you mean by that?"

"Just let me do my job: to run the proceedings and set the tone. As long as you pay attention and follow my lead, everything should be okay. Basically, just stick to the truth, minus the most embarrassing parts, and don't volunteer any information you don't need to. Do you think that'll be doable?"

I review the program Doko's laid out for the presentation once more. "Nothing here seems too problematic, at least in concept. I was hoping to get a chance to catch up with Owlhoot, though."

"That's fine, just don't do it in front of the cameras and microphones. Time for all that after we get through the glad-handing portion of the program, Quick. Just grit your teeth and it'll all be over before you know it."

"Let's hope." Something tells me it won't be that easy, though. It never is.

* * *

"Welcome back to CN News' coverage of the New Fighters press conference—I'm Roger Walters reporting. We're currently at four minutes past the hour and as of yet, no sign of either the New Fighters nor their self-proclaimed representative, Agent Ric Doko of D.E.A.P. As you can see in the footage from our live feed, dozens of media representatives have gathered here for what we have been promised will be the formal introduction to the New Fighters, a team whose previous incarnation was yesterday recalled only dimly except by aficionados of superhero trivia and history buffs—but as I say, that was yesterday. Today, despite few concrete details being known—even the specific membership has not been disclosed as of yet—at the moment, the New Fighters are nonetheless the name on everyone's lips. For more, we return now to Betsy Carmichael, on the scene at Master Mystic's tower fortress. Betsy?"

"Thanks, Roger. While as of yet there has been no sign of movement within the New Fighters' presumed headquarters, we are expecting this press conference to begin at any time..."

Doko huddled just inside the door, watching the coverage taking place just outside on his phone's screen. The display told him he should have been out there five minutes ago, if not before—the fact that no one had been there to greet the attendees was sure to have already put certain members of the press corps on edge. Reporters were such self-important prima donnas, if everything wasn't to their expectations they'd take it out on the subject they were supposed to be objectively reporting on in a heartbeat. Careers had been destroyed for less.

Then again, he told himself, if they were going to tear him apart, it was doubtful a mere display of punctuality would have dissuaded them in any case. Reinhart, for one, was undoubtedly champing at the bit for the opportunity to grill Doko over any perceived weaknesses or inconsistencies in his story. Who knew what seemingly insignificant items of trivia he had dug up, polished off and pocketed, just praying for the chance to spring them in front of the world, raising his own profile at the expense of the New Fighters' grand introduction—and therefore, the safety of millions.

Doko grimaced. *Okay, that might be pushing the argument a bit*, he admitted to himself. Even as a lifelong government employee, he knew the threat posed by vigilant oversight was often the only factor containing the lazy, corrupt, or dishonest tendencies inculcated within certain agencies or divisions, even his own. Yet the distrust and antipathy he faced daily in many citizens occasionally caused him to rethink the wisdom of his career choices.

Sighing, he recalled the period right out of college when all vistas had seemed wide open, his freshly-minted criminal justice degree and outstanding honors serving as his passport to any number of law enforcement careers—why, in another world perhaps he was an FBI agent or an undercover detective, keeping deadly weapons or drugs from reaching the lives of unsuspecting Americans. Instead, here he was, playing glorified emcee for a bunch of costumed amateurs, most of whom who hadn't remotely approached earning the appellation which was about to be applied to them so indelibly that after this day, it would undoubtedly appear within the first sentence of their obituaries, regardless of whatever else they managed to accomplish during their lives. No matter if one founded a multinational corporation, authored a best-selling book, or cured a disease that had plagued mankind since the dawn of civilization, once a body was publically known for wearing a costume and using extranormal abilities in public, that was how the rest of the world would think of you for the rest of your days—regardless if those abilities were used for the right or wrong reasons.

What Doko really found disheartening was that sometimes, it seemed to him that by and large, nonpowered individuals tended to prefer the villains. It wasn't just his perception, either; among D.E.A.P. agents, it was such a common complaint that it had long since passed into the type of stock gallows humor typically shared over the water cooler or around the lunch table: "How do you get a civilian to volunteer to help a D.E.A.P. mission? Tell them you work for the Alliance."

There were many theories as to why this type of antipathy seemed so prevalent, but to Doko the most likely explanation was the simplest: powers or no powers, most people didn't trust that other people would make the right choices—often rightly. So when superhuman abilities were added to the equation, people naturally got even more nervous, almost uniformly expecting misuse of those abilities to follow. In some cases, it had become a saddening cliché, as a number of young heroes had flamed out publically, embarrassing both themselves and D.E.A.P. before a planetary audience, wasting millions of dollars and agency man-hours thanks to their apparent total lack of self-control.

When he thought back to those incidents, Doko was heartened: whatever their faults, the New Fighters were at least not the products of the type of intense media coaching and show-business environment from which the members of D.E.A.P's last few team efforts had arisen. And hopefully, that artificiality was the factor that had set the teeth of America's citizenry on edge; although he hadn't known them long, he appraised an honest approachability in the New Fighters that he hoped would carry through the camera lens to the hearts and minds of the millions watching that day.

In the dark of night, though, Doko feared a darker truth lay at the heart of the matter: people feared powered individuals, whether hero or villain, because they coveted their power. And deep down, they secretly hated the heroes for not exploiting their abilities the way they imagined they would, and therefore putting the lie to that cynically self-serving perspective on the world. At those times, Doko felt that if power were to be bestowed upon any randomly selected person, it almost didn't matter what type of person was chosen or what kind of background they came from—if infinite power corrupted infinitely, surely smaller amounts were just as corrosive in their own ways. So no matter where they started out, in the end they always seemed to end up just about where one would expect.

Perhaps things were different in the days when everyone was limited to a common set of abilities, Doko mused, but he suspected not. Even then, the relatively minor differences between people would likely have been seen as the most alien and terrifying possible, even over something utterly benign and insignificant—hair color, say, or foot size. But in any case, the world they had was the world they had to deal with, and like everyone else, Doko had little choice but to deal with it on whatever terms made sense to him at the time.

So how, then, did he now find himself preparing to deliver an awkward introduction for these gifted freaks to a worldwide audience, his every word about to be beamed around the planet and beyond before being transcribed, translated, and torn apart? Sweat trickled down his temples as he recalled the famous moon landing transmission, Armstrong's verbal error preserved for all time, turning his intended profundity into a nonsensical mishmash for lack of an article he would swear for the rest of his life he'd pronounced.

"Jesus Christ. Are you still in here?"

Doko jumped and spun around. "American Rose. I—"

"Don't call me that. Didn't Jon make that clear? The only reason I'm here is to promote my brand, and American Rose is most emphatically not part of that."

"I know, I know. I'm sorry." He waved the paper clutched in his damp fingers. "I have you down here as Sloan Webster, of course—I just have the Fighters monikers on the brain. As agreed, I'll only be making one reference to the American Rose name, in the context of introducing you and the other legacy members. I still wish you'd reconsider—"

"No," she interjected, unceremoniously cutting him off. "I won't be associated with this group in any way after today, even as an inactive 'reserve' member or whatever you want to call it. Don't get me wrong; I do appreciate your making Owlhoot the same offer, even though he's clearly in no condition to be much help to anyone. The benefit payments and stipend that position provides will make a huge difference in his quality of life, though, particularly since he squandered away what little retirement savings he had years ago." She shook her head. "Poor dumb Larry. He was like a neon target for every con man in the country once he let his identity slip."

Doko narrowed his eyes. "Does Jack know you've been taking care of Owlhoot's expenses for the past few years?"

Unused to being taken off-guard, Sloan gaped at Doko for a moment, but managed to recompose herself almost immediately. "Of course he doesn't. What I do with my money is certainly none of my ex-husband's business, and hasn't been ever since I agreed to stop holding him to the terms of our separation agreement. After all, it hardly seemed charitable to continue taking his well-intentioned child-support checks once my show was syndicated across the continent."

"After all," Doko repeated. "Well, after all the troubles the original Fighters faced toward the end of your run, I have to say I'm pleased you were willing to rejoin the group, even if only for this one occasion."

"I'm not re—"

"I know, I know, you're not rejoining the team in any formal manner. But regardless of the circumstances, to see you, Owlhoot, Jack and Mystic in the same room back there, well…I can't deny it sent a thrill up my spine."

"Why, Mr. Doko," Sloan grinned. "You're not a fan by any chance, are you?"

Doko looked away. "Not a fan, really, I just…I'm just old enough to remember a time when heroes meant something more than an endless series of fights, dismemberment, destruction, and death. I remember when heroes stood for ideals that seemed universal and inspiring. I'd like the New Fighters to be the group that brings that feeling back for a new generation, and I'm proud to be in a position to do what little I can to make that possible, if not necessarily likely." He blushed. "Also, I, er...feel I should confess that when I was a teenager, I had that poster of you in the blue outfit on my wall."

"The picture in front of the Statue of Liberty?"

"No. The, uh...the one on the Lamborghini."

"Oh, no. Not the one with the torch between my legs?"

"That's the one."

"Oh, dear. Well, admittedly that picture used to mortify me somewhat, but I'm afraid after signing several thousand copies over the years, I've grown immune to the embarrassment. More than anything, I'm mostly just sorry I don't look like that anymore—and that I didn't manage to hold on to the copyright to that image, much to my regret."

Doko looked up shyly. "You don't have anything to be ashamed of. Either then or now."

"I wish that were true. If you manage to live long enough, we all accumulate our shames, both public and private." She set one hand on Doko's shoulder. His heart nearly leaped through the ceiling, but he managed to contain his surprise as he met her warm gaze, and she smiled wearily. "I may not have known you long, Doko, but it seems like your intention's in the right place. I certainly hope so, for Jack's sake as well as those other poor souls you've managed to convince to sign on."

Doko grimaced. "You think I talked them into joining up?"

"I know you did, in at least one case. And having dealt with you myself, I know your powers of persuasion can be considerable."

"Even if they left you ultimately unmoved? You're not wearing the costume, are you?"

She smiled. "No, but I'm here. That's far more than anyone else has ever been able to pull off."

"Only because you want to be here. Just like those people back in that room: if they truly didn't want to be here, nothing I could say one way or the other would have made the slightest bit of difference."

"Maybe, Doko. Maybe. But don't dismiss the power of your words so readily." She waved the briefing in front of his nose. "I mean, this isn't poetry, but it's clear, concise and comprehensible. I wish I could say the same about a hundredth of the press releases I've been subjected to. You pull this off, and you change the narrative on the Fighters from this point forward."

"If I pull it off."

"I can't tell you it'll be easy, Doko. Even after all these years, I still get butterflies in my stomach every single time I get ready to head out onstage to tape a new episode, so I can't even tell you it'll get easier. But I can tell you this for certain: if you're the type of man that can look me in the eye after admitting to my face that you whacked it to my picture on the regular when you were a pimple-faced teenager, nothing that could possibly happen out there in front of the press corps could ever be a fraction as awkward. Right?"

Doko's face was crimson. "I...suppose you're certainly right on that account."

She grinned. "Oh, come on. You didn't think I was under the impression all those sales came purely from appreciation of the car's fine engineering? I had to meet and shake the hands of those people getting their posters signed, Doko. I made a pretty penny investing in hand sanitizer around that time; no great surprise, since I was already buying it by the barrel."

"Prudent," Doko agreed. "Well, no sense further delaying the inevitable."

"That's right. The longer you wait, the worse it's going to be." She pointed toward the door. "It's past time to face the music. Remember, this whole thing was your idea."

"Ugh, that's right," he muttered. "Me and my big ideas."

"Oh, stop complaining. It'll be fine. What's the worst that—"

"Don't say it," he interrupted.

She smiled. "All right. Break a leg, Doko."

"If I'm lucky."

* * *

Doko stepped up to the platform, thankful the last-minute construction job seemed to have been done to spec. At least, it didn't immediately collapse beneath him—he'd have to remember to have a box of donuts or a pizza or two sent over to the workmen in appreciation. Maybe even a case of beer, if they all somehow managed to get through the event free of disaster.

He swallowed hard, his throat dry as he reached the podium and turned to face the sea of upturned faces and lenses, his eyes squinting against the glare of the brilliant stage lights. He coughed and jumped six inches in the air, startled by the amplified sound of his own cough reverberating back at him.

Suddenly his mouth was dry and his mind was blank. Why was he there? What was the point? What had he hoped to accomplish with all this? Doko blinked twice and stared down at the briefing in his hand. The letters seemed to swirl before his eyes, the words as foreign as alien hieroglyphs.

Looking up in desperation, he seized on a familiar face hovering before him—Reinhart. The man's expression wavered between delight and alarm; he'd clearing been slavering over the chance to grill Doko further, but now the fact Reinhart might actually be concerned worried Doko. *What must I look like*, he thought? *Is it that obvious I'm drowning up here?* He wasn't sure how much time had passed since stepping up to the stage—less than a minute? A half hour? Eons?—but he knew he'd have to say something soon.

Clearing his throat, he leaned forward and tapped the microphone, buying himself a few precious seconds while he feigned a technical error to cover his momentary lapse of reason. Of course, few in the expert media crowd would be fooled, but hopefully once the presentation finally got rolling all thoughts of its awkward beginning would be forgotten—or at least muted, somewhat.

At the amplified sound of Doko's finger brushing the mic, the crowd fell silent. The few eyes that hadn't already been directed his way fixed upon him, microphones inched ever closer, and the last few camera lenses dialed in. Smiling widely, he opened his mouth to speak, praying what came out made sense—but just at that moment, a familiar voice rang out, shattering the quietude.

"You bastard!"

On the far side of the crowd, Jack Frost Junior stood atop the roof of a decade-old Ford Taurus, pointing as dramatically as possible at Doko. Cameramen whipped around frantically, tripping over themselves in their rush to refocus and capture the interloper's image as Frost recited his undoubtedly well-rehearsed dialogue, grinning with satisfaction.

"You thought you could deny me my revenge, Fighters? Well, revenge is a dish best served cold—as you're about to find out."

Smile frozen on his face, Doko breathed a sigh of relief. *Thank god*, he thought, *thank fucking god*.

* * *

"Well, I suppose that wasn't a total disaster," Sloan ventures.

"Are you kidding?" Doko asks. "Frosty's timing couldn't have been better if I'd choreographed his arrival myself. Lucky for me, that sense of theatrical timing for impact apparently infects even the worst of us."

"Sense of self-aggrandizement, more likely," Sloan scoffs. "If Frost'd had the sense to wait until the cameras had dispersed, his chances of winning would have been a hell of a lot better."

"Well, sure," I concede. "But surely he didn't really ever think he was going to win, do you think? I mean, yes, before anyone else rushes to point it out, he did get the jump on me the other day, I've come to terms with the fact that I'm never going to live that down. But in my defense, he was a completely unknown factor at that point, and it was only me."

"Let it go, Jack," Sloan sighs. "No one was going to say anything."

That's nice of her to say, but given how quick Doko has been to put me in my place all along, I suspect her intuition might be slightly off on this one. Nevertheless, I let it go for the sake of not further derailing the conversation.

"But my point is, before attacking today he'd seen the whole team in action already and even run away once. He had to know the whole team was right inside just waiting for Doko's cue. Surely he wasn't dreaming he'd be able to take us all out?"

"No, most likely not," Sloan admits. "This was probably more about trying to establish himself in the public eye as your preeminent archfoe, or some such juvenile horseshit. I suppose it's possible he had some ace up his sleeve that he never got a chance to pull, but it's just as likely not. Maybe that moment in the spotlight was his only goal, in which case, mission accomplished." She rolls her eyes. "Many a dumb asshole has done far more for much less attention, and that one sure didn't seem any too bright."

"Just like his dad," I add.

"Lucky for us," Doko agrees.

"Lucky for you," Sloan counters, smiling. Doko blushes slightly; I consider asking for clarification, but something tells me I'd be wasting my breath. If I know anything about my ex, it's that she's unsurpassed when it comes to keeping other people's secrets—I suppose that's what makes her so easy to talk to. Probably what makes her so good on TV as well.

"Very lucky for me," Doko confesses. "Not only did he obviate the need for awkward one-by-one introductions, but the assembled press corps got a front row seat to the team acting as a unit to take down a dangerous threat to their own well-being. Even a stalwart skeptic like Reinhart will have to take a more sympathetic tack on the team now—it's hard not to when one's own life is among those the team might have saved."

"Certainly no one was in any mood to dispute the minor details of your little presentation after a display like that," Sloan says. "Even the typos in your info handout will probably go unremarked upon, thanks to the juicy story Frost managed to drop right in their laps. And as for you, Doko, I'll give you credit for bringing it all back together in the aftermath of the chaos and reestablishing as professional an atmosphere as possible within only a few minutes of a serious threat to everyone's safety. Others would have been too thrown by the disruption of their schedule to make hay of the opportunity, but you improvised like a pro. I know from personal experience how hard that can really be."

Doko blushes again. "Well...thanks, Sloan."

"Not a problem. You deserve it. I'll admit, when you first called I was more than a little dubious whether you'd be able to turn this thing around in such a short time, but you actually pulled it off."

"We pulled it off," Doko corrects her. "Your presence definitely helped lend the event a sense of gravitas we might otherwise have lacked. I hope you were able to get what you needed from your appearance."

"I will have once that footage goes around the world and back. If we don't end up seeing a full ratings point increase by next week, I'll be shocked." Sloan sinks into the chair emblazoned with her old American Rose logo, and I smile, relishing the nostalgic image. "Ugh," she moans. "I hate to admit it, but this old chair actually feels awfully comfortable.

"How comfortable?" I ask.

"I knew I shouldn't even have said anything," she sighs. "Don't get any ideas, Jack. I'm still not planning on putting any version of the American Rose costume on, ever again."

"I wasn't—"

"I know you weren't. Not yet, anyway. But I know how your mind works, and sooner or later you would have twisted that one little offhand comment into a sliver of hope. And then you'd take that sliver and you'd use it to dig and dig until you'd carved out enough space to consider the impossible. Isn't that your typical modus operandi?"

I hang my head. "All right, all right. I'm not going to argue."

"I appreciate that, but that's only because you know I know you better than you know yourself. Trust me, Jack, heading off that train of thought before it leaves the station is better for everybody's peace of mind."

"I know, I know." I collapse into my own chair, intending to slump in resignation, but instead I feel unexpectedly...good. "Man, you weren't kidding, were you? These old chairs feel fantastic. I don't recall them being this comfy back in the day. Do you?"

"Can't say I do," Sloan says. "But then, I can't say I really appreciated the pleasures of a really fine place to sit until I crested the half-century mark, myself."

"Tell me about it," I groan, rubbing my feet ruefully.

"Oh, please," Sloan scoffs, waving her hand dismissively. "Don't even start up with that."

"What are you talking about?"

"Oh, come on, Jack. Get on Facespace and look up your high school graduation class sometime. How many of those people are in the shape to squeeze into the same running suit they wore thirty years ago? There certainly can't be many doing much running at all, super-speed or no. Hell, you know perfectly well that Jon is over two decades younger than you are, and while I'm sure you've been too wrapped up in your own issues to notice anything, I've had to tolerate a seemingly unending series of bitchy little jealous comments from him ever since you showed up back at my office. Poor Jon works out two hours a day just to stay on top of things, whereas you vanish into your house for over a decade and come out looking basically the same except for a slight thinning of your hair and a few extra pounds? That just doesn't happen."

"I suppose I have been pretty lucky."

Her eyes roll to the ceiling. "Luck has nothing to do with it, Jack. A seventy-year old man simply doesn't look the way you do without the help of something a lot more powerful than luck."

Ellie spits her soda across the table. "Holy shit. You're seventy years old?"

Doko frowns. "Language, Ellie."

"Sorry. But seriously, I thought you were like, fortysomething, max." She plops down across the table from me, addressing the sullen lad perched on the chair next to her. "Didn't you, E?"

"To be honest? I d-don't think I ever thought about it. Forty is pretty old anyway, though, isn't it?"

"Thanks, kid. No danger of me getting a swelled head anytime soon around here, I guess."

"Sorry." He doesn't look sorry.

Owlhoot slaps his leg. "Har har har! This young'un sure don't hold his tongue, does he? You've got a lot of spirit, little whippersnapper. You remind me of someone, kinda." He gets a quizzical look on his face. "Can't quite place it. It's been nagging at me like a piece of barbeque stuck in my teeth, but it'll come to me."

E doesn't look like he wants to know who he reminds Owlhoot of. Having been introduced to a few of Owlhoot's friends over the years, I can't say I blame him.

"Where did the others go, Doko?" I ask. "I was hoping to get a, er, group photo while everyone was here. You know, something we could put up on the wall."

"Should have told me a while ago then, Quick. Electrikid and Tekno Knight both had other obligations, so they took off right after the press corps did. It is a weekend, after all, and some of us do still have the vague remnants of a personal life to which to attend."

"I suppose you're right, after all," I agree, leaning back in my seat. "Ah well, plenty of time for pictures and all that later."

"Oh, don't be silly," Sloan scolds. "Don't you think maybe one of those thousand or so cameras pointed in your direction might have caught an image or two of the team while you were taking Frost Junior down? I'll just have my assistant keep an eye on the news photo streams, and we'll send the best pics on over after we stumble across a few appropriate choices. Don't worry, Jack, I know what you like—classic images of heroism will go to the top of the list. Anything that looks like it might have been a great magazine cover, back when that actually meant something."

"Thanks, Sloan." I allow myself a weary smile. "Even if we're not exactly on the same team, it's nice to be on the same side again."

"Oh, Jack. I'll always be a Fighter; there's nothing I can do about that. It's in my past and it's in my blood. I'll never be an active member again, but I can't deny what I was—what I am—either. So while I certainly can't say this has been all fun, I'm glad it hasn't been a total disaster."

At that moment, Mystic walks into the room bearing a smile on his face wider than I've ever seen. As warm as it looks, I can't help feeling a chill.

"Ah, my old compatriots. My heart is gladdened to see you assembled here once more in our hallowed hall, where in days past we did meet so many, many times."

Sloan grimaces. "Please spare us the 'o' word, Mystic. In my industry, we like to refer to those of us getting long in the tooth as 'honored legends'."

Owlhoot walks around to stand behind the dusty chair emblazoned with his own self-designed logo—a cartoon owl wearing a cowboy hat, God help him. "Legends we may or may not be, missy—that ain't for me to say. I can tell you for damn sure that it's an honor for a dusty old cowpoke like me to have served with fine people such as yourselves. And them days was a long time ago no doubt, but they wasn't so long I don't remember. What do ya say? After all that ruckus, one picture of the old gang reunited for one last time?"

"After all this time," Sloan sighs, "I'm not sure I have the strength left to resist. I suppose I can work up the energy to plaster on one more fake smile, if it'll make you all happy."

"It will," I confirm. "After all, who knows how long it'll be before we have this many of the, er, classic Fighters together again?" Looking over at Owlhoot, I frankly wonder whether he'll last long enough to make it to another reunion, no matter how soon.

As he sits, the relief of the visible strain on his weary bones sets my mind momentarily at ease, and I smile at Mystic. "Boy, if you'd gotten this kind of reaction from these guys the first time you sent out the call, maybe there wouldn't have been any need to send out the call for New Fighters at all. Eh, Mystic?"

"That is correct, Jack Quick," Mystic intones, pulling his chair out from the table. "And now that we have finally reassembled something far closer to the group I had initially envisioned, there will be no further need for much of anything."

Master Mystic seats himself triumphantly, grinning like the devil as twin forks of blue fire burst forth from his eyes in a V shape, striking Sloan and Owlhoot square in the center of their chests, then shooting back towards E and me. With my accelerated vision, I can just see the mystic azure bolt before it strikes me dead on, but there's nowhere near enough time for me to move. Instead, I'm forced to watch helplessly as it pins and paralyzes me, blasting back at Mystic to form a flaming pentagram among we four original Fighters—and E, strangely enough. I don't have time to wonder further about that, though, as I feel my consciousness receding, almost as if I was falling asleep. But instead of fatigue, every molecule of my body is suffused with mortal terror—terror I see reflected back at me in the faces of Doko and Ellie as my eyes roll back in my head and everything goes dark.

EPISODE SIX: AFTER ALL

"Jesus Christ," Doko exclaimed. "What the hell just happened?"

"I don't think Jesus has anything to do with this," Ellie said. "But from the looks of things, hell just might."

"This isn't one of your projections, is it?"

"I wish. This is as real as it gets." Ellie peered at her five fellow Fighters, frozen seated upright at the table. "Even this blue fire, despite the fact it doesn't seem to be burning the tabletop."

"Magic," Doko spat. "Damn it. This was all a setup by Mystic to get the old Fighters together in this room. After nobody but Quick answered his first call, he must have known he'd have to get tricky." He waved his hand in front of Master Mystic's face. "But to what end? He seems to be as helpless as the others."

"Somehow I doubt that," Ellie warned him. "If this had really been as intricately planned out as you say, I can't imagine he would have left himself vulnerable."

"I know it," Doko admitted. "I was trying to convince myself as much as anything. Hell, the tower itself is probably able to protect him alone."

"We can't give up, Doko," Ellie pleaded. "We have to try something to help."

Doko looked around the room, then at Ellie. "I...I wish I had something to tell you. But honestly, this is out of my depth. Maybe I was crazy to think this would ever work. Look at what's happened in just a couple of days! If I hadn't let this go as far as I did, we wouldn't be in this fix now. God, I'm so stupid; I played right into his hands and delivered up everything he wanted on a silver platter. And now, all we can do is sit and pray everything will turn out all right." He hung his head sadly. "I've never felt so damn useless in all my life."

"Not useless," a voice from the darkness enunciated precisely. "Prayer is of no use only to those who have no faith."

Startled, Doko and Ellie's heads spun as a familiar figure stepped from the shadows.

"Mom!" Ellie exclaimed, excitedly dashing over and embracing her. "I'm so glad to see you! But what are you doing out of the house?"

Doko clucked, "Never mind out of the house—how the hell did you get here?"

"It's really quite simple, Mister Doko," Angie responded. "Henry told me where you were headed after you picked Ellie up this morning, so we watched the whole thing live on the television, then the minute it was done he drove me over to congratulate you in person. Oh honey, you looked so beautiful! I'm so proud of you."

Ellie blushed. "Thanks, Mom."

"I admit, I did catch my breath when that awful Jack Frost showed up out of nowhere, but Henry explained it was all a setup to make the Fighters look good."

Doko shook his head. "No, no—I mean, how did you get into the tower? I know that door was secure. I turned the lock myself to make sure no pesky reporters would be sneaking in for an unapproved exclusive."

She smiled. "Oh, child. Not much can keep a mother from her daughter in her time of need." She looked at the other Fighters, still frozen statuelike in their seats. "And even this tower's eldritch power cannot contain the evil that has been unleashed here, today. When the compact was broken, I could hardly help but feel it in my heart and my bones. At that moment, I knew where I had to be."

"They're totally unresponsive," Doko said. "Has Mystic dragged their astral bodies off with him? Can you tell where they are?"

"They are right here," Ellie's mother answered. "To this one, man is but an obstacle," she said, indicating Mystic's still form, "and some children never grow up, but only get taller," she added, shaking her head over Jack Quick. "Others are running, but the smaller ones crawl."

Doko rolled his eyes. "And here for a second I thought you were actually going to give me a useful answer." Ellie scowled, reminding Doko of their circumstances. "I'm sorry, I shouldn't have said that. Let me try again: I can see their bodies are here, but they aren't able to hear us or respond to anything, let alone wake up. Is there anything you can do to help us with that?"

"I might," she allowed. "And I appreciate you asking nicely."

"No problem," Doko said, nodding as Ellie smiled. "And I hope I'm not being impertinent when I say that you seem much more, er... present than the last time we spoke."

"I have my good days and bad days," she said. "As do we all, in my experience."

"You're right there," Doko admitted. Now was not the time to push the issue, in any case; if Ellie's mother was determined to be opaque to his questioning, he wouldn't learn anything anyway. Whatever morsels of knowledge she was prepared to dish up, he'd better be grateful if they helped point anyplace remotely helpful—because otherwise, he had a feeling things were going to get much worse. How much, he didn't know—but he suspected he wouldn't like the answer.

For the second time in far too short a period, I awake having no idea where the hell I am. At least this time I seem to be free to move, which I find comforting until I look up and see the orange skies above, as unearthly as anything concocted for the wildest science fiction spacescapes in the history of film.

I stand and shade my eyes from the harsh glare of the bluish light from above, trying to get a sense of my surroundings. The horizon stretches on forever in all directions, unimpeded by terrain or obstacles—as far as I can see, it's nothing but flat, featureless terrain all around. At my feet lie the motionless forms of Sloan, Owlhoot, and E—all breathing comfortably, as far as I can tell, but no matter how I try, I'm unable to wake any of the three.

I wonder briefly why I alone managed to stave off the slumber that holds them captive, but only briefly. I've learned the hard way that if answers aren't immediately obvious, it's unlikely I'll be the one to ferret out the truth, no matter what questions I ask.

Instead, I do the one thing I really know how to do: I run. I run in every direction for miles and miles, never seeing anything, never accomplishing anything but making myself tired. Each time, after around a hundred miles or so I turn around and go back the way I came, afraid to lose my bearings entirely in this surreal landscape and terrified I'll never find my way back to the others if I take too many turns.

Eventually, I realize I don't have any choice: I have to run further and faster if I'm to have any hope of figuring out where I am, let alone escaping. Hoping the oxygen content of the air is enough to let me pull this off, I take a few minutes' worth of deep, invigorating breaths, and then take off like a shot. I run as fast as I can in one direction, never turning—I figure if worse comes to worst, at least this way I can run directly back the direction I came. Hell, depending on where Mystic transported the four of us maybe I could even wrap all the way around the planet, but that assumes I'm even on a round planetoid, or that the physics of this place work similarly to those of Earth. And at that point, it's more variables than I can contend with, so I don't try. Instead, I think about nothing—nothing but running.

My legs start to ache, then hurt, then burn. I ignore it and push through the pain, which works for a while, but soon it starts to feel worse than any pain I can ever recall feeling.

I don't even slow. Instead, I transcend the agony it in a way I've never done before, shoving it from my awareness until all physical sensation seems like a distant transmission only dimly received. I run and run and run until I lose track of time, of place, of identity. I run until it's all I am, all I can remember ever doing, all other aspects of my life faded like dissipating bits of tissue in the face of a torrential downpour, washed away as if they never existed.

Finally, I spot something that shocks me back to my senses: it's Nelson, from the looks of things also running for his life, with what look like a pair of shadows hot on his heels. The sight shocks my brain back to consciousness and every fiber of my being aches for relief, but I can't give in now. Instead, I swallow hard and dig into my last reserves of strength, putting on a burst of speed that pushes me ahead of the shadows, gathering Nelson into my arms as the momentum carries us miles away from them in less than a microsecond.

Every last erg of energy in my body spent, the two of us collapse into a heap on the ground. My legs feel like numb rubber and my throat burns, but the shadows are nowhere to be seen. Bracing myself on my elbow, I force a smile onto my face as Nelson gapes at me. "Sorry to break up the party without an invitation, Nelson, but it looked like things might be getting a tad unruly between you and your friends back there."

"Jack?! What the hell are you doing here? Go back, go back now—you'll ruin everything!"

The corners of my mouth turn down. "Well, I guess a parade was a little much to expect, but a simple 'thank you' is always appreciated."

"You don't understand, Jack. If you're here, then—oh. Oh, God. Tell me you're here alone?"

"I—no." I point back the way I came. "Sloan, Owlhoot, and a kid you don't know are lying in a pile somewhere back there, too."

"Oh, God, Jack, no. You don't know what you've done."

"At least I got you away from those shadows that were chasing you, though?"

Nelson holds his head. "No, Jack, you couldn't have. Those demons are just manifestations of Grantu's will, conjured to keep me from getting in his way." He spreads his hands wide and turns in a circle. "Everything you see is an extension of Grantu's will."

"Wh—where the hell are we, Nelson?"

"We're nowhere, Jack. This is the limbo my spirit goes to when Grantu—Master Mystic—takes over my body. So if you're here, you and the others are under Grantu's complete dominion, and he's already won." Nelson waves his hands, drawing some arcane design on the molecules of the air—a simple spell of remote viewing I recall him casting at least once per mission back in the old days. A portal of fire opens before us, and I hear Nelson sigh in resignation. "Just as I suspected: we've lost. Everything is lost."

I peer through the ring of fire and gasp at the sight of my own motionless body sitting bolt upright back at Mystic's tower, a foreboding pentagram of blue fire coruscating between the five of us. Somehow, it looks like Mystic is growing.

"What the hell is this, Nelson?"

"Like I said, Jack, it's Grantu. It's always been Grantu."

"What does he want?"

"He wants to end everything. And when you put his mantle on my shoulders, you handed victory to him on a silver platter."

I hold my head. "Oh geez, Nelson, I'm so sorry. But how could I have known?"

"I know, Jack. I don't blame you, not really. Mystic had this all planned too well, subtly influencing dozens of people's actions over decades of time to bring this all about. No one could have seen it coming, not without sharing the perspective of a near-immortal—Grantu plays the long game on a scale you and I can't even imagine. To him, years are like seconds, eons like afternoons."

"Still, Nelson—you were my friend. I should have seen through the empty liquor bottles and pizza boxes. It was just that you were in such a state, and I was just trying to get to the bottom of the problem, the way we used to in the old days."

"I don't claim to be perfect, Jack, and I've made plenty of mistakes on my own to fuck up my life, believe you me. But the worst might have been letting my alcohol use sneak up on me over the years until I was exactly the way Mystic—Grantu wanted me. After all, no one believes a drunk, much less a mentally unstable one, so once I earned the reputation of a drunk, he would be free to operate unhindered. Eventually, the combination of the alcohol and Grantu's magic influence just wore me down until I had nothing left to fight with."

"After all," I repeat. "That phrase."

"Yes," Nelson confirms. "Grantu's been imperceptibly shaping the thoughts and actions of everyone who came within the sphere of influence of the tower to bring about his own ends. You couldn't sense it, of course, but the human subconscious inevitably reflects that stimulus one way or another."

"I should have known. Damn it!"

Nelson shakes his head. "No, Jack. You shouldn't blame yourself. You can't. This was all my fault, no matter how you look at it."

There's a tone in his voice I've never heard before, and somehow, I believe him. "What...what did you do, Nelson?"

"Nothing I didn't do with the best intentions, for what little that's worth. But I was a fool who couldn't face the fact of what a fool he truly was. I knew from the beginning that the power of Grantu is far too much for any mortal to bear for long—I saw what it did to the last guy who tried. I saw the haunted look of his face as his withered fingers handed me the mantle, moments before his ancient, tortured body crumbled into dust right before my eyes. And yet...I couldn't force myself to put it down—then, or later. Eventually, after a decade of wielding the mantle's power, I could no longer ignore its deleterious effects on me: each morning, I'd see shadows of the previous mantle-bearer's burned out husk staring back at me from the mirror. But by then...it was too late. Grantu had grown exponentially more powerful during my custody, and if I'd ever had a choice to put the mantle down, well...it was all too evident that time was long, long past."

"How did he—it get so powerful?"

For a moment, Nelson doesn't reply. I know he knows better than anyone how limited our time must be, so the fact that he pauses at all truly worries me.

Finally, he sighs and answers, "It was our Fighters missions, Jack. Each time the team went out, he'd siphon whatever free-floating energy he could from our opponents. Those 'mystic bolts' that I—Master Mystic used to hurl weren't just offensive blasts; they implanted something awful in each of our opponents. Something that would transmit a portion of their might to Grantu without their knowledge—without anyone's knowledge—for the rest of their days."

Despite myself, I gasp. "Good lord. All of our foes? From the beginning?"

He nods sadly. "From the very beginning. So you see, after a while he'd sunk his tendrils into most of the villainous population of the planet—and a good number of the heroes as well, I'm ashamed to say. You know how it goes."

I do. It's a sad commentary that heroes fight each other nearly as much as we fight the supposed bad guys.

"But....why?"

"It's how Grantu works; it's his very nature. He's a parasite. Despite his 'magical' trappings, he creates nothing. Every erg of energy he expends was siphoned off from something else. From someone else. That's how he's managed to survive so long, hopping from one host to another, each of us thinking himself the master...when in reality, to him we were nothing but a pair of shoes to be run into the ground and then discarded without a second thought."

"My god, Nelson. I never had any clue."

"Of course not. How could you? Who could have a hope of understanding what even I, the person who knew the most about Grantu in the world, was incapable of apprehending?" Nelson has a hint of that wild look in his eye again. "He—it—is an immortal entity that's existed as long as anything in this universe. We have as much chance of comprehending the thoughts of Grantu as a microbe has of understanding astrophysics."

"I'm amazed you managed to keep the lid on all this time, if he's really as bad as all that."

"Oh, it wasn't that bad at the beginning. Like I say, he hadn't managed to accumulate that much power up to that point—none of his hosts traveled nearly as far or wide until me. But once the Fighters started taking on the potential world-beaters, well...." He moans. "At least when Ingrid was around, the two of us managed to keep things under control, working together. She'd keep watch while I was asleep, letting me rest, truly rest...but once Grantu managed to solve that problem, things began deteriorating rapidly."

"I never got a chance to ask what happened to Ingrid before."

Nelson's eyes are large and watery, like a decrepit basset hound. "I... wish I could tell you it was just Grantu. But that wouldn't be accurate. You know how it used to be, Jack—you know how guys like you and me were raised. I thought it was my role to be the Master, and it was her role to support me in that. Grantu took advantage of that and encouraged my bullheadedness and inflexibility year by year. And once the Fighters broke up, it didn't take long for the situation to become...problematic."

I get it. Cooped up in that tower with a steadily deteriorating Nelson and an insane god twenty-four hours a day, seven days a week with no end in sight? That's tough to ask of anybody.

"The problem was, once Ingrid was gone I knew I wouldn't be able to keep control over Grantu much longer. Deluded as I was, I could still read the writing on the wall: I was getting weaker with every year that passed, while Grantu only grew stronger. But I figured if I could somehow cut his power back, I could manage to keep the lid on long enough to figure something else out.

"So the power got...divided. Split up and placed in certain individuals for safekeeping: the only people I knew could be entrusted with such power, even if they weren't aware of it." Nelson taps my chest. "I mean, after the way the Fighters ended, I figured it was the safest bet in the world that a majority of us would never be in the same room at the same time again, let alone back in that damned tower."

"You put this...thing in me without my permission? In all of us? This thing that was killing you? How did you know it wouldn't knock us dead?"

Nelson shakes his head. "Oh, no. I was much smarter than that, Jack, or I thought I was. No, in my arrogance I actually managed to convince myself I was acting in your best interest by figuring out how to split the power down to manageable and even beneficial levels—that's what's been keeping you looking young and spry, Jack, not your speed. Same with American Rose, Owlhoot, and the others."

"Owlhoot? Are you joking? Have you seen him? He's a broken-down wreck of a man."

Nelson smiles at me as one would at a child. "Jack, Larry is a hundred and sixty-five years old. He never was just pretending to be a cowboy—he's one of the originals. All those jokes about looking good for his age weren't just comic relief."

"I...guess I kind of get it. What better safeguard against yourself than your friends?"

"That's kind of you to see it that way, Jack. But yes, that was the idea. I mean, getting two of us together seemed undoable at the time. So five? Seemingly an utter impossibility—but only in our limited imaginations."

I shake my head. "No. This doesn't add up, Nelson. What about E?"

Nelson looks genuinely confused. "E?"

"He's just some kid who randomly posted the ad online that helped this whole thing along. E is just what he calls himself. Why did Mystic bring him here along with me, Sloan, and Owlhoot?"

Nelson grimaces. "Randomly? I doubt that. Things in this world don't work that way. Tell me: is this kid's name Edwin?"

My mouth falls open. "How did you know?"

"Even he doesn't know this, but the boy you know as E is the offspring of the man you and I fought alongside as the Red Angel."

"Mark? Mark Forbes?"

"That's right. I know not what motivation Edwin's mother has for keeping this information from him, but the portion of Grantu's power that had been placed within the Red Angel passed down to his son, when...well, you know what happened."

I do. It still hurts, even after all this time.

Nelson puts his arm on my shoulder. "I know, Jack. It pains me that we weren't able to help our friend in his time of need. But that wasn't your fault, nor mine." He looks around. "This...this is. These last thirty years, Grantu's just been biding his time, waiting for the right moment to strike. Hell, he probably had this all figured from the moment I got the mantle in my damned hands way back when—in Grantu's terms, executing a fifty-year plan is like the blink of an eye, even yours. I thought I was so smart, Jack, but to ever think I was outsmarting Grantu was utterly deluded." He hangs his head. "And now that he's unlocked the spell and reclaimed the missing fragments of his power, I can't imagine any way we can stop him from getting what he wants."

"Come on, Nelson—we're Fighters. You know even if it looks like all hope is lost, there's no giving up until the last bell rings. Right?"

Nelson looks like he wants to argue the point, but instead a wan smile creases his face. "Same old Jack. What do you propose?"

"Well, let's go back to the basics: what is it that Grantu wants? And how can we get in the way of him getting it?"

Nelson's smile disappears. "Oh, after all this time I know Grantu all too well, and he wants only one thing: to stop."

"Stop?"

"Yes. He's older than everything, Jack, at least everything living. And he's tired of it all."

"So he wants to kill himself? Okay. What can we do to help that part of the plan along?"

"It's not that easy. Grantu can't die in the conventional sense. But if all universal motion ceases, he can...stop."

Suddenly it dawns on me and my throat freezes. "But...the only way that happens is..."

"That's right: the universe ends. Certainly it was always a given that it had to happen sometime, but Grantu just wants to bring that time forward a few trillion years."

"Jesus, Nelson. Oh Jesus."

Behind Nelson's head, a cloud of shadows appears, coming our way fast. Looking all around us, the horizon in every direction is blotted out by clouds of demons, all careening in our direction faster than I'd have thought possible, and the orange sky darkens to a burnt umber.

Nelson smiles again, very faintly. "Looks like the time for chatting is done, Jack. Time to run."

* * *

"Your friends are...not doing well, daughter." Ellie's mother folded her hands. "In fact, I would venture to say that they are suffering more than they have ever before."

"It doesn't take any powers to see that," Doko sputtered. "Their breathing gets shallower and more labored with every minute that passes. What is happening to them?"

"The entity you know as Master Mystic is draining their very life essences. Their consciousnesses are as yet undamaged, but for how much longer, I cannot say."

"Mother," Ellie said flatly. "We need to help."

The woman looked down at her daughter. "You are still but a child, Elspeth, and that which your friends face is no less than the Great Destroyer. How long think you will last in the fact of such opposition?"

"And how long will we last after they fall? Please, mother," Ellie pleaded. "We don't have any choice but to help. It's…it's only human."

"Perhaps…perhaps there is a way to lend your friends our strength." Ellie's mother frowned. "It will require full participation from all of us to have even a prayer of working, though. How say you, government man?"

Doko clapped his hands together. "Just try and stop me."

"Glib words will not win this day, I'm afraid."

"Fine. But if this is as serious as you say, perhaps it's time to push the panic button," Doko said, pulling his phone from his pocket. "Give me thirty seconds and I can call in the cavalry—for real, this time. The Alpha Guns, the Black Terror, maybe even Stardust or Thor—whoever might be able to help."

"There is no time whatsoever to spare, I'm afraid. Fate has dictated that this duty fall upon us, and us alone. As well, I feel it behooves me to allow that this undertaking is not without significant risk to all of us, body and soul alike."

Doko set his jaw. "That's the job, lady. Let's get started, we're wasting time."

"As long as you understand." She stepped to the other side of the table, between Sloan and Owlhoot, and took one of each of their limp, dangling hands in her own. "We must complete the circuit connecting your friends to each other—for now, they fight alone. But if we can close the gaps…"

Ellie grasped Owlhoot's left hand and E's right; Doko took Sloan's right and Jack Quick's left. Almost immediately, they felt the power coursing through them.

"Hey, this tingles," Doko exclaimed.

"Hold tightly to your friends, if you would. Soon, it will do much more than tingle." She began to chant under her breath, words low and dark and incomprehensible; Doko felt his eyes close, and for just a microsecond before everything went dark, he wondered whether the choices he'd made throughout his life had truly been his own, or if he'd been led to this moment by forces beyond his imagination.

* * *

I lift Nelson onto my back piggyback style and take off, racing away from the approaching demon shadows, but wherever I look, more and more of the damned things are pouring into the air.

I turn and shout back over my shoulder to Nelson. "We're running out of options here fast, buddy!"

"You said he brought Sloan, Owlhoot, and that E kid here with you? Where are they now?"

"Doesn't matter," I answer. "They were out cold when I left them, and it didn't look like that was changing anytime soon."

"Either way, they're still tethered to our reality, Jack," Nelson bellows. "Can you get us back there?"

"I—sure." I was about to explain that heading back that direction would take us directly through the thickest cloud of shadows speeding at us, but as our choices have diminished down to this one I decide to save my breath for running.

I'm not sure how long it takes us to get back to the other Fighters—the longer I'm in this weird limbo, the less meaning time seems to have—but eventually we make it back to find them lying just as I left them.

"Yes!" Nelson shouts, right by my ear. "Can you feel that?"

"I…can." Even though my leg muscles are like spaghetti at this point, I feel stronger all of a sudden, like I could run around the world twice without blinking. "I didn't feel anything like that before."

"Someone must be trying to help us back in the real world, Jack—thank the cosmos. Here, take their hands—we have to complete the circuit!"

I grasp Sloan's and Owlhoot's hands, and immediately feel like I plugged into a wall socket—but in a good way, if that's possible.

Nelson's teeth grit against the flow of power, and just for a moment, I think we might have a chance.

Unfortunately, that moment ends quickly. The sky fills with dark shadows, blotting out the weird, eerie light from above, and what sounds like the loudest thunderclap I've ever heard shakes the heavens and firmament alike.

Finally, with a high-pitched, earsplitting screech, the shadows merge into one gigantic, terrifying mass of swirling darkness, and I think this must be what being at the center of a tornado is like. Blasts of wind buffet us relentlessly; Nelson shouts, "Don't let go!" at the top of his lungs, but his instruction is hardly necessary. I'm already trying as hard I can to hold on—what other choice do I have now? Here, with my friends, will be the site of our last stand—whatever the consequences.

The air currents build to near-hurricane strength, but I'm used to maintaining traction against tremendous forces thanks to decades of running against the wind. And despite his disheveled—if not debilitated—state, Nelson is putting up more of a fight than I might have thought possible. Give the guy credit: fighting that lonely, internal battle all alone for all that time would have been more than most would be able to stand. Yet here he is, managing to rally his strength enough to stand against forces powerful enough to cow men twice his size.

The sky splits with a terrible crack and the hellish winds cease, more suddenly than would be possible for natural currents. I don't slacken my grip even a fraction, though—grit and determination or no, it's clear that it's only the power being transmitted among the circuit of Fighters allowing us to hold fast.

Above us, the whirling mass of ebon clouds coalesces, condensing into what looks like a tight ball with a sheer black surface that hurts to look at—no, not black, not really. It's as if it's totally devoid of color, as if light cannot exist in its vicinity, like a hole at the center of my vision. It's something hideous and wrong, something against every law of physics and nature, something that exists inside and outside our universe simultaneously. For the first time I truly understand what we're dealing with, and fear freezes my veins from my head to my chest to my groin.

I hear a voice louder than any noise I've ever heard, a massive sound resonating through my skull and rattling my bones, and the most frightening thing about it is that despite its crushing volume, its tone is calm and familiar.

"AH," it says. "I SEE ASSISTANCE FROM BEYOND IS PROTECTING YOU FOR THE MOMENT. EASY ENOUGH TO RECTIFY."

Suddenly, my arms are burning as if they'd caught fire, but I don't let go even as the pain expands, traveling up my arms and throughout my frame until every molecule of my body burns with terrible energy. I cinch my eyes shut against the agony and just manage to hang on, for what feels like hours, but must have been only seconds, if time has any meaning in this miserable limbo.

Eventually, I feel the torture blessedly recede. Though my every cell rejoices at the torment's cessation, I feel like weeping.

Nelson moans, "I'm...sorry, Jack. I held on as long as I could."

"It's...it's okay, buddy," I gasp. "You gave it your all. That's all anyone could ask."

"THE CIRCUIT HAS BEEN BROKEN," the voice of Grantu pronounces. "NOW LET ALL HOPE FADE, AS THOSE WHO DARED STAND AGAINST GRANTU JOIN YOU."

Nelson screams at the heart of the storm. "Grantu, no! Don't!"

"MORTAL, IT IS ALREADY DONE."

I hear a sickening snap and the air before us turns inward upon itself. A flash of blinding energy forces my eyes shut for a microsecond. When I open them, Doko, Ellie, and a woman I don't recognize are standing before us, and my heart sinks with dismay, knowing all is lost.

"Looks like the gang's all here," I say. "Sorry I didn't lay out coffee and danishes for you, but our hands have been a bit full."

"Jack? Mystic?" Doko asks, clearly discombobulated by the trip.

"Not Mystic. Nelson," I correct him, pointing to the sky. "That's Mystic—or Grantu, more appropriately. Nelson here is—was—Master Mystic's human side."

"And now that that connection has been severed, there's nothing holding him back," Nelson laments, slumping to the ground in defeat. "The circuit is broken."

"THAT IS CORRECT," Grantu's voice resonates all around us. "AND JUST AS YOUR LIFELINE HAS BEEN SEVERED, SO SHALL JUDGMENT COME TO ALL OF EXISTENCE."

"Come down and face us, coward!" Doko yells at the sky. "How dare you pretend to pronounce judgment on us from above, like some benevolent God—you're nothing but a piece of crap!"

I'll give Doko credit: that one sure has some balls on him. Most people would be curled up in a ball on the ground crying for their mothers in a situation like this, but he wades right into the thick of it—and miraculously, it looks like he managed to provoke a reaction.

My vision shimmers and blurs, and I rub my eyes before realizing the problem is with reality, not my eyeballs. My brain aches with dissonance as suddenly the imposing form of Master Mystic stands before us once more, despite the fact that Nelson remains on his knees.

"Hello, Jack Quick. Government Man. You wish to address me, one last time? I shall grant your request—I understand your species' attachment to the concept known as the last request all too well. I have taken the form most familiar to you to facilitate our interaction—but I forewarn you, your fates are sealed irrevocably, once and for all."

"Mystic," I gasp. "Why?"

He smiles warmly. It's the most evil sight I've ever seen in my life.

"Why? Why, to bring about Armageddon, Jack Quick. It is simply nature reasserting itself, correcting an imbalance that has existed since this universe's inception. And I shall take the opportunity offered by this cosmic disruption to end my suffering—along with everything you have known as existence."

"I still don't understand, Mystic."

"I would not expect you to. These events are far beyond the scope of what your mammal mind was designed to comprehend; it is simply necessary to reestablish the balance. The slate will be wiped clean—that is all. Any more explanation would be lost on your primitive consciousnesses."

Ellie cries, "How can you do this to us? To all those innocent people back home?"

Mystic looks at Ellie. "Girl," he intones ruefully, "you understand nothing. As always, you humans desperately overestimate your own importance in the grand scheme. Earth is but one planet in billions, in one galaxy in billions, in one universe in billions. It is less to me than the smallest bacterium is to you, and you kill bacteria in the trillions for what you consider the 'greater good' every day, in the process of simply digesting your food.

"This is no different. Earth is a rotting sore that must be cut out. From your limited perspective, you perceive this world as everlasting and crucial to existence. I can assure you that this is not the case—because I know the truth. This world is younger and more fragile than you could possibly know; every week, hundreds of worlds no different than this one are wiped out, and it is of no consequence whatsoever."

Tears rim her eyes. "But this one's mine," she says. "That's the difference."

"Unfortunately, that is of no consequence to the forces of which I speak, girl, nor to me. For that, you have my condolences."

"You arrogant piece of shit," I hear a woman screech, and something flies past my head, almost too quick for even me too see. "How dare you talk to her like that?" Her stance is defiant and rays of bright white light pour from her hands as she tears fearlessly into Master Mystic's form with such force that for a moment, I dare to allow myself to hope she'll succeed—but only for a moment.

"Ah, I see some fight still remains in humanity—how refreshing. However, I note that you are attempting to injure me with energies that were stolen from me by my pathetic host—and therefore your attack only adds to my strength. I also sense you are using this power to manipulate the senses of those around you, an irritant that is ultimately of no consequence but one I confess I mislike. Here, woman," Mystic intones calmly. "In one stroke, I shall reclaim the last bit of my diverted power and crush your last hopes."

He gestures with one hand, sending the woman's battered form tumbling toward the ground. I dash to try and break her fall, too late—she hits with a sickening thud.

"Mom!" Ellie screams. "You bastard!"

I reach Ellie's mother before she does, of course—but when I do, I start in shock.

"My god," I gasp. "Ingrid?"

Nelson lifts his head. "Wh-what?"

Doko squints. "I thought your name was Angie. And you look...different."

The woman faintly smiles, the light in her lidded eyes fading with each moment that passes. "Oh, child. You thought what you needed to think, and saw what you needed to see. It is our nature."

Ingrid looks at her daughter, her eyes wide, and the girl kneels to cradle her mother's head, tears streaming down her cheeks. "H-her name is Ingrid Angela Carrefour."

With what seems like great effort, Nelson pulls himself to his knees and crawls over to her side. "Lord," he says. "It really is you."

"Yes," she coughs. "I'm sorry, Nelson. I really thought I could stand by your side even against the tide of Grantu's infinite enormity until time ran out. But I...I was wrong. Wrong about so many things. And when I discovered I was pregnant, I was terrified, of so many things—I just ran."

"You have nothing to apologize for—I'm the one who's sorry. I got us all into this mess. And for that, I can't tell you how sorry I am—but I have to know, Ingrid. This girl, is she...I mean, am I..."

"Yes, Nelson," she whispers. "Ellie's your daughter."

Nelson and Ellie look at each other, the conflagration all around momentarily forgotten.

"A touching scene," Mystic sneers. "Had I either heart or soul, I'm sure both would be aflame with emotion." A scornful grimace creases his face. "Though truthfully speaking, you should thank me for finally bringing the two of you together in these, the concluding moments of existence. If you do so, I might even be convinced to delay the end slightly. What say you, my former host? Go on, then—bow down before me. Bow and beg for a last few precious seconds in which to make peace with your friends and family."

Still staring openmouthed at Ellie, Nelson slowly turns to face first Ingrid, then me. His face is blank and helpless.

Mystic snaps, "Now—my infinite patience is at an end. Grovel before me or die now—though in either eventuality, like everything in your wretched little reality, it makes no difference whatsoever."

Somewhere deep in Nelson's expression, I see a tiny flicker of red flame. "No difference? No goddamned difference?" As if against incredible gravitational forces, he stands, looking directly into the face of his lifelong captor and tormentor.

"How dare you, mortal?" Mystic asks, blue flame crackling and swirling around him. "Out of respect for our history, I was prepared to offer you a mercy above that offered to any other creature in existence. But instead, you slap away the hand of kindness? I suppose I shouldn't be surprised—you humans always seem determined to make things worse for yourselves." He shakes his head. "Now you will be the first to know the pains of nonexistence."

"No!" Ellie screams, loud enough to visibly startle both Nelson and me, if not Mystic.

Nelson looks back at them as if truly seeing for the first time. His teeth grind against each other and he lowers his head as Mystic raises both arms, hands pulsing with eldritch energies.

"Farewell, Nelson Kendall. As you pass into oblivion, rest assured that your life was not meaningless—for by your association with me, you gained significance beyond any other among your wretched species."

"No," Nelson mutters, almost too quiet to hear. He raises his head, his jaw set boldly against Mystic's terrible energy, and my heart swells with pride at the sight of this fellow human facing his end with dignity —until suddenly, scarlet fire pours from Nelson's eyes, ripping into Mystic with startling ferocity. I hear a bellow of pain, and it takes a moment for me to register that it belongs to Grantu, not Nelson.

"No!" Nelson yells, and the syllable resonates throughout every corner of this limbo. "Damn you, Grantu. You took everything else from my life, you ruined everything and drove everyone away one by one—and I let you. But you will not take this from me!"

My spirits soar as Master Mystic flickers and withers in the face of Nelson's assault, and I dare to hope Nelson somehow managed to reserve enough power to force Grantu back into submission. But even as Mystic's pseudo-form shimmers and vanishes, the dark hole in the sky reappears, reminding me of Grantu's true nature and crushing my hopes before they can take root.

"NOW," the voice of Grantu bellows all around us. "EVERYTHING DIES."

The black hole compresses slightly, turns a vivid cerulean blue, and expands rapidly until it's so bright I'm forced to cinch my eyes tight against the blinding glare, never expecting to open them again.

But after a moment, I catch my breath and realize I'm still alive. Cracking my eyelid, I see Nelson standing firm in the face of universal conflagration, a crimson sphere of energy encircling us, just managing to hold back the tide of azure death all around.

Grantu bellows angrily, "YOU CANNOT HOPE TO WITHSTAND MY INFINITE POWER LONG, FOOL. AND ONCE YOUR PITIFUL SHIELD CRUMBLES, YOU SHALL LIVE JUST LONG ENOUGH TO WATCH AS I CONSIGN YOUR FELLOW HUMANS TO ETERNITY."

Nelson doesn't even blink. "No," he says quietly, "You won't." He turns, with wide eyes, and faces the rest of us. "Please," he implores us. "I know you all have your own reasons not to—some of you, very good ones. But trust me just this one last time?"

With what looks like great effort, bracing herself with Ellie's help, Ingrid stands and takes Nelson's right hand. Once she's sure her mother isn't going to fall, Ellie takes her father's other hand, smiling shyly, and Nelson's breast swells as our protective sphere darkens and expands, pushing away the evil that surrounds us.

I take Ingrid's hand, Doko takes Ellie's; the shield strengthens visibly, causing Grantu to thunder with frustration. Surprisingly, his voice has diminished to near-tolerable levels—he must be diverting enormous amounts of power to try and crush Nelson's spell—and out of the corner of my eye, I see Sloan, E, and Owlhoot stirring as Grantu entreats with Nelson.

"Host," Grantu implores. "This should not be. Mere moments ago, you were willing to lie passive while your world was erased. This makes no sense; this girl is no different than millions—billions—you were willing to let die. From whence, now, have you gained the strength to resist the inevitable?"

Nelson squeezes Ellie's hand, and his voice comes quietly but emphatically: "This one's mine. That's the difference."

I beckon to Sloan and the others with my free hand. Give them credit: even in the face of oblivion, they don't hesitate for a moment—not even E. In moments, we stand together, united: Owlhoot, E, Doko, Ellie, Nelson, Ingrid, myself, and Sloan. I feel the power course through us, more than I've ever dreamed of, and I give myself over to it, allowing my soul to commingle with those of my fellow humans, and we share an instant, intimate knowledge of each other that causes my heart to soar with boundless love.

Vermilion streams of unfettered power emanate from us in all directions, dissolving Grantu's stolen energies wherever they come into contact. Nelson, Ellie, and Ingrid are glowing brighter than a thousand suns, channeling the vitality of billions of lifeforms back home through the circuit Grantu unknowingly created by pulling them here—and for the first time in memory I allow myself to truly smile with blessed relief, knowing with a final comfortable certainty I never thought myself capable of attaining that in the end, no matter what, everything is going to be all right.

"Come on!" Nelson yells, loosing his hands and drawing a flaming circle upon the air as Grantu howls in dismay. "We only have a few seconds, if that. Everyone, dive back through this portal to the tower—Ellie, help your mother, if you would," he instructs, but the girl is already halfway through, one hand in her mother's and the other supporting Owlhoot. Doko is right on her heels, Sloan's arm in his as she limps across the gulf between worlds, while E hustles behind by himself.

"Go, Jack," Nelson cries. "I can't hold it much longer—go now!"

"No way, buddy—thanks to that magic linkup you rigged, I know what you're planning. And there's no way I'm going to leave you here to face that thing alone."

"It's the only way, Jack. I have to pay for what I've done—and someone has to make sure Grantu doesn't escape. It only stands to reason that responsibility should fall on my shoulders." He looks down. "My only regret is that I won't have more of a chance to get to know my daughter—but tell her I love her and I'm sorry things had to be this way."

"Tell her yourself," I reply. "Because for once, I'm the one who gets to save the day."

Before Nelson has a chance to protest, I sweep him up in my arms and race for the rapidly shrinking portal, just ahead of Grantu's violet tendrils, desperately grasping for us from every direction.

"Get ready," I shout. "We're going to hit the threshold in minus three…two…one…now!"

I shut my eyes tight as we plunge into the magic circle and a flood of energy pours from Nelson's hands, searing my back and shoulders with pain—but I don't even whimper. Conversely, behind us I hear a soul-searing wail of defeat that starts as a deafening roar before quickly diminishing down to a shriek, then a muffled yell—and finally, vanishing into a silence sweeter than any music I've ever heard.

EPILOGUE

When I dare to open my eyes again, I find myself back in the meeting room, surrounded by smiling faces.

"We did it," Nelson says, "I never would have been able to drain Grantu's energy so completely without you racing me away at the last microsecond like that. Have to hand it to you, Jack—that was some quick thinking on your part."

"For once, anyway," I laugh, rising from the floor and slapping him on the back. "I guess that glimpse of universal consciousness or whatever when we were all linked up gave me just enough inspiration to help get us all home safely."

"Well, don't expect it to last," Nelson warns. "Now that the limbo dimension is sealed off forever, any advantages we gained there will fade rapidly."

Sloan and I exchange glances; I notice her look over at Owlhoot as I ask the question on both our minds; bless Larry, I still don't think the potential implications have dawned on him. "What about the, uh, rejuvenation effects we experienced over the years? Do we need to worry about all that time catching up with us?"

Nelson shakes his head. "No, I didn't screw that up too badly, at least. Grantu had just enough energy to maintain us all at our current levels, as well as allow me to continue to act in public as Master Mystic—though I concede, it will be at much reduced strength. And from this point forward, we will resume our natural rate of aging—but only at the same rate as everyone else."

"Well, don't tell anyone else outside the Fighters, for God's sake," Doko admonishes him. "But presuming you're saying you'd like to remain with the New Fighters, I think we can come up with a few strategies to make public perception work to our benefit, for once."

Nelson glances over at Ellie and Ingrid. "I would like to stay. I know I have a lot to make up for, but I'd like to try, if you'll have me."

Biting her lip, Ellie looks up to her mother. "Is it okay if he stays, Mom?"

Ingrid smiles. "I think it might be good if you spent some time with your father. What do you think, Henry?"

Before anyone has a chance to ask what she's talking about, a man I don't recognize walks in. Ellie rushes into his arms; Doko steps up to shake his hand as she releases him from her loving embrace.

"Henry. Good to see you. But how did you get in? I didn't think you had Ingrid—er, Angie's abilities."

"I don't," Henry drawls. "But I've got eyes to see that front door blowing right off its hinges and brain enough to figure out that might mean you guys needed some help in here. Is everything okay?"

"Everything's great, Henry," Ingrid answers, stepping to his side. "My mind is clearer than it has been in years. And even though I told you it would never happen, you were right—Nelson finally came to his senses."

Nelson walks over to Henry and tentatively extends an open hand. "Henry, is it? Happy to meet you, Henry. And thank you for watching over these two."

Henry grips Nelson's hand and shakes it twice, heartily, then releases it. "That ain't a duty, it's a pleasure. And it's one I don't aim to give up any time soon, but I can't say as I mind sharing the joy, assuming you all agree to protect this little jewel like the gem she is while you teach her to use her powers properly, as well as abide by whatever Ellie's momma says."

"I appreciate that, Henry," Nelson says. "Because the fact that you were able to get in here so easily means we may be quite busy rounding up and correcting more of Master Mystic's various mistakes over the next few weeks."

"Ken!" I exclaim, slapping myself upside the head. "Oh shit, he's probably long gone, huh?"

"Him and a hundred others Mystic's power had kept confined to the fortress," Nelson confirms.

"There goes my trip to San Diego," Doko mutters. "Sure you won't stick around to help us out, Sloan? Owlhoot?"

She shakes her head. "I don't think either of us would be of much assistance, Doko, particularly as time continues to advance, as it tends to. But what if you could add American Rose to the ranks anyway?"

I see a spark in Doko's eye and his lip curls in a smile; apparently he and Sloan are already on the same page, but I'm still struggling to catch up.

"Why, that sounds more than ideal," Doko answers, nodding warmly. "I suppose the only question remaining would be—who?"

"What do you say, Ellie?" Sloan asks. "Want to be the new American Rose?"

"M-me? Are you serious?"

"A hundred percent, honey," Sloan says. "I know you can use your power to make yourself look just like me, back when I looked the way people wanted to. Plus, the torch has some stuff built into it to help you in situations when your power can't, so you'll be safer. And as long as people think they're up against old-school American Rose and a fully-powered Master Mystic, along with Jack Quick, and the other members of the new class, the element of surprise will be firmly on the New Fighters' side."

"Well...when you put it like that, how can I refuse?" Ellie smiles.

* * *

And just like that, the untold secret origin of the New Fighters came to its conclusion. Of course, the team would go on to have many more adventures, with many victories and a few tragic losses, but chances are you know about most of those already—E's eventual acceptance of the

Red Angel's legacy, the unforeseen consequences of Ellie's favor, the disastrous outcome of Doko's long-delayed vacation, what happened when Edge got his own powers, and so forth. But I'm afraid if you were hoping for further information on any of those incidents, you'll have to seek it elsewhere at the moment—for right now, I'm scheduled to meet up with my children in ten minutes, on the other side of the country. And I don't like to be late where my kids are involved—so it's time for me to run.

THE END

ABOUT THE AUTHOR

A. J. Payler is the author of the novels The Killing Song, World of Heroes: The Untold Secret Origin of the New Fighters, Lost In the Red, and Terror Next Door, along with many short stories.

He currently lives in California with his family.

The author does not participate in social media.

Visit http://www.ajpayler.com for information on currently available books and sign up for the A. J. Payler mailing list to receive email notification when new books are released.

ALSO BY A. J. PAYLER

The Killing Song

Lost In the Red

Terror Next Door

Lightning Source UK Ltd.
Milton Keynes UK
UKHW010609210722
406171UK00001B/264